IF THE SHOE FITS

The Liberty Lawrence Series: Book Three

Bea Stevens

Table of Contents

Copyright

Copyright © 2018

All Rights Reserved Worldwide

Any unauthorised reprint or use of this material is prohibited. No part of this book may be reproduced or transmitted in any form, or by any means, electronic or mechanical, including photocopying, recording, or by any information storage and retrieval system without express written permission from the author.

This book is a work of fiction. Names, characters, businesses, organisations and places or events, are either the product of the author's imagination or are used fictitiously. Any resemblance to actual persons, living or dead, events or locales is entirely coincidental.

ISBN13: 978-1912913077

Spellings are in British English

Dedication

I'd like to dedicate this book to those who helped make it happen: Natalie, Nicola, Helen, Charlotte, Lou and Maria—I honestly couldn't have done it without you. I owe you a drink—or a bottle—or a keg—or a... you know what I mean! Thanks so much, guys, you're the best! Xx

I'd also like to acknowledge the kind support of the group REBEL, https://www.rebelbaroque.com who generously allowed me to use them as a catalyst in this novel. I really appreciate your help, guys, and hope you enjoy the book as much as I enjoy your music. X

1

Think nice thoughts, I tell myself over and over as I hop about from one foot to the other, my knuckle poised millimetres from the door. I'm trying hard. Right. Concentrate. I stare down at my shoes. Louboutins. You can't get nicer than those. These are shiny, black courts. Expensive. Not quite as expensive as they would have been had I not bought them on eBay, but still a lot more than I told James they were.

And speaking of James, another nice thought just pops into my head. We actually did it... Friday night, believe it or not. He has been in such a foul mood with all that business with his ex-wife, Suzanne, that I didn't expect it to happen at all. The cow's only gone and moved into his flat. He was livid, but there wasn't much else he could do under the circumstances. If he hadn't let her stay at his place, she would have only made him pay for a hotel—and Suzanne doesn't do cheap.

She obviously knew he'd say yes because she'd brought all her stuff. James promptly packed a bag of his own, and after we'd gone over to their house in Richmond, he came back to mine—well, mine and Cassie's. Cassie Beaumont is the best flatmate and friend anyone could ask for. She didn't bat an eyelid when I explained that James was staying for the weekend. She did wink, though.

Suzanne had neglected to get a crack mended in a pipe in their bathroom, and the damn thing had burst, sending water cascading all over the first floor of their gorgeous home. It wouldn't have been so bad had she bothered to turn off the water before gathering her belongings and heading over to Fulham to disturb James and me at a most inopportune moment. By the time we got over there, the living room ceiling was already sagging, and the upstairs carpets were ruined.

James switched off the water, but it was too late to do anything about the mess. We just locked up and went back to my place. It was great. The whole weekend, I mean, not just... you know. Although that was amazing, too. More than amazing, actually, it was...

'Arghh!'

Someone just opened the door in front of me, scaring me half to death.

'Did you want something?'

My hand's still in the air, mid-knock. I quickly put it back to my side, clearing my throat while I unscramble my thoughts.

'Good morning. I heard you wanted to see me.' Phil Peerless frowns at me. Nothing new there. 'Right. Yes. Come in.'

He looks as flustered as I feel.

'Thank you.'

I straighten my back and walk into the office, taking deep breaths to steady my nerves.

He looks out the door, and I can't help suspecting he was probably on his way to the loo. Now, he'll have to quickly decide whether to keep me waiting or delay his visit. I read somewhere that people make their best decisions while bursting for a pee. I believe it's something to do with the urgency, which doesn't give you time to over-think, so you just impulsively choose the best course of action.

'Is everything okay?' I ask, not wanting to sit down in case he thinks me rude, but at the same time, not wanting him to disappear and have time to think about sacking me. Not that I've done anything wrong, exactly. Well... not really.

All I did was solve a mystery—well, several actually. But I thought my boss, Dave Chandler, was a crook and nearly got him into trouble with the police. Well, how was I to know he had an identical twin brother? And then I inadvertently threatened to take my story to the press if the *Daily Chronicle* gave me the sack because of it. I hoped I'd get away with it, but the management decided to wait until after the weekend to make their announcement about my fate. And so, here we are.

He jerks around to face me. 'Yes, of course.'

He closes the door and walks around to his side of the desk. 'Sit down, Libby.'

I do as he says. *So far, so good!*

I'm about to ask him if he had a good weekend but think better of it. If he didn't, he might dwell on it and be in a bad mood and much more likely to sack me—especially if he thinks it's my fault. Which it isn't. Wasn't. Can't have been. Or he might ask how mine was, and if it was better than his, he'll be even more annoyed. And I have a feeling mine was *much* better than his. After all, I'll bet he and his wife didn't spend nearly all their time in bed and... No, I don't think he'd still do any of that at his age. If ever.

'Mr Stratton and I had a long talk on Friday evening,' he says.

I lean forwards, trying to read his expression. When that fails, I try for his mind. Even emptier.

Mr Stratton is the owner of the *Daily Chronicle*, the newspaper I work for. Or, at least, I *hope* I still do.

'Right.' I can't think of anything else to say.

He clears his throat before taking a sip of water from a crystal glass on his desk. 'We've decided to move you to work on *Woman Matters*, the ladies' supplement.'

My stomach lurches, and I want to jump up and give him a hug, but I refrain. Not just because he might change his mind, but he smells a bit weird. Sort of old mannish.

'Right.' I try not to sound too thrilled, but inside, I'm doing cartwheels—which is a bit of a miracle because I could never do them on the outside. I swallow hard, keeping my hands firmly clasped over my knee.

'Siobhan O'Leary will be your mentor, and your chief editor will be Valerie Fulton-Coombes. The position will be for a trial period of one month. After that, we'll see how things stand.'

See how things stand? I think he'll find me standing firmly rooted to the department—maybe even running my own section. I'm just imagining it when I remember he's awaiting a response.

I nod. 'Thank you.'

'Melanie will be starting her maternity leave next week, so you can begin over there today. Hopefully, she'll be able to hand over the reins before she goes.' Phil looks very stern, and I wonder if he would have preferred to sack me after all. I can't help speculating about just how much say he had in the matter.

'Right, thank you.' I stand and lean over to shake his hand like the true professional I am.

He raises his eyebrows but shakes my sweaty palm as he gets up. He follows me out the door, and I walk to the lift as quickly as I can. Once inside, I fist pump the air. That's when I realise, I'm not alone. Kevin Stratton is standing behind me with a couple of very important-looking ladies.

They all glare at me. I smile and give a nervous little laugh. I actually hear one of the snooty women tut. I stare at her, just to let her know I've heard and turn to face the door, willing it to open soon.

Both women are well-dressed, one in a bright-green Prada suit, which brings out the colour of her eyes, and the other in a navy shift dress I think I recognise from Monsoon. It doesn't excuse their lack of manners, though.

I desperately want to text James, but I daren't get my phone out with the big boss standing right there. *Damn!* I know he'll be worried about me, too, despite how optimistic he was this morning. I honestly don't know how anyone can be so cheerful first thing on a Monday. He never ceases to amaze me.

To my horror, I let out a giggle. I was only thinking about how amazing James was and out it came. And now, I can't stop. I feel them all staring at me from behind, but I daren't look round. The more I try to stifle it, the worse it gets. I think I'm about to burst. Suddenly, a loud snort overtakes me. Gosh, this is awful. That woman's just tutted again, but I daren't stare at her this time. Just the thought of those stuck-up faces makes me worse. I'm praying for the doors to open so I can escape. What if I get sacked for this? Oh, no, just when it looked like it was all going so well. Even that idea doesn't stop the onslaught, and suddenly, I do a laugh-snort-cough thing just to really finish it off.

As soon as the doors open, I hurl myself out of the lift, bumping headlong into a couple of photographers.

'Hey, watch out!'

'Sorry.'

I hear another tut behind me and spin around to see that Kevin po-faced Stratton and his women have followed me out. Oh, no. I was only getting off here to escape them. I don't even know which floor I'm on. Taking a deep breath, I head down the corridor until I see a sign for the ladies' loo and dive in. Surely, those annoying, tutting women won't follow me in here? I don't even look back to check. I just find an empty cubicle and lock myself in.

I sit down with a massive sigh. Oddly enough, now that I'm away from that lift, I don't feel like giggling at all. It must have been nerves that caused it. And relief. I'm so glad I've kept my job—for now. I can't believe they're putting me on a month's trial, though. *What does that mean? If I don't fit in, they'll move me? Or sack me anyway?*

A lead weight sinks to the pit of my stomach. I'm not out of the woods yet. But there's hope. If I keep my nose clean and do well in the women's supplement, they're bound to want me to stay. If not, I dread to think what'll happen.

I stand and straighten my dress. It's my black Karen Millen skater with the white trim. It's a bit loose as I must have lost weight with all the running around I had to do while working in the newsroom. I've teamed it with a white jacket and a little black shoulder bag borrowed from Cassie. The bag's a Gucci. That just shows how good a friend she is.

I'm on a mission now to make everyone in the new department like me. That way, they won't make me leave when my month's up. In fact, I'll be so popular, they'll beg me to stay.

I wash my hands and check my hair and make-up. Apart from being a little flushed, I look okay. Now, if I can just work out which floor I'm on, I might be able to find the office, which is on the fourth floor. As I turn to leave the room, I hear a tut behind me and swing round to glare at the culprit. It's the woman in the green Prada suit. I frown at her.

'Is there a problem?' I ask as politely as I can manage. She raises her perfectly shaped eyebrows, looking quite taken aback.

'I beg your pardon?' She sounds very posh.

'That's the fourth time you've tutted at me today,' I tell her. 'I wondered if you have a problem with me?'

She shakes her head disparagingly. 'My dear girl, I don't even *know* you. However, I do find your behaviour more than a little... shall we say... *distracting*? I don't know which part of the building you work in, but in my department, I expect my staff to show far more decorum.'

With that, she rolls her eyes at me and leaves.

No decorum? How dare she say I have no decorum? I'm filled with bloody decorum. Well, the rum bit anyway, James and I drank quite a bit of it over the weekend. I want to go after her and give her a piece of my mind, but I don't. I need all my mind pieces to impress my new boss. It's a good job she's left, though, or she would have heard exactly what I think of her.

'Snooty, stuck-up bitch!' I mumble, staring at the closed door.

A tut from the washbasin makes me jerk around, and I stare at the woman in the Monsoon navy shift. Shit. I hadn't realised anyone else was in here. She looks down her nose at me, daring me to retaliate. Instead, I huff loudly and leave the room.

Looking up and down the corridor, I don't recognise this area at all. I head back towards the lift and discover I'm on the fifth floor. Luckily, the lift is empty this time so I quickly text James on my way to the fourth level.

Hi, James. I'm going to work with Siobhan! Hope you're okay. Lxx

There's no need to worry him about the temporary bit. With any luck, it won't be an issue anyway. I'm determined to make a go of it.

I smile as I open the door to the large office where Siobhan and her team work for the fashion section of the *Daily Chronicle's* female supplement, *Woman Matters*. There's a large table in the middle of the room with desks all around the wall. It's very light and spacious, and everyone's bustling around excitedly. Rails of clothes line one end of the room, and a couple of women are looking at them. Someone else has laid an outfit on the table and is frowning at it. I recognise one of the girls as Tammy. We met on a night out recently when I joined Cassie and her boyfriend, Rob. There was a gang from the newspaper with them, and we all got on famously. Her gorgeous, dark-red hair is shorter than the last time I saw her. It now bounces in natural waves on her shoulders, looking lovely. Her Prada glasses make her look very intelligent and enlarge her bright-blue eyes. She carefully pins a dress onto a mannequin, her tongue hanging out in concentration.

'There you are! I thought you'd got lost,' Siobhan calls over to me with a smile. She has an immaculate black bob and perfect make-up. Utterly stunning. She's with Francesca, the girl I met the other day. Francesca's much more natural looking, with tight, orangey curls cascading over her broad shoulders.

I grin at them, not wanting to admit that I *did* actually get a bit lost.

'Hi.' I go over, suddenly feeling a little nervous.

'Welcome to the mad house,' Siobhan says, gesturing to the room. She even smells gorgeous.

'Thank you. I'm so excited to be here.'

'We're just waiting for a new collection to come in,' she goes on. 'It's called 'Fame' and is all about brandishing your name on your clothes. You know, getting your name out there, sort of thing. It ties in with the current trend of selfies and self-promotion. I think it's supposed to encourage confidence and self-esteem.'

My stomach flips with excitement. 'Sounds great. I love the idea.'

'The delivery's been a bit delayed but when they arrive, I want you and Francesca to work on them. Melanie's had to go home poorly, so it's great that we have you. I need to know all about the quality, workmanship, and wear ability. It's something that's taken off in a big way over in the States, and we're the first to see it over here. Apparently, the collection's set to make a lot of money.'

'Right.' Sheer joy bubbles up inside me. This is what I wanted to do all along. This job is just perfect. I'm right on the cusp of something massive.

'First, let me introduce you, though,' Siobhan says. She raises her voice, looking very efficient in her royal blue bodycon dress. I've no idea how she can walk properly in something so fitted, let alone work in it, but she looks great. 'Okay, girls, listen up. This is Libby, who's come to join us. I know you'll all make her welcome and give her any help she needs.'

There's a chorus of hellos as everyone looks over and smiles at me. They look like a bunch of models—they're all so pretty. I smile back. This is so lovely, although a little intimidating. I didn't get anything like this in the boring old newsroom.

'I won't go through all the names now, as it can be a bit overwhelming, but you'll pick them up as you go along. And don't be afraid to ask questions, Libby.'

'Thank you.'

'Come on, I think Valerie's back in her office. She's the boss. I'll take you in.' Siobhan ushers me towards the corner where another office hides behind a glass door. The door has blinds pulled down, and I notice this place has windows overlooking the main room. Again, those blinds are down at the moment as well. I can imagine it'll be a great way for the boss to be included with what's going on without being intrusive. There's a good sense of cohesion about it.

Siobhan knocks, and a voice calls for us to go in.

'Hi, Valerie. I just wanted to introduce you to our new recruit,' Siobhan says, as I follow her into the large office. 'Valerie Fulton-Coombes, meet Libby Lawrence.'

When Valerie stands to shake my trembling hand, her eyes flash at me and widen. My stomach churns as I take in the green Prada suit, the immaculate hair, and the disparaging look. Judging by her expression, she's recognised me, too.

Oh, shit!

2

I offer Valerie an anxious smile, which isn't reciprocated. There's some classical music playing softly in the background, but it does nothing to alleviate my nerves.

'Thank you, Siobhan,' she says before my only ally leaves the room. It's one of those moments when you just want the earth to swallow you up. 'Sit down, Liberty.'

I take a seat and spend the next ten minutes—which feels more like ten years—hearing about the kind of behaviour she expects from employees in her department, even those who are only temporary. In fact, the word 'temporary' seems to crop up a lot more times than I'd have liked during her dreary—and frankly, quite frightening—speech.

'I'm a plain speaker, Liberty,' she says.

And a boring one. I nod, not quite sure what I'm supposed to say to that.

'And if there are any problems, you can rest assured I will tell you.' She finishes with a warning look that makes me go all hot.

'May I say something?' I ask in a shaky voice.

She nods, her chin-length auburn hair bouncing slightly.

'When you saw me in the lift earlier, I'd just heard I was going to work in your department. I was so excited at the prospect, I might have acted with less decorum than usual, but it was only because I was so thrilled at the opportunity. I'm sorry if I gave you a bad impression.'

'You did,' she replies bluntly.

I say nothing, disappointment oozing from my pores. I had hoped she'd say something like *'Oh, it's all right, Libby. I quite understand. I'm glad you're so excited to be working with me. I'm thrilled to be working with you, too,'* but she doesn't.

Her attention has returned to some papers on her desk. The frown on her face suggests they might be something relating to me. She tuts. *Yep, they're definitely about me.*

'I notice from your CV, you don't have any experience in the fashion industry,' she says.

'Not exactly on paper,' I tell her, my hopes of impressing her swirling down the drain. 'But I do *like* fashion. In fact, I love it. I wear fashionable clothes all the time, and I always like to keep up with the latest looks.'

She eyes me up and down as if noticing my outfit for the first time. I lift the Gucci bag a little higher in my lap to give her a better view.

'I'm glad to hear it,' she says in a very unimpressed sort of way. *Tough crowd!* 'And do you foresee any problem with getting along with the rest of the girls in the department?'

I balk, wondering just what Phil bloody Peerless has been saying about me. Or Kevin Stratton.

'Absolutely not,' I assure her. 'In fact, I've already met Siobhan, Francesca, and Tammy, and we all get along extremely well.'

She looks surprised. I'm not quite sure how to take it, to be honest, so I carry on talking. 'I loved the feature you ran recently in conjunction with the paper's 'House and Home' campaign. Building a capsule wardrobe for moving house was ingenious.' I want to go on and tell her that I helped Fran choose the outfits, but I wouldn't want to get her into trouble.

For the first time since I walked into the room, Valerie's face actually softens.

'Yes,' she says. 'One of my best ideas.'

A massive lump hits the pit of my stomach. I'm sure it was Siobhan's suggestion.

'Anyway...' she says, before I can object. 'Siobhan will explain your duties. She is in charge of the office out there. I believe you will be working on a new collection. We're all very excited about it, so you need to convey that in your report.'

'Of course.' I nod, smiling to try to show my own excitement at working with the brand—which I've never even heard of, incidentally—though Valerie doesn't seem to notice.

She stands, and I follow her to the door. She pulls up the blind and catches Siobhan's attention before opening the door and offloading me.

'Isn't she lovely?' Siobhan beams at me, leading me over to a clothing rail covered in plastic.

I can't lie, but I'm amazed my new mentor has such a high opinion of the boss. 'She has a surprising taste in music.' I think that's a safer way to put it. I like classical music that's not too slow and boring. My grandad used to play lots of Bach and Vivaldi when I was growing up, and this reminded me of that sound. It was nice and had a cheerful, jaunty tone—unlike Valerie.

'It's Baroque. Quite the in-thing in certain areas, I believe,' Siobhan informs me.

I'll remember that.

***

We reach the other end of the room. 'This is the new collection I was telling you about,' Siobhan continues, opening the zip and pulling the plastic cover from the rail.

I reach over to help her and grab hold of the cover, yanking it back over the clothes. As I do so, the teeth of the zip catch on something.

'Is everything all right?' Siobhan asks from the opposite side of the rail.

'Yes, of course.' I give it a good, hard tug, and hear something tear. *Oh, shit!* Then it frees the fabric, and we manage to remove it. No one seems to have heard the rip over their chattering, so I say nothing, though my heart's hammering.

After I've helped Siobhan fold up the cover, we stand back to take in the new range. There's an array of pretty pastel colours.

'Gorgeous!' I enthuse.

'Wow, aren't they just?' Francesca appears behind me, smiling.

Siobhan takes a pale-blue sweatshirt from the rail. It's in a child's size and has the name 'HANNAH' emblazoned across the back in bold, white, capital letters. On the front, left-hand side, the name appears again, but this time smaller and in a swirly font. The first 'H' is capitalised, but the rest is in lowercase.

Some of the other girls gather round to take a look, and there are whoops of delight as they all pull items from the rail and examine them.

'I think I might have to change my name for this one,' one of the girls shouts. She holds a pale pink T-shirt with the name 'Amelia' on it. 'This is so cute.'

A very glamorous woman with thick, dark, wavy hair picks out a green hoodie with 'Eva' printed on it.

'Oh, look, they've got my name!' she squeals excitedly. 'I might have to have one of these.'

It's hard to imagine her in casual clothes, though I'm sure she'd look just as lovely—she's one of those women who'd even look good dressed in a bin bag.

'It's a lovely colour,' one of the others says. 'Do they do them in adult sizes?'

'Yep,' Siobhan pipes up and passes her a peach-coloured 'Sophia' T-shirt.

The girl takes it from her and immediately removes her jacket to try it on. 'Wow, they're so soft,' she says. 'They feel like good quality.'

'Good to know,' Siobhan calls over. 'Libby, you'll need to make a note of that.'

'It's a generous size, too,' the girl tells me.

'Duly noted,' I tell her with a smile. 'Is it the right name?'

The girl laughs. 'I wish. I've never found anything with 'Beulah' on. It's one of those names no one bothers with—apart from my parents, of course. I think they must have hated me.'

'I think it's a lovely name,' I tell her.

She smiles, dimples appearing on her flushed cheeks. Her dark-brown hair brushes her shoulders in glossy waves, her hazel eyes sparkling. She's wearing a taupe shift dress with cream trim, which had a matching jacket until a few minutes ago when she replaced it with the peach T-shirt. She's ever so pretty. 'I still think I'd prefer Sophia,' she says with a giggle. 'You're Libby, aren't you? Is that short for Olivia?'

'No.' I shake my head. 'It's Liberty.'

Her eyes widen. 'Wow! You've got great parents,' she says. 'I'd love a name like that!'

I shrug. *She's obviously never met my folks.* I've never truly considered whether I like my name; it's just sort of... there. 'Thanks,' I say.

'I'll bet they don't do a T-shirt with your name on, though,' another girl interjects with a grin.

I laugh. 'No, I don't usually see my name on anything.' I turn back to Beulah. 'I know how it feels.'

'They've got mine.' A blonde girl pulls a tiny T-shirt from the rail. 'Now, if I were only...' She checks the label. 'Six to twelve months old, I'd have this.'

We all laugh as she holds up the cute, lilac shirt with 'Alice' emblazoned across it.

'What's going on?' Valerie's voice pierces the hilarity, and suddenly, the room is silent.

'We were just checking out the new line,' Siobhan explains. 'I think everyone's very impressed.'

There's a chorus of yeses and a lot of head nodding as the girls stand back to allow Valerie access to the rail. She gives the clothes a cursory glance, then frowns. She pulls out one of the larger hoodies and holds it up. There's a tear on the top of the shoulder.

'Has this been reported?' she demands from Siobhan.

The black-haired girl looks horrified. 'No, I hadn't noticed,' she admits in a small voice.

'You're supposed to check the complete order as soon as it arrives so that this sort of thing is picked up right away.' Valerie sounds vicious. 'It's your responsibility to ensure that any damage is documented and reported to the distributor immediately, so we can't be held liable. Now that you've allowed everyone to help themselves to the collection, how can we possibly prove this wasn't done by one of our staff?'

My stomach lurches. Part of me wants to shout, *'It was my fault. I did it.'* The other part wants to keep my job. I narrow my eyes at Valerie. She's not being very fair to Siobhan, berating her in front of all the staff. Especially as she's not the one to blame.

'How will the distributor *know* we've all handled them?' I ask. 'And besides, we were only examining them individually. Once we'd got to that one, we'd have noticed the damage and reported it.'

Everyone stares at me, and I feel myself getting hotter by the second. I know I shouldn't rile my new boss, but I can't stand by and watch her castigate Siobhan—especially as she's innocent. *Unlike me.*

Valerie glares. 'Are you questioning me?'

'No, of course not. I'm sorry if you see it that way, but I honestly wasn't,' I reply, my voice trembling as much as the rest of me. 'I just think that maybe it's not as much of a problem as it seems. We can still report it. After all, *you're* the only person who's touched that one.' I hope she'll see me as offering a solution, but the look on her face suggests something very different. *Damn!*

'How *dare* you?' Her voice suddenly booms, and there are gasps from the girls around me. 'Get into my office. Now!'

I'm shaking so much I can hardly walk. I get some very sympathetic looks from the girls as I make my way through the little crowd and down to the end of the room. I stand in front of Valerie's desk, a feeling of impending doom overtaking me. *I get that a lot, for some reason.*

Some sort of upbeat, triumphant music plays now, and I can only hope it sends a positive vibe to my boss.

I stand tall, glancing around the office. One entire wall looks out onto the larger room, and I now realise it's so she can spy on the girls. When I came in earlier, all the blinds were down but now they're up, and I can feel my colleagues staring at me through the glass. They seem like a lovely bunch, very friendly and supportive. Valerie, on the other hand, seems to hate my guts.

She slams the door behind her, making me jump. I half-expect the glass to shatter, but it doesn't. *Pity. It would serve her right.*

The atmosphere between us is thick and heavy as she walks around to the front of her desk, her Manolos clicking on the tiled floor. She sits down and presses a button on a pad that closes all the blinds. Another switch halts the music. This doesn't look good. Neither does she, actually. Her face is tense, and her frown shows up her wrinkles. I'm surprised a woman in her position hasn't had some sort of cosmetic surgery. I might suggest it to her—another time.

She gives a loud huff before speaking. 'You haven't been here five minutes and you're already in trouble, young lady.'

I want to object, but my mouth's gone dry and my throat's closed up. Besides, I'm not entirely sure what to say.

'I was warned that you always seemed to be at the centre of the drama at the news desk, but I hoped it wouldn't be the case here. I see I was wrong.'

I stare at her. If I'm going to be sacked, at least I'll defend myself first.

'May I ask what drama you're referring to?' I frown at her quizzically. Then I realise I might get wrinkles like her, so I quickly raise my eyebrows to counteract the effect.

'I'm sure you know.' She gives me a condescending and slightly confused look.

'I know I was accused of doing things I didn't do, and when I proved my innocence, I received apologies from everyone in the office, as well as Mr Peerless,' I reply calmly, forcing the words past the lump in my throat. 'I suppose that would put me at the centre of the incident but only as the injured party.'

She looks rather taken aback, and her eyes flash at me. 'Yes, well...' she mutters.

'I hadn't done anything wrong,' I reiterate.

'Well, you've certainly done something wrong now,' she says, more forcefully. 'Answering back to a superior isn't exactly the best way to ingratiate yourself in any department—especially mine.'

'May I speak?' I ask.

'No. You may listen for a change and hopefully learn something.'

I clench my hands together as well as my lips.

'When Mr Stratton asked... no, *pleaded* with me to allow you to join my department, I wasn't sure. My team works beautifully together and individually. Having heard about the disruption caused in the newsroom, I was concerned that the same might happen here. However, *I* keep a close eye on things to ensure this sort of thing doesn't occur in *my* section. If I find anyone unsettling my girls, I weed them out. Do you understand?'

Weed? She's calling me a weed? Damned cheek.

'Yes, I do,' I assure her. *But I'm still not a flaming weed.*

'It's fortunate this has happened so soon after you joining the department,' she goes on. 'At least you haven't been able to cause too much disruption yet. But I think you must realise this can't continue.'

She's expecting me to simply agree with her, but I can't. I'm not certain what she's saying, to be honest. I clear my throat.

'I'm not entirely sure I understand the problem,' I say. 'I asked you a question in there. One I hoped provided the solution to the unfortunate situation. I was trying to help. I wasn't being rude or disruptive, and I certainly didn't intend to cause any offence. Why would I do that on my first day in a department I've been longing to work in since I started at the *Chronicle*?'

She squeezes her lips together in outrage. I take a deep breath, preparing for the onslaught.

'For a start, it wasn't your place to speak up when I was questioning Siobhan, your superior. And furthermore, how dare you imply that I was the one who damaged the garment!' Her teeth are gritted as she struggles to contain her anger.

I stare at her. 'I'm sorry if I spoke out of turn,' I say, a little more quietly than I intended. 'But I certainly didn't mean to imply that *you* had caused the damage. Quite the opposite. When I pointed out that you were the only one who had handled the garment, I meant it as a compliment. I mean, as it was *you* who touched it that confirms the damage *must* have been done beforehand—*you'd* never do such a thing. It was an endorsement that we couldn't be held liable. I'm sorry if you took it the wrong way.'

She swallows hard, seemingly digesting my claim.

'I see,' she says at last.

'And Siobhan didn't exactly let everyone handle the clothes, it just sort of... happened. We were all so enthusiastic about the fabulous new range, we couldn't wait to check it out. It's only because we're all so passionate about our work. No one meant to undermine Siobhan in any way. Please don't be cross with her.'

Valerie stares at me, and I wonder if I've overstepped the mark. Perhaps, I should have left it there, but I couldn't stand by and let her blame Siobhan.

'I should think my feelings towards Siobhan O'Leary are the least of your worries right now, Liberty,' she says. 'At least, if you want to keep your job that is.'

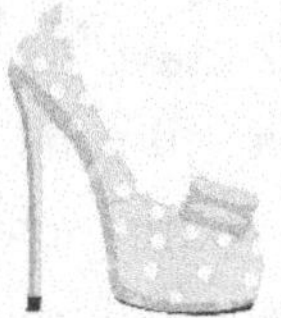

3

The feeling of dread I felt when I walked into Valerie's office has just turned to one of blind panic. I *need* this job. I need to maintain this lifestyle somehow. What would James, my dreamy boyfriend, say if I were suddenly unemployed? He has enough to cope with paying for the repairs on his house, thanks to his ex. That's assuming they still own the house, of course, after Suzanne—his ex-wife—signed some legal papers for her con man boyfriend who's now in prison.

And that's not to mention my own fabulous life living in swanky Chelsea with my bestie, Cassie. She's wonderful, such a lovely person and loads of fun. Although she never flaunts it, she's actually from quite a rich family and has loads of lovely designer clothes and shoes that she lends me from time to time. Like the Gucci bag I'm using today to impress my new boss. Although Valerie doesn't look all that impressed right now. She looks more... outraged.

'I'm so sorry,' I say, not entirely sure what I'm apologising for, but hoping it might sway her a little.

She sighs. I think it's working. I say nothing for a few minutes, which I have to admit, is a real strain. She seems to mellow a little and takes a sip of water. I momentarily consider coming clean about the hoodie I ripped earlier. Maybe she'll admire my honesty. Maybe she'll warm to me and feel sorry for me. *Or maybe she'll sack me on the spot,* I think, with a huge lump in my throat.

She sits back in her chair, narrowing her eyes at me. My legs are getting tired now. I'm sure Christian Louboutin didn't design his lovely shoes for standing around for hours in front of the boss' desk while she decides whether to sack you or not.

'Liberty, I'm a fair person and I promised Mr Stratton I'd give you a proper trial in my department. Unfortunately, we seem to have started on the wrong foot. I'm prepared to give you another chance as long as you realise that backchat and insolence won't be tolerated here. I expect my staff to act with impeccable manners at all times. You take direction from your superiors without question, and you do not speak out of turn. Do you understand?'

She sounds like my old headmistress from school—not that I was hauled up in front of her *that* many times, of course—and it takes great effort not to roll my eyes.

'Yes,' I reply, sensing a glimmer of hope. I also sense that she doesn't want to appear a failure in front of Kevin Stratton. Or Phil Peerless. If she had to sack me within an hour of me arriving in her department, it wouldn't bode too well for her management skills, would it? And I already know she's a glory-seeker. She's worried about her own damned reputation. The thought empowers me a little—though not enough to open my big mouth and ruin it all.

'Then I'm prepared to drop the matter. But I have to warn you, any repeat of the sort of behaviour you displayed this morning will see you getting your P45 and disappearing out that door for good, understood?'

Crikey, she knows how to milk a situation!

My mind's whirling. What flaming behaviour? I only asked a question. Siobhan told me to ask away when she introduced me to everyone. Maybe she didn't include Valerie in that. It's something worth remembering.

'Yes.' I daren't say any more than that. I'll only shoot myself in the foot. *I do that a lot, though I've no idea how.*

She stands and ushers me out the door. Siobhan comes straight over to us, her eyes wide with worry.

'I'm giving her another chance,' Valerie announces to a hushed audience. There are gasps all around me, but no one dares speak.

Siobhan smiles.

'Keep a close eye on her,' Valerie says, as though I'm a two-year-old. 'Any repeat of that type of behaviour, and I'll reconsider my decision.'

I gawp at her. Talk about rubbing it in. She's determined to make me look stupid to the entire staff. Unfortunately, I can't retaliate as *I'm* determined to keep this damned job. *And she knows it!*

Valerie returns to her office like a bear retreating to its cave, and Siobhan leads me back to the other end of the room.

'Well done for surviving,' she whispers, her back to Valerie's office. 'I've never known anyone escape from there with their job intact after a summons like that.'

In whispers and hushed tones, the other girls congratulate me, which is a massive relief, as I was afraid they'd think I was as stupid as Valerie had just made me look. I welcome their support and am surprised at how stunned they are that I still have a job. Maybe I had an even luckier escape than I thought.

'First, let me show you how to fill in the admin forms for the delivery,' Siobhan says, leading me over to her desk. I hadn't expected to be form-filling. For some reason, I just thought, or rather, hoped to be checking out the clothes right away. We have to match each item to the delivery note, and there's a separate form for the faulty top. All the details of the fault need to be recorded, including the size of the tear and its position, as well as a veritable essay on its description and how we think it might have occurred. Of course, I keep very quiet about the zip getting caught in it, and Siobhan writes a piece about it being like that when it arrived. It's like an interrogation, and I can imagine some fancy designer shining a bright light in my eyes and demanding to know what *really* happened. Honestly, you'd think it was done on purpose or something. I have half a mind to suggest they get better zips put on their covers in future—or use Velcro—but on reflection, decide it's best to say nothing.

We then have to double-check by counting every garment and ensuring the figures match the list. It's quite tedious, but I can see how vital it is to do all this stuff. In fact, I feel quite important to have been given such a responsible job. I still think it's one of those tasks I might delegate to someone else once I get my own section, though. And that can't come soon enough.

It's a relief when lunchtime finally arrives, and I find a quiet spot to call James.

'Hi, how's it going?' I ask, hoping he's having a much better day than me. Not that I'm not enjoying the new job, of course, it's just rather... precarious.

'I'm working on a horrid case right now,' he says. 'A missing child.'

'Oh, no.' My stomach cramps. I can't think of anything worse. James is a police sergeant and obviously has to work on whatever crops up, but some cases are far easier than others.

'And I have more workmen down at the house,' he says with a sigh. 'It's going to be a massive job.'

Since early Saturday morning, the plumber has spent most of the weekend replacing the broken pipe. Not only will it cost James a fortune in repairs, but his flaming ex-wife, Suzanne, who caused all the trouble, doesn't seem at all bothered. She's even taken over James' bedroom while he has to sleep on the sofa.

'Did you call your solicitor?' I ask, biting my lip.

'Yeah, they're looking into the business of Suzanne trying to sign the house away to that crook. And I had to tell the estate agent what's happened with the pipe. The buyers pulled out right away, concerned about what other damage there might be. We'll never sell it at this rate.'

'Oh, no. That's awful!' It's taken almost a year to find a buyer for the house. Suzanne has been putting people off so she could continue living in the luxurious residence, and now this has happened.

It wouldn't be so bad, but the house isn't even hers. James inherited it from his uncle a few years ago. I think it's caused some sort of rift in the family, but he won't talk about it. Of course, as they were married at the time, he signed half of it over to Suzanne—probably at her insistence—but it still doesn't give her the right to do this.

Poor James. He's been trying not to think about it too much all weekend, as we won't know the extent of the damage until the assessment is done. Also, the legal stuff about Suzanne trying to give the damned place away won't be investigated until today. I thought I did quite a good job in keeping his mind off it all, hence hardly getting out of bed for two whole days. But we had to face reality at some point, and it seems that point is now.

'Suzanne's going over to the house during her lunch break to find the papers so we can send them straight to the solicitors.' James sounds fed up. 'There's no point worrying until we know exactly what she's agreed and whether it's legal.'

'But you shouldn't have to pay for the repairs if the house isn't yours,' I point out. 'Surely, it's Reynolds' problem to sort out?'

Oliver Reynolds was Suzanne's con man boyfriend. She fell for all his lies and might have signed the house over to him. Honestly, how can you not know about something like that? Apparently, she just signed some papers he gave her and didn't pay too much attention to what they were for. Rose-tinted glasses and all that. And probably lots of rosé wine.

Anyway, he's now in prison, where he belongs, leaving poor James to sort out the whole mess.

'The solicitors think it's highly unlikely that she signed over my share of the house, even if she gave him her half,' James explains. 'And the longer the repairs are left, the more damage it will cause. I'm having all the carpets and furniture removed this afternoon so we can try to dry the house out structurally. We'll need a new ceiling in the living room, and the walls will need re-plastering for a start.'

'But how long will all that take? Suzanne's going to have to find somewhere else to live in the meantime.' Even as I say the words, I know what James' reply will be. Suzanne doesn't have the money to buy a new house, and she won't rent anything that's not up to her impossibly high standards. That means James will have to pay her living expenses, or she'll continue staying in his flat in Fulham *with him*.

'Look, I'm sorry, I have to go,' he says hurriedly, and I hear voices in the background.

'Okay. I'll call you later,' I promise.

James is a lovely man, but he never uses terms of endearment—well, not outside the bedroom anyway. He has an important job and needs to keep professional while he's at work. Previously, I'd been a bit worried that maybe he didn't feel the same way about me as I do about him, but this past weekend has allayed all those fears. I smile at the thought. James is very much into me. He's the strong, silent type, but actions certainly speak louder than words. I'm just remembering some of the action we shared when Fran bounds up to me.

'Aren't you coming for lunch?'

'Oh... er... yes.' I used to bring my own lunch when I worked in the newsroom, but it meant I needed a bigger handbag. Now, I can dress nicer for this position, I don't want to be limited with my bags. I'll give the staff canteen another try. It was a disaster last time, but I'm determined to master the art of juggling food, trays, and money without breaking my teeth. *It's a long story!*

James doesn't know I'm now spending money on lunch. He's not mean but he's always careful with his money. Now that he might have lost the house and is having to pay out for its repairs, he's even more worried about his finances. His flat in Fulham is quite pricey, and although he's a detective sergeant, he doesn't earn *that* much, apparently. He's also been subsidising Suzanne, as she couldn't afford all the bills for the big house in Richmond.

It seems everyone in the building has lunch at the same time, and the canteen's heaving when we arrive. I look around, and my heart sinks. It'll take forever to get through the queue, and we'll be lucky to find a seat at the end of it.

'We're over there,' Fran says, pointing excitedly.

Siobhan, Tammy, and some of the others are sitting around a large table over by the window. I follow her over, glad to see they've saved us a couple of seats.

'You can have chicken salad or ploughman's,' Tammy informs us. 'We thought it safer to go for something cold as we weren't sure how long you'd be.'

There's an array of cakes and puddings, as well as pots of coffee and tea lined up along the centre of the table, and the two main meals have been placed in front of the empty seats.

'You choose,' Fran says with a smile.

'I'll take the salad, please,' I say, and we both sit down.

'It's a nightmare getting a decent seat around here,' Siobhan explains, 'so the first one down nabs the table. We weren't sure where you'd got to, so we thought we'd better get you some food sooner rather than later. You'll have to let us know what you prefer for future reference. Hope you're okay with the choice.'

'Great,' I say, surprised. They all seem to eat quite healthily, which is what I'm trying to do, but it's a relief that they like their sweets, too.

'We got a couple of extra desserts so you can take your pick,' Tammy pipes up. 'But mine's the chocolate éclair.'

The girls all laugh.

'Nothing new there, then,' Fran says, rolling her eyes in jest.

'There's nothing wrong with being a creature of habit,' Tammy says.

'Talking of which, you seem to have a great habit of winding Valerie up,' one of the girls says, nodding at me. She's striking, with long, straight, chocolate-brown hair and flawless skin.

'Don't be so mean, Kiki. It's not her fault.' Beulah leaps to my defence.

'She's right,' I admit, tucking into a piece of tomato. 'I don't mean to, but everything I say seems to be wrong.'

'We've noticed,' Kiki says with a grin. 'We've never seen so much entertainment in that office.'

'You have to be careful, Libby. Valerie's a powerful woman. You need to get on her right side if you want to stay in the department.' Siobhan reaches for the coffee pot.

'I know.' I sigh. 'But it's not on purpose. She just seems to pop up at all the wrong moments. *And* she takes things the wrong way.'

'Try to blend into the background a bit,' Siobhan suggests.

Hmm. Blending into the background isn't exactly my forte, but I can see I need to keep a low profile for a bit.

'I *am* trying,' I tell her.

'That's the trouble,' Siobhan says with a giggle.

I roll my eyes. Mum always says I'm a very trying person. I've no idea why. It has taken me years to realise it wasn't a compliment.

'You can start getting some notes together this afternoon for your report,' Siobhan tells me. 'Valerie's eager to make it a good one.'

'How come Valerie's so keen on the range?' I ask her. 'She seems very protective of it.'

Siobhan shifts in her seat, staring into her coffee. 'It's just a new client. She wants to make a good impression.'

I'm not convinced that's all there is to it, but I daren't rock the boat. I think I've done enough of that already. Instead, I finish my lunch, enjoying the banter of the girls around me. The atmosphere is much lighter than that in the newsroom, and they're all so friendly. I round off my meal with apple crumble and cream, which is nothing short of delicious.

'Right, I'm going back,' Siobhan announces, gathering some of the empty dishes onto a tray.

'Me too,' says Beulah, 'Though I need the loo first.'

'Same here,' Eva pipes up, stacking some plates.

Soon, we're all getting up and heading for the nearest ladies'.

After touching up our lippy and doing other 'necessities', we return to the office. Valerie still has her blinds down so there's no telling if she's there or not, but I quietly go back to my desk and get on with the report, just in case.

4

We settle into our work, the murmur of conversation and the odd chuckle keeping the atmosphere light and friendly.

'I've made a few notes on the new line,' Francesca tells me after a while, showing me her notebook. She's used bullet points to list all the advantages:

· colourful
· unique
· clear fonts
· suitable for adults and kids
· suitable for males and females
· machine washable.

I frown, taking the pad from her. 'Are they really suitable for men?' I query. 'I mean, do men *want* their names on their clothes? And what about the colours? There are more shades here for females than males. Even the blue and green are very soft, pastel shades. Wouldn't men prefer bolder colours? Maybe with black and grey, too?'

'I hadn't thought of that,' she admits, looking a little despondent.

'They're pastel because they're a spring collection,' Siobhan explains.

'But aren't they missing a golden opportunity?' I frown. 'Christmas would be a great time to buy kids stuff with their names on. They're a practical gift but also fun because of the novelty of the personalisation. Surely, they could do some in bold colours for the winter? That would be a much better marketing strategy because people would still have the option of the paler colours if they preferred them but would be more likely to buy brighter colours for Christmas. In my opinion, anyway.' I add the last bit rather hastily, in case anyone thinks I'm being critical of the new range.

'You've got a good point there,' Siobhan says. 'That's worth feeding back to the designer.'

'Is it?' I gape at her. 'I wouldn't want to offend anyone. I mean, it's only an observation. My personal opinion. And I love the pastel colours.' I'm on edge now, in case I'm perceived as a troublemaker. Everyone was so enthralled with the range, I'm sure no one else has thought of questioning it. 'I'm just trying to look at it from all angles,' I go on. 'Sort of... playing the devil's advocate. Because members of the public are bound to find downsides to everything. It's best to get them ironed out so we've got an answer for them if they do.'

'Absolutely,' Siobhan says. 'Well, I'll leave you to it. Make a list of pros *and* cons. We'll run it by the designer before we print anything, though. We don't want him to think we're being negative.'

Francesca and I take another look at the clothes on the rail. I pick out the damaged one and examine it closely.

My stomach churns with guilt. I know I should own up to damaging it, but what good would it do now? I'd only get the sack and then the department would be left short-staffed, with Melanie going on maternity leave. Besides, no one was hurt. The offending item will be written off along with all the other rejects, and no one will be any the wiser. I'm sure the manufacturers can afford to lose one measly top in the grand scheme of things, and the *Chronicle* will be in the clear. Thinking about it logically, I'm actually helping by not admitting it. If Francesca had to do this job on her own, she'd never have thought of all the ideas I have. How could she? No one's brain works the same way as mine. I think about that for a moment. I'm not sure if it's a good thing or not.

'Has the paper worked with this client before?' I ask, running a finger over the tear.

'No. That's what's making it so exciting. They're new. Valerie's keen to make a good impression, especially with their range being so popular in the States. We're the first to feature these in the UK.

They're bound to be a big hit, and she wants us to be at the forefront of their success.'

'I don't see how a regional newspaper can benefit that much from introducing a new clothing line, though?' I pout. 'I mean, I get we'll be paid for the feature, and we might get repeat business when they bring out their next season's line, but apart from that, we're not making anything from it, are we?'

'If it gets onto the telly that we've introduced this successful new brand, we'll get the publicity,' Francesca explains. 'The *Daily Chronicle* will be on the news and mentioned in all the national papers. Anything that raises our profile's a good thing, but this could go global.'

She sounds very enthusiastic, and I get the premise, but I'm not convinced. 'What's stopping them being featured in other regionals as well as ours, though?'

She shrugs. 'They'll have signed a contract awarding us exclusivity.'

'I suppose,' I concede. 'It still seems a bit of an odd way to publicise a new brand. You'd think they'd want it in *all* the papers to get the word out.'

'Valerie's very particular about what gets into *Woman Matters*,' Francesca explains. 'She'll have insisted on it.'

'She seems to be a shrewd businesswoman,' I admit.

'I'd love to be as good as her one day,' Francesca replies wistfully.

I gawp at her. Francesca's a pretty girl, with wild, red curls and a sort of boho style. Today, she's wearing a lovely blue and white maxi dress with boots. It skims over her figure, flattering her curves. I can't believe she'd want to be anything like the staid, stuck-up Valerie Fulton-Coombes. I get that the woman's successful, but she doesn't seem happy. Even if she does have good taste in music.

I turn my attention back to the damaged hoodie. The tear seems to be getting worse with the loose thread just running an even bigger hole. Furthermore, the thread itself is very thin, making for a rather flimsy top layer of fabric.

'I don't think they'll be very hardwearing,' I observe. 'Look at this, Fran—er—Francesca.'

She smiles, walking towards me. 'It's only Francesca when Valerie's around,' she says. 'She insists on calling everyone by their full name. To everyone else, I'm usually Fran.'

I nod. I'd noticed Valerie's penchant for calling me Liberty and thought it was just her way of being condescending. After all, I'd been introduced to her as Libby. It's obviously just her way.

'I always think of you as Fran,' I admit. 'Francesca seems far too formal for someone like you.'

She gapes at me, and I wonder if I've offended her. 'I mean—you're like a free spirit. Not tied down with conventional fashion or ideas.'

She raises her eyebrows.

'In a good way,' I explain quickly. 'You've got your own sense of style, a unique look. A brilliant one, of course.'

'Thank you, I think.' She's frowning quizzically now.

'You're welcome. Look.' I hurriedly show her the garment, eager to change the subject. 'See how this just keeps on running?' I hold up the thread. 'It's not going to last long on a child. The fabric needs to be much sturdier. Even for an adult, I don't think the quality of the material's good enough to withstand normal wear and tear.'

'What do you think you're doing with that?' Valerie's shriek makes us both jerk around. Her face is bright red, and she's scowling at me. 'You've just added to the damage, you stupid girl! It wasn't that bad before—it's totally ruined now!'

My whole body burns hot and feels like lead. I can't move. I'm totally stunned. The room is silent yet again. And that familiar feeling of dread has just overtaken me. *Shit!*

'I w-was examining the quality and workmanship,' I stammer. 'I think there might be a problem with it.'

'I think I know *exactly* where the problem lies, young lady,' Valerie snarls. 'And I'm *looking* at her.'

My heart sinks. 'But look.' I hold up the garment. 'The thread shouldn't just keep on pulling. It should be fastened off at regular points to avoid that happening. And see how thin it is? It won't be durable enough for regular use.'

Not for the first time today, Valerie looks furious. In fact, she looks like she's about to burst. Not her best look, to be honest, but I don't think I'll mention it right now.

She marches over and wrenches the hoodie from my hand. 'This range has been highly praised all over America. How *dare* you suggest it's poor quality?'

'I'm sorry. I didn't mean to insult it. I'm just doing a critique for the feature. We've been told to list all the pros and cons that's all.'

'Are you answering me back?' Valerie's lips are so tightly squeezed together, her pink lipstick seems to have turned white.

'No.' I swallow hard. 'I was just... answering.'

Siobhan steps forward. 'She's right, Valerie,' she says firmly. 'I asked the girls to make a list. We must be seen to give a fair assessment of the range. Of course, we'll run it by the designers before anything goes to print. We won't be publishing anything derogatory about them or their product. But it's only right to give a fair review. Don't you agree?'

Valerie stares at her, but Siobhan just smiles politely.

'Well... er... yes, yes, of course. What I meant was, why was Liberty making the damage worse? There was no need to add to the tear.' It's odd to see Valerie so flummoxed, and I guess people don't stand up to her too often. I'm pleased Siobhan had the guts to defend me, though.

'I think the thread just ran even farther when she picked it up,' Siobhan says. She points to the garment in Valerie's clenched hand. 'If you look, you'll see that the top layer of fabric is a very fine knit. As Libby said, if it hasn't been fastened off, it'll just run and run. It's unfortunate, but you can't argue with the facts. We can speak to the designers about it, though. Maybe promote it as a luxury item for occasional wear instead of everyday fashion. There'll be a way around it.'

I wish I had Siobhan's confidence. She sounds very matter of fact and not at all concerned at the 'just about to explode' expression on Valerie's beetroot-coloured face.

'Right, well... I'll leave you to sort it out,' Valerie replies through gritted teeth.

She hands the garment to Siobhan and returns quickly to her office, the heels of her Manolo Blahniks clicking noisily across the tiled floor.

I decide to keep my head down for the rest of the day, in an attempt to also keep my job. I type a report of pros and cons of the clothing range, keeping my findings firmly on the computer screen and off my lips.

I take the opportunity to text James on my way home. I've missed him badly today.

How's your day going? Lxx

He answers right away.

Okay. The missing child turned up safe and well, but we're still investigating who took him. Jxx

Thank goodness. Are you coming back to my place after work? Lxx

I hold my breath while I wait for his reply.

Yeah, I'd love to. Need to go home first for a change of clothes and see Suzanne. Seems all the paperwork got soaked in the flood. Jxx

Oh, no! He'll be even more stressed now. He relied on her getting that information to the solicitor today.

Is any of it salvageable? Lxx

Not sure. She's taken a pile of it back to the flat to try to dry it out. We'll know later. Jxx

I huff. As soon as Suzanne gets him back in that flat, she'll find all sorts of stuff to talk about to stop him from coming out with me. Poor James is having a tough enough day as it is, without having to spend the whole evening with her. *Not to mention the night.* My stomach twists at the idea. I never thought I was the jealous type, but the image of her spending the night in his flat with him just makes my blood boil. What makes it worse is that *I* haven't even spent a night there with him yet.

I'm kicking myself now for ever discovering that Suzanne's new lover was the con man, Oliver bloody Reynolds. If I'd just kept quiet, she could be still making a damn fool of herself with him while James and I would be free to have some fun.

I sigh as I board the Tube. Of course, it wouldn't have been as easy as that. It never is in my life.

An hour later, when I'm lounging in front of the TV, it comes as no surprise to hear my phone ping with another message from James.

Really sorry, but I'm not going to make it tonight after all. We've got paper scattered all around the flat on radiators and in the airing cupboard. Even tried a hairdryer but it's soaked through. Not sure any of it will be readable once it's dried out. I'm trying to get some sense out of Suzanne about what was actually said about the house, but it's like pulling teeth. I'm going to keep trying. I'm truly sorry, but we need to sort this out as soon as poss. Miss you. Jxx

'I knew it!' I slam the phone down angrily on the sofa.

'James?' Cassie frowns at me in sympathy.

'Yep. Suzanne's got him dangling on a piece of string now.'

'Does that mean you're not seeing him tonight?'

'Yep.'

'Aw, sorry, hon. If it's any consolation, Rob's working late tonight so I'm staying in, too.'

She comes over and gives me a big hug.

'It's not his fault,' I say with a sigh afterwards.

She snuggles down onto the opposite sofa. 'What's she done this time?' Cassie shakes her head.

I go on to explain about the wet paperwork and then text James back.

Hi J. It's okay. You need to get it done. I understand that. Can't wait to see you again, though. Hope it's soon. Good luck with the dentistry tonight, lol! Miss you. Lxx

I giggle at the thought of him ramming his knee into her chest and yanking out her pearly whites with a huge pair of pliers.

Cassie leaves the room to make us a cuppa and comes back with chocolate biscuits as well.

'You can have two, then I'm putting the tin back,' she says, handing me my cup.

'Spoilsport.'

'You wouldn't thank me if you ate the whole packet and couldn't fit into your dress tomorrow.'

She's right. I always like to plan my outfit beforehand, and I've put aside a smart, cherry-red shift dress with a matching jacket to wear tomorrow. It's from Dolce and Gabbana, and it's absolutely gorgeous.

It was one of Cassie's that she bought to wear to an event and never wore again. I get lots of my clothes that way. She's such a lovely friend.

'Okay,' I say, taking two biscuits from the tin.

'And for not moaning about it, I might just let you borrow my Pigalles to wear with it,' she says with a smile as she takes the tin from the table and disappears into the kitchen.

I nearly spill my tea with shock. She's talking about her Pigalle Follies Patent Agathe, a beautiful pair of Louboutin court shoes in a swirly pattern of shades of dark red and ivory.

'You can also use my ivory bag to match,' she says, coming back into the room sans biscuits.

'You are the absolute best,' I tell her, reaching up for a hug as she passes my sofa.

'I know,' she says with a modest smile and gets back to her own tea and biscuits.

'I don't know what I'd do without you, honestly,' I tell her. 'I mean it.' The thought of not being around her makes me want to cry, and my voice suddenly goes wobbly.

'Hey, don't worry, I'm not going anywhere,' she says, surprised. 'Don't cry, you'll set me off in a minute.'

'It's true, though.' I compose myself. It's silly. Neither of us is going anywhere—I hope.

Cassie sprawls out lazily on her sofa and moans. 'This is great.'

We're both in our loungewear, watching *The Devil Wears Prada* for the umpteenth time. It's one of our favourites.

'You mean, you wouldn't rather be out somewhere nice with Rob?'

'No. I mean, I really like him, don't get me wrong. And I love going out and spending time with him. He's so lovely. It's just that it's nice sometimes to be at home with you.'

She's right, I realise. I shouldn't get so het up about James. I know his work is important, and this business with Suzanne is upsetting him just as much as it annoys me, but it can't be helped. *Or rather, it could be, but murdering her would only land me in prison. Then I'd never be with James.*

'I agree.'

She balks, 'Seriously?'

She's staring at me now, over her mug.

'Yes. It's like old times, just you and me.'

'Oh, no! Now, we just sound like an old married couple.'

I know she's spending more and more time over at Rob's, and I wouldn't be surprised if one day she announced she was planning to move in with him. I mean, it's what people do, isn't it? But I can't bear to think about it. Not now. I couldn't manage this place on my wages, and I wouldn't want to live here alone. I push the thought to the back of my mind. It's not happening. Not yet, anyway.

'That woman reminds me of Valerie,' I say, using my biscuit to gesture at Meryl Streep on the TV. She's playing the part of the horrible boss.

'She can't be that evil, surely?' Cassie looks horrified.

'No, not in that way. She just seems quite manipulative. Siobhan seems to like her, but I don't think Valerie cares about her one bit. Valerie even made out that one of Siobhan's ideas was her own.'

'Siobhan should leave, then.' It all sounds so simple when Cassie says it.

'No, she shouldn't. She should be running the place. She's great, and she knows all about the business. She'd make a fantastic boss.'

'Maybe that's what Valerie's worried about,' Cassie says, pursing her lips.

'I think you're right.'

'Did you know she wants to get married?'

'Valerie?' I stare at her, almost choking on my chocolate digestive.

'No, silly. Siobhan.'

'I knew she was in a long-term relationship but not that she was engaged.' I sit up a little straighter, my legs still outstretched across the sofa.

I've only been out with Siobhan socially once, and I liked her straight away. She's part of a gang that often joins Rob and Cassie on nights out, so my bestie knows her better than I do.

'She can't afford the wedding yet, but if she got promoted, she might have a chance,' Cassie says, nodding. 'They want to buy their own house, too, but again, they need the money. At the moment, Siobhan gives practically every penny to her mum to pay for her dad's nursing home. He has Alzheimer's and some days he doesn't even seem to know who she is.'

I gape at Cassie incredulously. Siobhan never talks about personal stuff at work. I had no idea she was going through all this.

'Will her dad get better?'

Cassie shrugs. 'Who knows? I think it's doubtful. That sort of thing usually gets progressively worse, not better.'

'What about her mum?'

'She's riddled with arthritis, apparently,' Cassie says, glumly. 'She has a part-time clerical job but doesn't make enough to keep herself *and* pay for her husband's care. Siobhan said she pays for his home because she's the one who insisted he have somewhere half-decent instead of what her mum could afford. She takes full responsibility for him and ensures that he always gets visitors.'

'That's awful.' I feel so sad for Siobhan and her family and even worse because I had no idea about any of this. 'Is her fiancé supportive?'

Cassie nods with a smile. 'Yeah, he sounds brilliant. He doesn't earn a huge amount, but he does the best he can for all of them. Siobhan's head over heels about him. They're trying to put aside as much as they can between them, but she reckons it'll be years before she can walk down the aisle.'

Siobhan always looks immaculate and is the most organised and unflappable person I know. She seems to have everything—the looks, the job, the clothes. I never would have guessed she had to save up for things the same way I do. Well, maybe not *quite* in the same way I do. I can't imagine Siobhan O'Leary shouting at her VISA operator because they won't raise the credit limit on her card, for a start. It just wouldn't be her style. But I'm still amazed and horrified. Poor Siobhan.

5

'I've made a list of all the pros and cons of the new range and written a report on it, like you said,' I tell Siobhan as soon as she joins us in the office the next day. She's smiling, as usual, and my stomach churns knowing what she's going through.

'I don't know what you've got against that collection,' Kiki remarks. 'I think they're great. Even if they haven't got my name. I'd settle for Keira, but they don't even have that.'

'It's not that I've got anything *against* the clothes. I just have to weigh up both sides, and unfortunately, although they look nice, they've got far more cons.'

'I'd wear one,' Eva exclaims. 'They'd be great for the gym.'

I roll my eyes in disbelief. Even if they were top notch and produced by a bona fide designer, I couldn't see the glamorous Eva wearing a hoodie or a T-shirt even as exercise wear. Besides, one good stretch and they'd probably fall to bits.

'You need to take a closer look. I know they're very pretty, but the quality just isn't there,' I tell her, shaking my head. 'I'd hate to think how they wash. Do we get to test them?' I'm watching Siobhan sip her water. She looks thoughtful, and I hope she's not regretting helping me get the job.

'No.' She's clearly relieved.

I have to admit it's probably a good thing. Everyone wants me to write a positive article about them, but I can't lie.

'Shall we read each other's?' Fran suggests a few minutes later.

I've just added a few nice things about the collection, saying how cohesive it is, and the good variety of T-shirts, sweatshirts, and hoodies. It's damn near impossible to find some positives when I know that truthfully, it's rubbish, but I'm trying hard.

We print them out and swap reports. I can't believe I'm reading about the same clothes. Fran has gone into detail about the colours, the way the writing stands out in the white print, the gorgeous font—which I agree with, admittedly—then the softness of the fabric, the light, airy feel of the loose knit and the luxurious texture. She's also waxed lyrical about them being made in Britain, which I have to admit is a massive plus point these days.

'You haven't mentioned the tear,' I tell her, once I've finished.

She's staring at me. 'You seem to have mentioned nothing *but* the flaming tear,' she says, horrified. 'They won't be able to use any of this.'

'What?' Frowning, I go over to where she's sitting, staring at the paper in her hand.

'You've practically said the whole collection's crap,' she whispers. 'Look, it says it's *unsuitable for everyday wear because of the fragility of the materials used.*' She points to the phrase. 'Valerie will go mad if she sees that.'

'But it's true. I can't lie about it. And besides, Siobhan said she'll run it all past the designers before anything gets printed. They'll come up with some blurb about it being a luxury item for occasional wear, and we'll rewrite it all accordingly. This is just a brainstorming exercise.' I shrug, taking the paper from her. I haven't been downright rude about the product. In fact, I think I've put it very carefully and succinctly, but I had to tell the truth. If my name's going on the report, I want it to be accurate. What if someone bought a hoodie because I said it was a fabulous product and then it got ruined on the first wear? They'd sue me. Or at least, discredit me. I'd never work in fashion again. My whole new career would be over before it's even started.

'Girls, take a look at these,' Siobhan calls over from the central table. 'It's the photos to go with the article.' She's spread out some large pictures of various models wearing the new collection.

'They look great,' I admit, dropping the reports on the table to pick up a photo.

'This is what convinced Valerie to run the feature,' Siobhan says. 'See how this one brings out the blue of the little boy's eyes?'

The colours look soft, and the white stands out with enough contrast to easily read the names. I have to concede that they look absolutely great in the photos. They've been filmed against a soft-focus background of greenery and flowers, which enhances the gentle hues of the clothes beautifully.

'They are lovely,' Fran agrees.

I study the pictures carefully. 'We could do with a close-up of the fabric,' I suggest. 'They look like a much closer weave in these.' I go over to the rail and pick out one of the hoodies.

'This is all we've got to work with,' Siobhan says, biting the inside of her cheek.

I frown. 'Can't we get our photographers to take more? I mean, we could do with some more detailed stuff like the labels.' The only tag visible is one with the company name 'Rebel (London)' on it. I thoroughly check the inside of the garment but can't find any washing instructions. However, I do find a tiny label with 'Made in Bangladesh' written on it.

'I thought they were produced here in the U.K.?' I query, showing the others the tag.

'That's what it said in the press release,' Fran says.

'There's nothing here to say what the composition of materials is, or how to care for the garment or anything,' I point out. 'Just where it's made. Which *isn't* in Britain.'

Siobhan stares at the label. She takes the item from me and double-checks it, carefully turning it inside out. 'That can't be right,' she mutters and goes over to the rail to examine more of the clothes.

Her pale expression tells me they all state the same. I'm a little surprised that she finds it quite so important, but its origin is obviously a relevant attribute to the collection.

'I'm just going to have a word with Valerie,' she says, taking some of the clothes with her.

Fran and I return to our desks. 'I'd better change my report,' she says despondently. She pulls the article back up on her screen and taps at her keyboard.

I quickly check my phone. As I'd hoped, there's a text from James.

Really sorry about last night. Had a hard time with Suzanne and all that damn paperwork. Took all evening to wade through it. I've handed it to the solicitor but not sure it's what he needs. Waiting to hear from him today. Jxx

I feel so sorry for him. That woman's such a pain.

How about going for a swim later? Lxx

The idea came to me in a flash of inspiration. I don't get many of those, so I have to make the most of it. It'll be a good way to de-stress and might ease James' back after sleeping on that little sofa of his. Also, I get to see him in his trunks all wet and…

'They're coming.' Fran warns me just in time as Valerie comes storming towards us, closely followed by Siobhan.

I quickly pop my iPhone into my bag, pulling out a tissue at the same time so as not to arouse suspicion. I'm not sure what the rules are about personal calls here, but I don't think I've seen anyone else use a mobile since I arrived.

Valerie stalks straight past us and goes over to the rail. She gives the clothes a cursory glance, pursing her lips. I notice the click-clicking as she taps her foot, too. She's fuming. I'm not sure what the big deal is, but something's got her riled—and just for a change, it's not me.

Fran and I are given the job of wheeling the rail into Valerie's office, while Siobhan scoops up all the photos and follows us. I can see now why the boss has such a large workspace, as we position the rail near a window and Siobhan puts the pictures on her desk.

'Thank you.' Valerie's words are clipped, and we all leave as soon as we can. Her blinds are all rising as we go back to our work, and I guess she's going to spy on us for a bit.

'I'll do some research on the product's popularity,' I say. 'Maybe get some facts and figures for the article.'

'Good idea.' Siobhan looks impressed. 'Fran, see if there's anything similar on the market and make comparisons if there is.'

'No problem,' Fran says with a smile.

An hour later, I wish I hadn't suggested looking into the product at all. I can't find anything about it anywhere. I know it's supposed to be a big hit on the other side of the pond, but there doesn't appear to be any reports about it on the web. There are no photos, no write-ups, or reviews, not even an advert.

'This is crazy,' I say, shaking my head. 'For something as popular as we're led to believe, I can't find a single word about it.'

'Maybe you could ask him for more info,' Fran says, indicating a man who's just entered the room.

I have to look twice to convince myself it's not George Clooney. The silver fox beams at us, and the room goes quiet as we all take in his beauty. His teeth are perfectly aligned and gleaming. His copious hair is slightly wavy with streaks of silver and grey. He walks with the grace and confidence of a slightly older man, possibly in his late forties or early fifties. His Armani suit fits him perfectly, and his crisp, white shirt is unbuttoned at the neck in a slightly casual manner.

Siobhan goes straight over and shakes his hand before showing him into Valerie's office.

'That's the designer,' Fran whispers.

I think I've just had a Diet Coke moment. I'm still watching him as he shakes Valerie's hand and sits opposite her, chuckling.

'She doesn't look very happy,' Fran mutters.

I can't help thinking how hard it would be to remain cross at a guy like him. He seems so maverick and laid-back that everything would just wash over him. He's still smiling, although Valerie's pointing her finger and saying something I wish I could hear. She looks quite harsh, but he seems to be laughing it off. Talk about water off a duck's back!

'Don't stare.' Siobhan's just returned.

'Sorry,' I mumble, looking back at my screen. 'I can't find anything about this range being out in America. Will it be under a different name?'

Siobhan frowns. 'I don't think so.' She reaches over and presses a few keys on my computer, bringing up the glossy American magazines that report on the latest fashions. Nothing. She taps some more, but still there's no sign of it. 'That's odd.' She looks sideways to where 'George' is talking to Valerie.

'Maybe we'll know more when Valerie's spoken with him,' I suggest.

Siobhan nods. 'I certainly hope so.' We gaze towards Valerie's office. They're both smiling in there now, sipping coffee.

'So, he's the designer,' I say, half to myself. I can't help thinking he *is* rather dishy, though a bit old for me, and still not a patch on James.

'Yeah. That's Quinton Bellis,' she replies, her eyes narrowing at him.

'You don't like him much, do you?' I ask her quietly.

She stares at me.

'But Valerie seems to,' I continue in a murmur.

'That's the trouble,' she whispers, leaning closer to me. 'She hasn't known him five minutes. I think she's just taken in by his charm and good looks.'

I frown. Siobhan's either worried about Valerie or jealous of her. 'Is that a problem?'

'It could be.' She walks back over to her own desk.

I glance back at Valerie's office. The boss certainly looks happy and relaxed. It's the first time I've seen her smile. She actually looks quite pretty and much younger. She should do it more often.

'Well, it looks like I'll be here forever doing this,' Fran says with a sigh. She's scowling at her computer screen.

'Have you found a lot, then?'

'Loads, though nothing *exactly* the same,' she says, pursing her lips. 'But the idea's hardly unique, like the blurb claimed.'

I shake my head. 'Printing names on clothes isn't new, but is it a new-fangled font or material or something?' I can't help thinking no other company would use such cheap fabric and then try to charge such an extortionate price for them. I mean, who wants to pay seventy quid for a hoodie that falls apart the first time you touch it? It's doomed not to make money—particularly in the long run. And talking of long runs, I wonder if Valerie's shown him the torn hoodie yet. I just hope he doesn't twig that it was caused by the zip on the rail cover. *Or by me.*

Fran's sorting through files of fonts to see if any match those on the clothing. I'm pretty sure she'll find them—probably a couple of the free ones you can get from the internet. A thought occurs to me, and I quickly tap 'Rebel (London)' into my search engine.

The murmurs in the office suddenly stop, and I look up to see what's caught everyone's attention. The door to Valerie's office is now open.

'Ladies, I think you remember the designer, Quinton Bellis?' Valerie says, showing him off like a prize poodle.

'Hello again, girls,' he says, offering us a gleaming smile. He catches my eye. 'I don't think I recognise *you*,' he says, striding towards me.

Valerie picks up the pace behind him. 'Oh, no, this is our new recruit, Liberty Lawrence,' she says. 'Liberty, this is Mr Quinton Bellis, designer of 'Fame' and co-director of Rebel (London).'

He beams at me as we shake hands. He truly is gorgeous.

'Nice to meet you, Mr Bellis,' I say.

'Call me Quinn,' he says. 'All my friends do.' He winks at me, and I smile politely, although I can't help feeling a little uncomfortable. I'm not sure if it's the clamminess of his hand or the scowl on Valerie's face that causes it, but I wish they'd go away and leave me alone.

'This is the team working on the Fame collection,' Valerie says, ushering him away from me a little. 'You know Siobhan, and this is Francesca, whom I think you met on your last visit.'

They all smile and nod at each other, but Valerie doesn't give them time to speak before announcing, 'There was a silly mix-up with the collection we were sent, unfortunately.' She gives a little laugh. 'That was a rail of mock-up rejects, as you probably guessed. Mr Bellis is organising another set of clothes to be sent straight away.'

There's a collective sigh of relief.

'Well that certainly explains everything,' Siobhan says with a gracious smile. 'We knew Mr Bellis wouldn't have intentionally sent us anything substandard.'

'Of course not. I'll be having words with our distributors,' he says with a nod. 'Ladies, I can only apologise for all the time you've wasted.'

'Oh, that's not a problem,' Valerie assures him. 'These things happen.'

I can't help wishing she'd been so understanding with me earlier, but she's clearly captivated by the man's piercing blue eyes and perfect cheekbones. My mum would probably be just the same in the presence of such a hunk.

'Well, you have the information sheets, so perhaps you could use those for your feature in the meantime?' His voice is as soft as silk, and I can imagine it being hard to refuse him anything he asked. *But not impossible.*

'How soon can we expect the replacement samples, Mr Bellis?' I ask with a smile. 'Obviously, we can only take so much from the promotional material. Things like quality, cut, colour, and so forth can only be determined from the actual product, and of course, we want to write an accurate account of the collection.'

I continue to smile despite the look of indignation on the man's face, and the expression of horror on everyone else's. Valerie looks murderous. I can only assume his question was supposed to be rhetorical. *Oh, shit!*

'Of course,' he says with a nervous laugh. He's smiling at me, but I can see the strain in his jaw. His eyes are narrowed, and I suddenly don't find him as fanciable as I did. 'All I meant was, to save time, you might use the dossier while you await the new garments.'

'I'm sure Liberty didn't mean to cause any offence,' Valerie says coolly, her eyes flashing at me.

'Oh, no, I'd never do that,' I assure him, my smile firmly pasted in place. 'I was just hoping we won't have to wait long to see your fabulous range. We're all so excited about it.'

Flattery seems to do the trick, and Mr Bellis' face relaxes again, as does everyone around me, if the sighs of relief are anything to go by. Even Valerie looks slightly less fierce. *But only slightly.*

'Well, I'm sure Mr Bellis has better things to do than chit-chat around here,' Valerie says, ushering him away from us. Though I suspect it's *me* she's trying to get him away from.

I want to protest that I had lots more questions to ask, but I think it safer to keep quiet. I'm also aggrieved that she regards a perfectly reasonable query about the delivery as 'chit-chat.' I'm hoping she's already asked all the relevant questions and will fill us in once he's gone, but something tells me she won't have. Caught under his spell, I can imagine the duff delivery was the last thing on her mind.

It looks like I'll need to do some investigating of my own if I'm ever going to get the lowdown on this. I turn back to my computer, where the search engine is showing very little about the company. It seems that Rebel (London) is a limited company that designs, manufactures, and distributes quality clothing and accessories worldwide. I check out their listing with Companies House.

Oh, no!

My stomach lurches. I glance over to the door, but Valerie and her guest have disappeared. Siobhan is working at her desk. I minimise my screen and go over to her.

'Have you got a death wish?' she asks me. 'I thought Valerie was going to strangle you on the spot when you asked about the delivery.'

I swallow hard. 'I wasn't being rude. I just wanted to know so we could get on with the feature,' I explain.

'Libby, you need to be much more careful about when you open your mouth,' she says. 'Sometimes it's best to wait and see what happens instead of plunging in with both feet.'

'I'm sorry,' I say, thinking hard about what she's telling me. Maybe I shouldn't have mentioned the Bangladeshi labels or the poor quality of the garments.

After all, where did it get me? Everyone thinks I was insulting the range, and Valerie's even angrier with me than ever. Siobhan must be embarrassed by me, and everyone else regards me as the office entertainment. Quinton Bellis seems to have an answer for everything, and the charm to convince Valerie that black's white. Anything I say that puts Rebel, Fame, or the handsome Mr Bellis in a bad light will be taken as criticism—even if it *is* true.

I decide to keep my findings to myself, at least for the time being. I've got myself in enough trouble already, and it's only my second day here. I go back to my desk and try to keep my mouth shut for the rest of the day

The office is a bit quieter than yesterday, and I wonder if it's because I'm not saying much. I figure it's safer that way.

I sigh with relief when it's time to go home. Everyone says goodbye with a smile, and I'm glad to have made some good friends here, even if I have made at least one enemy. I'm looking forward to going for a swim with James tonight and it'll be a great way to unwind.

As I head for the Tube, I check my phone.

Hi Libby, hope your day went well. The solicitor just rang to say those papers Suzanne fetched were the wrong ones, so I'm taking her back to the house to retrieve the correct ones this time. I don't want to delay

any longer. We desperately need to know who owns the house. I'm so sorry, but it means we'll have to postpone tonight. Love the idea of a swim, though. Could we make it tomorrow instead? Can't wait to see you but can't rely on Suzanne to do the job properly. I promise things'll be much easier once this is all sorted. Jxx

My stomach churns. I knew Suzanne would try to ruin everything for me and James. She won't get away with it, though. He convinced me over the weekend that I mean much more to him than she does, and he can't wait to be rid of her. I know he'll be gutted about tonight, especially after last night, but he's right—she can't be trusted. If the house turns out to belong to Oliver Reynolds, there's no way James will be ploughing any more money into its repairs. Even if James only owns half of it, his solicitor will have to ensure Reynolds pays his share of the bills. Then it'll be even more legal wrangles to determine whether James can go ahead and sell it. This is all such a nightmare.

Hi James. Loads has happened, and I can't wait to tell you all about it. I understand though, it can't be helped. Hope you manage to resolve the issue this evening, and I look forward to seeing you tomorrow. I'll miss you again tonight ;) Lxxx

There. I'm proud of how grown up I'm being about it all, though I'm desperately disappointed. But I know it's not James' fault.

As I board the Tube, it occurs to me just how much blame I've put on James in the past. Mum always said I had a fiery temper, and I'm afraid I might have taken stuff out on him he truly didn't deserve. Crikey, I even implied he had a kid in front of all his work colleagues once. *Hmm, not my finest hour.*

I'm standing, as usual, while the world and his wife seem to be piling into the carriage. I'm being squeezed and prodded by passengers, but it doesn't stop the warmth inside my tummy as I think about James. I really like him.

'Ouch!' I shout, a sudden pain searing my left foot and shooting straight up my leg.

'Sorry.'

A stupid man with sweat patches and bad breath has just trodden on my Louboutin—or rather, *Cassie's* Louboutin. She'll go mad if it's ruined, and I'll never be allowed to borrow anything ever again. It's too crowded for me to look down and see if he's caused any damage to the shiny leather, so now I'll have to worry about it all the way home. I can't believe anyone could be so clumsy. The warmth in my stomach has turned to burning bile as I clench my mouth shut and try to murder the imbecile with 'Paddington' stares and looks of disgust. Trouble is, he's not even looking at me, so all my efforts are wasted. And so, the idiot lives to ruin another beautiful and expensive designer shoe—there's just no justice in this world.

6

I refuse to let Suzanne Harper get to me. I've missed James all night *again,* but today is a new day—and I have a plan. I'm seeing him tonight for definite—they found some papers last night that James thinks must be the right ones, so at least that's all sorted. He'll give them to his solicitors today and let them deal with it.

Besides, I have better things to worry about than his mouldy old ex-wife. I'm on a mission to make Valerie Fulton-Coombes like me. She obviously likes Quinton Bellis—though I've gone off him a bit, to be honest—so I won't be saying anything against him *or* his collection. Though I might *think* a few things.

I've borrowed a pair of Cassie's Manolo Blahniks to go with my blue shift dress with matching jacket. I swear that girl owns more shoes than Carrie Bradshaw. Not that I'm complaining, she always lets me borrow them, and I could never afford a collection like that myself. Luckily, the Louboutins were fine yesterday, so I didn't mention the clumsy oaf with the big feet.

Valerie wore Manolos again yesterday, so I'm hoping she might warm to me a little, having something in common. I even looked into Baroque music and found a group called REBEL who play that sort of thing on authentic instruments. I've ordered a CD of theirs for Valerie, being as how the group has the same name as the client we're working with. Although the musicians pronounce their name Re-bel after the French composer and capitalise it. I played some of their music on YouTube, and it's really good. I usually prefer modern pop stuff myself, but this was quite catchy. Cassie said her mum would love it—she's ever so classy and cultured, what with all her travelling and hobnobbing. I hope Valerie will appreciate it—and *me*.

My hair has actually behaved itself today and I've tied it in a neat bun with just a couple of loose wisps to soften the look a little, and my make-up is perfect—it should be, too, it took long enough.

I got up extra early today as I'm taking the Tube over to Fulham to surprise James before he goes to work. I know we won't get more than a few minutes together, but I badly want to see him and show him I'm supporting him through all this mess.

I arrive at his flat and press the buzzer.

'Hello?' Suzanne answers. *Damn!* I had hoped she'd still be in bed or on her way to work or something.

'Hi, it's Libby.' I try to sound friendly.

'Oh.' She sounds surprised. 'Come up.'

She opens the door when I reach the flat, and I follow her in, more than a little irked that *she's* inviting me into my boyfriend's home. Her coat and bag are hanging in the hallway as though they belong there, and I notice there are little knick-knacks all over the shelves and windowsills that weren't there before. I can even smell her perfume in the air. She certainly seems to have made herself at home.

'I just wanted a quick word with James,' I say, looking around the kitchen. Surely, he can't still be in bed.

'He's already left for work,' she says, after taking a sip of her coffee. 'Should I give him a message?'

She's wearing a Chanel suit, her hair up in the kind of perfect chignon I can only dream of wearing. Her scarlet lipstick shines under the bright spotlights. I thought I looked good, but she's gorgeous.

'No, it's okay. It's nothing important.' I feel sick. I wish I hadn't come. It had never occurred to me that he might go to work early. I wonder if it was an attempt to get away from her.

'Of course, it's not. You shouldn't keep bothering him, you know?' she says, shaking her head.

I was about to leave but turn to stare at her.

'He has so much going on at the moment, he doesn't need you hanging about all the time on top of

everything else,' she goes on with a patronising sneer.
The cheek!

'The only reason James has so much to deal
with right now is because of you,' I tell her, my heart
pounding. 'You've done nothing but cause him more
work and aggravation because of your selfish actions.
The poor man can't even sleep in his own bed because
of you. And it looks like you're taking over the whole
flat.' I wave my hand in the air, gesturing to the
cookery books on the shelf, the apron hanging behind
the door, and the large plant taking up half the counter.

'Well, I do live here, now,' she says with a
condescending smile. 'Of course, I've had to make the
place a little more homely for the two of us. It's what a
good woman does. And I've told James he's more than
welcome to share the bed. It'd be just like old times.'

'You don't *live* here!' My voice rises as my
blood boils. 'You're a guest in his flat and an
unwelcome one at that. Of course, he doesn't want to
sleep with you—you're his *ex*-wife for a reason. He just
wants the whole mess cleared up so he can get back to
normal.'

'It feels quite normal to *me* the way things are,'
she says airily. 'But then, you wouldn't know about
that, would you? In fact, I'm sure there are a lot of
things about me and James you wouldn't know about.'

Her smarmy face looks so slappable, it makes
my hand tremble. I won't give her the satisfaction,

though. Nor will I risk getting her Clarins Everlasting Foundation all over my fingers.

'You're a bitch, Suzanne Harper,' I say through clenched teeth. 'A bitch and a parasite. You need to learn to stand on your own two feet and stop relying on men to help you all the time. Why don't you just grow up?'

I leave, slamming the door behind me. Its echo surrounds me as I run down the stairs, my heart pounding and tears threatening my eyes.

I take deep breaths of fresh air once I'm out of the building and stride towards the Tube station. That cow won't make me ruin my perfect make-up any more than I'll let her ruin my relationship with James. I was right about her being a parasite—she tried to rely on Oliver Reynolds, but he ended up taking her for every penny she had, so she's back to relying on James to get her out of the shit.

My feeling of self-righteousness wanes as I wait on the busy platform. I think about how much I rely on Cassie for the roof over my head and the lovely clothes she lends me. *Surely, I'm not as bad as Suzanne?*

I intended to get to work a little early today in the hope of making a good impression. Unfortunately, this Tube is even more crowded than the one I usually get, and I have to fight my way through the other commuters to get on it. I can't risk having to wait for the next one as it would definitely make me late. As it is, I'm forced to stand right in the middle of the carriage, squashed between a young guy eating a greasy McDonald's breakfast and his friend who wears the largest backpack ever and keeps swinging it into my shoulder each time he laughs, which is far too often for this time in the morning, in my opinion. They're both looking at their phones and showing each other pictures while also describing them in loud voices. Just to cap it all, a man with terminal BO uses the grab pole as a leaning post while I totter and sway to keep my balance.

This has all the makings of a horrible day, but I, Libby Lawrence, refuse to let it all get to me. Positivity is the key. I *will* have a good day today—even if it bloody well kills me.

***

I'm glad to finally get to work and am surprised to recognise one of the ladies waiting for the lift. It's the woman from the other day in the navy Monsoon shift dress. Today, she's in a smart black trouser suit, which she's teamed with a cerise blouse. I suspect the blouse is from Chloé but have no idea about the suit. I recognise the shoes, though—Santonis. They're a similar style to the ones she wore the other day, with a square toe and block heel. She's certainly a woman of taste, even if she does tut a lot.

'Good morning,' I say, offering her a beaming smile.

She looks surprised, but answers with a quiet, 'Good morning.'

I don't think she's recognised me from Monday, which can only be a good thing.

'It's very cold today, isn't it?' I say. If she's a friend of Valerie, I desperately need to get her on side.

She raises her perfectly arched eyebrows and looks at me again, a little more intently this time. I feel the urge to look away—or even *run* away—but I stand my ground, willing her not to twig who I am. The ping of the lift is music to my ears, and I stand back to allow her to go in front of me—not just to be courteous but also because she's more likely to recognise my back than my front.

No one speaks in the lift, so I stand quietly by the wall, trying to figure a way to get to know the woman in the Chloé blouse. I'm glad to have something to focus on other than that row with Suzanne, to be honest, and at least this is productive. There are a few other people between her and me now so I'm hoping I don't look too conspicuous as I stare at the back of her head, telepathically telling her to like me. I'm normally quite good at this—at least, with Cassie—but I'm not sure how receptive this woman is. She just stares at the door in front of her. And I'm sure I just heard her tut.

I follow another couple of people out of the lift when we get to the fourth floor, but 'Chloé blouse woman' stays put. I smile as I pass her, but she doesn't smile back. It makes me wonder if she's recognised me, after all. Quickly, I scoot away from the lift, just in case she says anything, or heaven forbid, tuts again, and make my way to the office.

'Hi, Libby.' Kiki and Eva are already there, putting an outfit together on the table. They both look stunning, as usual.

'Hello.' I smile at them.

'What do you reckon? Pink or blue?' Eva puts a couple of gorgeous cashmere jumpers against a soft grey skirt.

'It's a hard one,' I say, wincing. 'They both look lovely.'

'That's the trouble,' Kiki says, shaking her head. 'I've been thinking about it all night, and I still can't decide which I like best.' She smooths her long ponytail, draping it beautifully over one shoulder. I wish I could tame my hair like that.

'We can only have one,' Eva says, pursing her lips.

'I love pink and grey,' I say, frowning thoughtfully. 'It's so feminine. But if it's for a more formal look, you may want to go with the blue?'

'Good point,' Eva says, raising her impeccably shaped eyebrows.

'Yep, I'd go with that,' Kiki agrees.

'Blue it is, then.' Eva sounds quite relieved that they've finally reached a decision.

I feel good knowing I've helped. 'Is Valerie here yet?' I try to sound disinterested, but I'm dying to know so I don't put my foot in it. *I know it's hard to believe, but I do seem to do that quite often.*

'Not yet,' Kiki says with a giggle. 'Probably had a heavy night with Mr Bellis.'

'In her dreams,' Eva sniggers.

'You don't think he's into her?' Kiki looks surprised. 'What do you reckon, Libby?'

My mind's whirling. It clearly wasn't just me who saw the effect the silver fox had on our boss, then.

'It's hard to tell,' I say. 'She seemed to be a different person when he was around. Not that I know her that well, of course.'

'Hmm. She likes him all right,' Kiki says, nodding. 'The question is does *he* like *her*?'

'Ooh, are we talking about Romeo and Juliet?' Beulah arrives, her eyes shining with excitement at the gossip.

'Who else?' Eva laughs.

'I'd like to see them get together. It would do her the world of good.' Beulah seems to have it all worked out.

'He seems a bit of a ladies' man, though,' Eva says, pinning notes to the skirt and blue jumper. 'Is he genuine, do you think?'

My mind immediately goes back to Suzanne Harper falling for Oliver Reynolds. I hadn't exactly met the guy, but he certainly seemed good-looking judging by his photos. It would be easy for a woman to be taken in by a handsome face and the kind of charm Mr Bellis portrayed yesterday. Although I don't like Suzanne one bit, I can't help feeling a little sorry for her getting hurt like that. I *don't* feel sorry that she's moved in with my boyfriend, however. Or that she's such a bitch.

I leave them chatting and go over to my desk to put down my bag. The rail of rejects hasn't been returned to the office, and I wonder if it's still behind the blinds in Valerie's room. I didn't see Mr Bellis take it with him, so I can only assume we're at the mercy of his distribution company, whoever they may be. *Hang on!* Didn't I read yesterday that Rebel handled their own distribution? According to their registration with Companies House, they do. Mind you, their entry also claims they design and manufacture their items, too— *not* have them made in Bangladesh.

The noise level rises as the rest of the girls pile into the room, and I admire Fran's calf-length boho dress. Siobhan, in sharp contrast wears a gorgeous suit with a pencil skirt, accentuating her slim figure beautifully. I wonder if I might look good in something like that now that I've lost some weight. I suppose I should be thankful to Dave Chandler in the newsroom for making me run all over town for those stories, although I can't help thinking that stint in the gym would have helped a bit, too—even though it was only one session.

'Are we working on the Fame range again?' I ask, a little warily.

Siobhan frowns. 'I'm not sure yet. I'll see what Valerie says when she gets in.'

Fran and I exchange a look.

'I know we can't finalise anything until we actually see the correct samples, but we could put something together out of the literature Rebel supplied,' Fran suggests. 'That might save some work later on.'

Siobhan purses her lips, looking towards the door. 'Good idea,' she says.

I'm not so sure. Something tells me it'll be a complete waste of time. And besides, I don't want to put my name to an article extolling the virtues of the range just in case—as I strongly suspect—the new batch of samples doesn't arrive. I don't know Valerie very well, but I hope she wouldn't sanction the article being printed anyway. Trouble is, while her personal integrity probably would dictate never doing such a thing, if she *is* dazzled by Mr Bellis' charm and good looks, she just might be persuaded otherwise.

'What if you cobble something together from the brochure while I see if I can come up with some sort of feature about the company itself?' I suggest. 'You know, the history of Rebel, a bit of personal stuff about its directors and their backgrounds that sort of thing? Make it more of a human-interest story than a sales pitch.'

'I like the way you're thinking, Libby,' Siobhan says with a smile. Then she lowers her voice, taking a step closer to me. 'Though you might want to rephrase your ideas, a little. I don't think Valerie would be too impressed at your suggestion of 'cobbling something together,' somehow.'

She winks at me, and I grimace. She might have a point there.

An hour later, Fran sits back and sighs at her screen. 'That's it,' she says. 'I can't think of anything else to write. I've practically re-written the whole leaflet *and* the press release. I've put that they're made in the U.K. and included a bit about them having them printed here, too. A company called BaROQ, apparently, but I can't find anything about them on the web. *And* I've included the photos. There's nothing else I can add.

'It doesn't help that we're not allowed to use our own pictures,' I say, rolling my eyes. 'I feel like our hands are well and truly tied. Is that normal?'

'It depends on the client,' she says with a shrug. 'Sometimes, we hardly get any photos, and we end up modelling the clothes ourselves so our guys can take whatever pictures we need. I don't think I've come across anyone quite as strict as Mr Bellis, though, not allowing us to take any additional ones. I presume he doesn't rate our photographers as highly as his own.'

I frown. 'Hmm, I wonder who he uses.'

'Have you dug up any dirt on them yet?' she asks, coming over to my desk with a mischievous smile.

'I wish. It's like this guy's just appeared from nowhere. And I can't find anything about the company at all. There are a couple of other companies called Rebel, of course, but not a Rebel (London) Ltd that I can find. They don't have a website or Facebook page or anything. Goodness knows how they advertise. I was thinking about asking Valerie if she had a phone number or address for their offices so I could ask them some questions, but she didn't look too happy when she came in so I thought it best not to.'

Fran's eyes widen. 'I wouldn't dare ask her anything,' she whispers.

Valerie did look quite unapproachable as she strutted through the office in her dark sunglasses earlier. Her stiff upper lip was a sure sign someone had upset her, and I couldn't help pinpointing Mr Bellis as the number one suspect.

'I'm a bit concerned Siobhan will think I've done nothing all morning,' I tell Fran.

'You'll just have to tell her you couldn't find anything. She can't blame you if there's no information available.'

I know it makes sense. I also know this is only my third day in the department, and all I seem to have done so far is offend the boss and throw up more problems than solutions. No wonder I've been labelled a troublemaker. Not that I *am*, of course. Well, not intentionally, at least.

'I'm going to speak to her,' I say, realising I truly haven't much choice.

'Valerie?'

'Siobhan.' It seems Fran underestimates my cowardice. I glance at the clock. '*After* we've had coffee.'

It's against the rules to have drinks in the office, apart from bottled water, which has to be kept closed and away from all fabric samples and computers, so we all head towards the canteen for our morning break.

My stomach's churning as I sip my drink. Most of the girls sit around a large table, chatting, while Tammy and Alice are over by the window, muttering quietly. Fran pats an empty seat at the end of the large table, so I join the crowd, though I'm not really in the mood for company. I need to get my thoughts together.

Siobhan sits quietly at the other end of the table, looking at her phone, while Kiki and Eva regale a humorous incident from last night's pub visit. I'm only half-listening to the conversation and manage to giggle when everyone else bursts out laughing, although I'm not even sure what was so funny. Perhaps you had to be there. Or perhaps I should have just paid more attention to the story.

I quickly send a text to James, hoping he's having a better day than I am.

Are we still on for tonight? Lxx

He replies instantly, making me wonder if he's been hoping to hear from me. Or maybe he's just getting lots of private calls today. I wonder if Suzanne's told him about my visit this morning. I hope not. He's got enough to worry about.

Yes, of course. Can't wait. Jxx

'Is it your boyfriend?' Fran asks, gesturing towards my mobile.

I nod. 'Have *you* got a significant other?'

'No, I'm between men.' She juts her chin out, and I can only guess that her last relationship ended badly.

'Lucky you,' I say with a grin, hoping to cheer her up.

She frowns, then blushes before bursting out laughing.

'I didn't mean *literally*,' she shrieks with a shocked expression. 'Though, maybe...' She looks thoughtful.

I roll my eyes, giggling.

Suddenly, everyone's moving, so I slip my phone into my bag and follow them back to the office.

'Siobhan, could I have a word with you, please?' I ask, catching up with her in the corridor.

'Yes, of course.'

'It's private.'

She frowns quizzically but nods. 'Come on over to my desk.'

We've just entered the office where everyone's still chatting away, and I can't help thinking there's not much privacy here. A loud peal of laughter tells me Fran's just repeated our conversation to Beulah and Kiki on her way back to her desk.

'I just need a couple of things,' I tell Siobhan.

I print off the information from Companies House that I found yesterday and quickly look around for another sheet of details. *Damn! Where did I put it?*

'Fran, what happened to the reports we wrote yesterday? The pros and cons.'

She looks over in surprise. 'I thought you had them.'

'No.'

I wrack my brain. 'Never mind, I can print mine off again, it's not a problem.'

But it *is* a problem. My truthful but rather scathing report is laying around the office somewhere for all to see. I hadn't worried about it at the time, but if someone saw it and thought...

'Siobhan!' Valerie's voice thunders through the room, making everyone stare in silence.

Red-faced, Siobhan quickly makes her way to her. Valerie is holding a pile of photographs, her face white with anger.

That's when I remember where I put the reports.

7

Less than a minute later, Siobhan marches out of the office, heading my way. *Shit!* Her eyes are wide, and she looks dumbfounded.

'Libby and Fran, Valerie wants you in the office now, please.' Her voice is curt.

Shaking, I stand up and follow Fran towards the office. Siobhan's heels click behind me. The room's silent as everyone watches us, open-mouthed. I feel like I'm being led to the gallows. As we enter the room, I realise I'm still holding the information from Companies House that I wanted to show Siobhan. I quickly fold it up and tuck it in my jacket pocket.

Valerie stands behind her desk with two pieces of paper in her hand and a murderous expression on her face. She gives the impression of a great ogre towering over us, teasing her prey before she gobbles us up. Her eyes look narrow and mean, and her lips are tight.

'I understand that you two were given the task of listing the attributes of the Fame collection,' she snaps.

We nod. I want to add 'not *just* the attributes' but I don't.

'And whose is this work?' She holds up Fran's copy.

'It's m-mine,' she admits.

'Good. You may get back to work.' Valerie doesn't have to tell her twice. Fran practically skips out the door. Not that I can blame her.

'Is this your version?' Valerie asks me, her face tense with rage.

'Yes, it is.' My voice is quieter than I'd hoped.

'Why am I not surprised?'

I want to reply, 'because you hate me,' but I stay quiet for a change.

She huffs, shaking her head at me as though I'm a tiresome child.

'Sit down,' she says after a few agonising moments.

We all sit down.

'Liberty, I realise that fashion isn't your forte and that you were sent to work here because of... *exceptional*... circumstances, but I think you'll agree that this really hasn't worked out, has it?' She sounds so condescending, my stomach churns with anger.

'No,' I say, my heart racing.

She gives a satisfied nod. 'I'm not sure if you'll be suited to another department, but I think that's for Mr Stratton to decide, so I'll…'

'I meant no, I don't agree,' I blurt out, seeing exactly where this is going.

She stops, mid-flow and stares at me. Siobhan gasps.

'What?' Valerie flashes her eyes at me. If looks could kill…

'Fashion *is* my forte,' I say, fighting to keep the tremble from my voice. 'I love great designers, quality garments, and innovative ideas.'

'But you need to understand business, too,' Valerie points out. 'Everyone is in this industry to make money, and we don't do that by decrying our clients' collection.' Her voice is clipped as she waves my report at me.

'I get that,' I tell her. 'But it's also about reputation and integrity. The *Chronicle*'s, the department's, yours, mine, everyone's. If we don't maintain that, we have nothing.'

'Right now, young lady, all *you* have is a reputation for stirring up trouble.' Valerie sounds vicious.

I shake my head, wondering how I'll ever make her understand. 'I honestly don't mean to.'

'Valerie, I need to point out that the object of the exercise was for the girls to list the pros *and cons* of the range. My intention was to highlight its attributes and investigate anything that could be construed as negative. We wanted to give a fair and balanced view.' Siobhan sounds quite firm, and I'm grateful to have her fighting my corner.

Valerie squeezes her lips together as though trying to stop herself from saying something. After taking a deep breath, she faces me again.

'Fame is a very successful clothing collection,' she says, slowly and precisely. 'Its producers are paying us a lot of money to convey that fact. We *need* this contract. We *need* to keep the client happy. We don't do that by questioning the designer and writing disparaging reports about their product.'

I swallow hard. I know she hates me. I know she wants to get rid of me, but I desperately *need* this job. And I want it. Working in fashion is what I always saw myself doing. Ever since I was small.

'I'm sorry that the piece I wrote was perceived as negative and derogatory,' I say, calmly. 'But it wasn't the report, nor was it finished. It was just a brainstorming exercise. I merely wanted to get everything down so I could analyse it properly.'

'You should just thank your lucky stars Mr Bellis didn't see it yesterday,' Valerie snaps.

'I do,' I admit. I know that would mean instant dismissal, no matter how unfair it would be. And it would be. *Very* unfair. 'It wasn't intended for his eyes, or yours. Or anyone's really. As I said, it was just a lot of thoughts put on paper, ready for unscrambling.'

'Nevertheless…'

'And how do you know the company's successful?' I add. *I might as well be hung for a sheep as a lamb.* 'Where's the evidence of that? I've trawled the internet and can't find a single mention of Fame or Rebel, or even Mr Bellis. Do they have a head office? A factory? If it's a limited company that information should be freely available, shouldn't it?'

Valerie looks astonished, and I'm not sure if it's because of *what* I said or just because I said it. Siobhan's frowning at me now, too.

'You couldn't find *anything*?' Siobhan asks, warily.

I take a deep breath. 'Well, actually, I did find *this*.'

I pull the Companies House information from my pocket and hand it to her. 'It's what I wanted to talk to you about earlier.'

Siobhan's mouth drops open as she reads the details. She stares at the paper and then at Valerie.

'What is it?' Valerie's voice wavers a little as she reaches out for the document. I watch her whole body sag as she reads it.

'No!'

'I'm so sorry, Valerie,' Siobhan says.

The older lady is still staring at the writing, horrified. 'Dissolved?' she whispers in disbelief.

'Last month,' I say, surprised at just how upset they are about the news. 'Although it only existed for five months, anyhow.'

'But he said...' Valerie gapes at Siobhan.

'I know,' Siobhan says, softly.

My mind's in a whirl. Something's going on. I mean, I know Valerie had a 'thing' for Quinton Bellis, but this looks far more serious than that.

Siobhan turns to me, biting her lip. 'Libby, can you go back to your desk please? And don't breathe a word of this to anyone, understood?'

I nod and stand hastily.

'We're trusting you,' she continues, as I walk to the door. 'Please. As a friend as well as a colleague. This is strictly confidential, okay?' Her eyes are wide and pleading.

'Yes, of course. You can rely on me.'

The blinds roll down before I even leave the room. My heart's hammering. Not only have I kept my job but I'm also privy to some top-secret information. It's not just that Rebel has gone bust, but Valerie is involved with Quinton Bellis a lot more heavily than everyone thinks. She couldn't hide her mortification that he's lied to her. And although I know she hates my guts, I can't help feeling sorry for her—even if she doesn't deserve my sympathy.

'Are you okay?' Eva asks as I walk to my desk.

'Yeah. I think I scraped through by the skin of my teeth, though.'

'You mean, you still have a job?' One of the girls—Brianna, I think—gazes at me open-mouthed. She's awfully pretty, with short, dark, curly hair that has red and dark-blonde highlights.

'Only just,' I admit. 'Thanks to Siobhan.'

'Was it that report?' Fran asks, wide-eyed.

I nod. 'Yep. I must have left them on the table with the photos yesterday, before they were taken to Valerie's office. She found it today and went mad. She said if ever Mr Bellis had noticed it yesterday, I'd be out on my ear.'

'You had a very lucky escape,' Fran says, shaking her head. 'I was certain she was about to sack you in there. She had a face like a bulldog chewing a wasp.'

'We were all watching,' Izzy calls over. 'How on earth did you turn it around? What were the papers you were all looking at?'

She's tall and slim with a white-blonde pixie cut, making her look beautiful but also a bit austere. I think she's the oldest of the girls—though still much younger than Valerie, of course. That's probably why I find her a bit intimidating. I get the impression she doesn't like me much, but I don't know why.

I feel hot inside. I'd forgotten we had an audience while all that was going on.

'Just some stuff I'd written,' I say, airily. 'She already knew I didn't think much of the range, anyway.'

'I don't know why you don't like it,' Fran says, incredulously.

'Yeah, what *have* you got against it?' Eva asks.

'It's nothing personal. I think it looks nice enough, it's just that it's not the quality you'd expect for the price that's all.' I shrug. These girls all look like they don't have to scrimp and save for anything. I, on the other hand, have to look at purchasing clothes as a long-term investment. I can't afford anything that will fall apart after the first wear. It's just false economy. *I think I may have been listening to James a bit too much, but I have to admit it makes sense.*

'Well, as long as it makes money, I don't suppose it matters to the company,' Izzy pipes up.

I smile and then get back to my work. I can't tell them my doubts that Mr Bellis—if that's really his name—is making any money at all. I keep my head down for the rest of the day, while everyone else gets on with their own projects. Siobhan and Valerie seem to spend the rest of the morning in the office, and then I think Valerie went home at lunchtime, as there's no sign of her when we get back from the canteen.

I feel like I have a secret with Siobhan, who's very discreet and doesn't give anything away. I like her a lot, and I admire her loyalty. I wish I was more like her.

8

My tummy feels all warm and bubbly as I shut down my computer and head out the door at five o' clock. I can't wait to see James tonight. I hadn't realised just how much I miss him. It seems like forever since we last kissed, not just a few days. I really think I'm falling for the guy in a big way.

My phone pings as I make my way to the Tube station.

Hi Libby, sorry but I'm going to be delayed tonight. I'll try to meet you at the pool around 7. Also, I'll pick up some groceries, and we can go back to yours afterwards. I'll cook. Jxx

Damn! Still, at least it looks like I'll actually see him tonight, so I can't complain. And it'll be great to watch him cook. It's a brilliant way of saving money too, instead of paying for a takeaway or eating out. He takes his finances most seriously, and I know he's worried sick about losing his nest egg.

Hi James. That's okay. Meet you outside the sports centre. Can't wait to see you! Lxx

He replies almost straight away.

Might be better to meet inside. Go ahead and get into the pool, just in case I'm late. Looking forward to giving you a big kiss. Jxx

I stare at the screen. James never writes stuff like that. He must be really missing me. I go all gooey at the thought.

'Watch it!' A woman with a large suitcase has just bumped into me, almost knocking me over.

'Sorry,' I say, suddenly realising I've stood still to gaze at my phone. The train is just coming down the track, and everyone's moving forward—except me.

She huffs, but I can't honestly blame her. I hate it when people stop right in front of me, too. I smile—I can't help it. She looks at me as though I'm mad, but I don't care. I'm not even bothered when I'm squished up tight against the cold window as everyone piles into the carriage. Nothing can faze me now.

I'm still smiling when I get home. Cassie's already there, whipping up an omelette. 'Want one?' she asks.

'No thanks. I'll just grab a sandwich. I'm going swimming with James later, and then he's coming back here to cook dinner.'

She raises her eyebrows as I open the breadbin. 'Will you have room for dinner after that?'

'Of course. By the time we've been for a swim and... whatever, I'm bound to be starving.'

She chuckles, giving me a knowing look. 'Yeah. Doing *whatever* always gives me a big appetite, too. How are things with him?'

I grin. We're usually on the same wavelength.

'Great. I think. He's hoping they've got the right papers this time and was taking them to his solicitor today.'

She shakes her head. 'He must have the patience of a saint, putting up with Suzanne.'

I agree. 'And me,' I add.

She chuckles but doesn't disagree, much to my disappointment.

'How's work?' I ask, reaching for the peanut butter.

She grimaces. 'Don't say anything, but I think Crystal might be in a bit of trouble.'

'Really?'

Crystal is the swanky fashion designer company that Cassie's been working for over the past few weeks. She loves her job and has even been allowed to help choose fabrics for their new collection.

She slides the omelette onto her plate, and I follow her into the living room with my sandwich.

'It's only a rumour, but some of the girls are quite worried,' she says with a sigh.

'But they make lovely clothes. And didn't you say they would be showing at London Fashion Week next year?'

'Yeah. One of the girls heard Meredith on the phone though, and she sounded doubtful about the cost of everything. It looks like Crystal might be going under.'

'That's awful.' I feel physically sick at the thought—though not quite sick enough to stop eating my sandwich.

'Nothing's been said officially, though, so we're just waiting to see what happens,' she says, shaking her head.

I'd hate to think of Cassie losing her job. It's the first time she's found one she loves doing, and it would be hard to get anything similar. Her dad would go mad, too. She's working hard to convince him that she can actually stick to something—he paid her a lot of money as a bribe to stop her from leaving her last place, which was the hotel we both worked at. Now that she's finally going to work of her own accord, it would be devastating for the company to fold.

'Maybe it's not as bad as it seems,' I say, standing up to take my plate back to the kitchen. 'Could your friend have got the wrong end of the stick?'

'I hope so,' she says, piling our plates into the sink.

'Me, too.' I give her a tight squeeze. 'Is Rob coming over?'

Her face brightens. 'Yeah, he should be here soon. We're going out with some of his mates tonight, so I won't be back.'

'Okay. Hey, maybe we could write a feature or something for the paper? Give Crystal some publicity. That should drive sales up a bit.'

'There's a thought,' she says, her eyes wide.

I glance at the clock. 'I should get ready.'

We go to our rooms to get changed. I throw my bathing costume and a large towel into my Stella McCartney Adidas holdall and comb my hair before fixing it into a much messier bun than I wore all day. It should be just enough to keep it from getting in my eyes while I'm swimming. I hate wearing swimming hats—not only do they make my head ache, but it's impossible to look glamorous in one. Not that I'll be looking that great tonight anyway as it's impossible to dress up to go swimming. I'm wearing loose trousers, a long Gucci T-shirt that I got half-price in Browns sale, and a thick Calvin Klein jumper with my flat Vivienne Westwood shoes.

Halfway to the Tube station, I regret not wearing a coat, too. It's early November and freezing. I'm glad the pool will be heated.

I'm disappointed to arrive at the sports centre with no sign of James. I'm a little early, but don't see the point in hanging around out in the cold, especially as he said he could be a bit late.

Luckily, the changing room is warm, though it's a kind of humid heat that makes your clothes cling to your skin, even when it's dry. I quickly get into my one piece and admire my slimmer figure. I've actually lost enough weight for it to show, and I love being able to look better in my clothes. Confidently, I strut out of the changing room and nearly trip over a couple of exuberant children on my way to the pool. I'd forgotten it's always a family session before eight o' clock on a weekday.

The water's cold at first but warms up a bit once I've swum a few widths. It's impossible to attempt lengths with so many people here, so I content myself with just bobbing about while I wait for James. The noise is deafening as the children's shrieks and shouts echo into the rafters.

I love being in the pool. I feel so light—not that I'm *that* heavy, of course, and I somehow feel the urge to suck my stomach in whenever it's not hidden by the water. I'm beginning to regret that sandwich, though, as I feel a bit bilious. I know I should've waited until after my swim, but I was starving.

It's hard not to keep looking at the big clock on the wall at the deep end. I know James is really busy with work and Suzanne, so I don't blame him for being a little late, but I do wish he'd get here soon.

A better idea would have been to meet in the café area. Trying to navigate around all these excited kids is a nightmare in itself, without constantly watching the door and the clock and trying not to look as self-conscious as I feel. Talk about Billy-no-mates.

I don't trust Suzanne. I get the impression she's trying to get her claws into him—it was no coincidence she got the wrong papers and had to go back to the house with James. She probably knew we'd planned to go out last night. I don't feel jealous, exactly, as I trust James, and know how fed up he is with the situation. But I can't help worrying about what Suzanne's up to.

***

After nearly an hour of struggling to swim with so many kids splashing about, I decide to get out. I'm getting tired, and I'm sure James will have rung by now to say he can't make it. Remembering to pull in my stomach, I climb out and go back to the changing room. There are only a few women in there when I arrive, but soon after I take my things from my locker, a whole crowd of kids and their mums swarm in. The family swimming session has obviously just ended.

I manage to grab a cubicle before the onslaught and quickly get dried and dressed. There are rarely enough for everyone, and I hate changing in the communal area. The noise is horrendous as I leave the sanctity of my cubicle and go over to the vanity unit to comb my hair and touch up my waterproof mascara.

'Rebecca!' a mum shouts as her little red-headed girl bashes into my legs.

I poke my cheek with my mascara wand, smearing a big, black streak across my face. *Typical!*

'Sorry,' the little girl says, looking up at me with massive brown eyes.

'What did I tell you?' her mum scolds as she comes over to retrieve her daughter.

'It's okay, no harm done,' I say, wiping the mess off my face.

'Sorry,' the harassed woman says.

'Honestly, it's fine.' I smile, feeling sorry for her, as she's clearly struggling with three girls to get ready as well as herself. Even if there were a free cubicle, I doubt it'd be big enough for all four of them.

'Go and put your T-shirt on,' her mum tells Rebecca, handing her the pretty pink garment. She turns to her other children who both seem a little older than Rebecca, who I'd guess to be about five. 'Maisie, hurry up and get your vest on.

Suddenly, there's a loud scream from Rebecca, whose face is bright red with tears streaming from her beautiful eyes. She points at a large puddle of water on the floor. In the centre of it, drenched, is her little pink T-shirt. Her tiny world seems to have ended.

'It's all right, you only dropped it,' her mum assures her, hugging her tightly. 'It's just wet that's all.'

'She can borrow this, though it might be a bit warm while we're in here.' Rebecca's other sister holds up a lilac hoodie. 'I know it'll be a bit big, but it should be okay to go home in.'

'Thanks, Emily.' Their mum takes it from her with a grateful smile. 'Look, Rebecca, you can wear this for now, and we'll get your T-shirt dried when we get home.'

Rebecca gives a big sniff and nods her head, still simpering. Her mum puts the hoodie on her. I gawp at it. It's a very familiar design, with Emily's name emblazoned across the back and then in a smaller font on the front.

'Wow. That's lovely,' I say, going over to them. 'Did you get it locally? I'd love one for my niece.' *Not that I have a niece; I'm just a damn good actor.*

The girls' mum smiles at me as she fastens Rebecca's trainers for her. 'We got it on holiday in Margate,' she says. 'Everyone was wearing them down there, so Emily just *had* to have one. She's only eight, but she's quite the fashionista these days.' She chuckles.

'Well, I'll have to look out for them next time I'm down that way,' I say, my mind reeling.

'I'm all hot,' Rebecca complains, pulling at the hoodie.

Their mum looks over to Emily. 'If you're ready, Em, could you take your sister outside to wait for Daddy? Here, get yourselves and Maisie some sweets from the machine.' She hands her some money, and the girls pick up their swimming bags and head for the door.

I follow them out, glad to be free of the humid atmosphere. Once out in the foyer, I check my phone. James had texted earlier to apologise that he'd been held up. I'm disappointed but not surprised. There's also another message from a number I don't recognise.

You won't win, you know? Bitch!

At first, it makes me go all hot and worried, but then I realise it has to be a wrong number. I don't know anyone who would send me anything like that, and I'm certainly not the competitive or gambling type, so I know I won't be winning anything any day soon.

'Wait there and look after this,' Emily instructs Rebecca, who stands against a wall just outside the changing room. 'And keep an eye out for Daddy.' Her sister puts her own bag next to Rebecca and goes over to the confectionary machine on the opposite wall.

I notice a man waiting near the vending machine. My heart leaps for a second, as I hope it's James come to pick me up and take me for a drink, after all. But it's not him. This guy's in black jeans and jumper and has sunglasses on, which seems a little odd. His hair's quite long and straight, which gives him a slightly scruffy appearance. He seems to watch Emily and then approaches Rebecca.

'Hi, Emily, do you remember me? Uncle Jimmy? Your dad asked me to pick you up tonight.' He swiftly picks up the swimming bags from the floor and grabs Rebecca's hand. 'Come on, we have to be quick. We don't want to keep him waiting, do we?'

Rebecca just stares at him as though totally bemused.

I suddenly go all hot as he takes a stride towards the door.

'Stop!' I stand in front of him, barring his way. 'That's not your child.'

I'm glad I can't see his eyes as his whole body heaves in anger. Several people look over, including the receptionist.

'He's trying to take this child,' I shout at the top of my voice, and the man pushes me. Luckily, I'm not the lightest of people—not that I'm overweight or anything—and I lunge my body back at him. It slows him down long enough for another man to reach us and tackle him to the ground.

Everyone around us is screaming and shouting.

I grab Rebecca's shaking hand and quickly take her over to Emily, who's crying hysterically. Their mum suddenly comes out of the changing room with Maisie, and she looks horrified at her children screaming while two men wrestle on the floor of the lobby.

'That man said he's their Uncle Jimmy,' I tell her hurriedly as she hugs all her children at once. 'He tried to take Rebecca.'

'Did he now?' A male voice booms behind me, and a tall, muscular man goes straight over to the fighters and thumps 'Uncle Jimmy' hard on the nose. Blood splatters all over the floor, but the guy continues to wade in and puts his hands around the man's throat.

Even the wail of police sirens isn't enough to smother the tirade of expletives exchanged by the men, but very soon, a couple of burly coppers drag them apart.

'He tried to kidnap my kid!' the muscular guy shouts as they pull him to his feet.

The copper holding him tightens his grip, glaring at 'Uncle Jimmy', whose glasses have come off in the fight, showing he already has a whopping black eye. His colleague hauls the bastard to his feet and cuffs him.

'That's interesting,' he says. 'We wondered where you'd disappeared to, Johnson.'

'I didn't do anything.' The man struggles, but the copper holds him firmly.

'We'll let the court decide that one,' the cop snarls.

The other man who was in the fight runs his hand through his hair. 'I didn't see anything, but that girl shouted, so I jumped in.'

'Well done, sir,' the first copper says with a nod. 'I wish there were more people like you.' He turns to me. 'We'll need to take a statement from you, Miss.'

***

Over an hour later, I finally leave the sports centre. Another couple of cops had arrived to help out, and one of them stayed behind to take statements from everyone involved. I received a big hug from Angela, the girls' mother.

'I can't thank you enough for intervening, Libby. Not many people would have done something like that,' she says.

'It was the fact the guy got her name wrong that alerted me that something wasn't right. I wouldn't have taken any notice otherwise.'

'Well, I'm glad you were there,' Angela says, 'and I'm going to bin that hoodie, fashion or no fashion.'

I've given my details to the police, who will be in touch if and when they need me again. I might even have to appear in court, though I certainly hope not. I'd rather forget all about it. I can't stop trembling. And anyway, I'd have nothing to wear. What do you wear for a court appearance? I'd have to go shopping and find something appropriate. Hmm, perhaps it wouldn't be so bad, after all...

The copper offers me a lift home, but I desperately need to get some air.

'I'll be fine,' I tell him.

It's nearly ten o'clock, but I badly want to talk to James about it all. I didn't realise how shaken I was by the whole thing, but it's really affected me. I was a bit nauseous earlier, too. And I can't help feeling miffed that he's stood me up, leaving me to freeze to death in that overcrowded pool. I send him a quick text.

Is it okay if I pop round? I need to see you. L. Xx

I shudder at the cold as I step out into the street. My phone vibrates.

Yes, of course. I'd love to see you. J. Xx

Relieved, I head for the Tube and take the next train to Fulham. It's not too crowded, and I'm pleased to be able to sit down and relax for a short while until we arrive. I breathe deeply, trying to steady my nerves, my heart hammering like mad. I feel relieved, sad, and angry all at once, and still can't stop shivering.

It's only a short walk to James' flat, and he buzzes me up right away. The events of the evening whirl through my head and I can't wait to be in his reassuring arms. The door's been left ajar, so I walk straight into the flat. I stop suddenly.

There, in the kitchen, Suzanne is dressed in a silky negligee that doesn't leave much to the imagination, kissing James with her slender arms wrapped tightly around him. Her long, red curls trail down her shoulders, and I can just make out her bright-red lipstick when she moves her head. I can't see James' face, which is probably a good thing.

I want to be sick all over again. But I don't vomit. I run.

9

Anger and hurt well up inside me, weighing me down as I race down the stairs. I can hear James' voice, but it seems so distant, it disappears into the ether. The urge to get away from there is too strong to ignore, and I don't stop running until I've slammed the door to the flats and burst out into the cold, night air.

The street's quiet, and I can hear every breath I heave into my lungs. I tremble as hot tears stream down my cheeks. I quickly wipe my face, angry because I'm crying and crying because I'm angry. The vision of James in Suzanne's arms taunts me as I slow down and walk towards the Tube station.

My phone rings, and despite my inclination to ignore it, I pull it from my bag. It's James. My head tells me not to speak to him while I'm so riled, but the temptation is too much to bear as it continues to ring.

'Libby. Don't go home. I'm on my way to you,' James blurts the words out, and I'm momentarily stunned by his breathless urgency. I can hear the desperation in his voice, the silent plea for me to understand. And in that moment, I do.

'There's no need.' I give a sigh of resignation. Not because I think I've lost him, but because I can see that I've been taken for a fool.

'There's *every* need.' He sounds very firm, and I can hear him panting. He's running.

I stop and look behind me. He's there, racing towards me. I can see the vehemence in his face. The fear, almost. My heart skips a beat.

'Libby. It's not what you think.' He slows down as he reaches me, his eyes wild and intense.

'Oh, I hope it is,' I tell him.

'What?' He looks horrified.

'*She* was kissing *you*, not the other way around.' The image in my mind's eye is perfectly clear. It was all her. He wasn't holding *her*. He wasn't even kissing her.

In the light of the streetlamp, I can see his face slowly relax. 'Yes. I thought she'd gone to bed. I was opening a bottle of wine for us and left the door open for you to come in. She must have been listening and just grabbed her chance—grabbed *me*.'

I knew it. Something deep inside told me he wasn't being unfaithful. He was being used. *The bitch!*

I nod, anger giving way to realisation. James takes me in his warm arms and holds me tight. His whole body feels hard and tense until his lips meet mine, making us both melt.

It feels like hours later when he finally releases me, and I feel almost bereft as he takes a step back.

'I've told her I want her out,' he says, calmly.

My stomach flutters. 'Really?'

He nods. 'She's trying to come between us, but I won't let her. I've given her a week to find somewhere to stay—somewhere *I'm* not going to pay for.'

I stare at him. He doesn't look angry, just determined. She's upset him as much as me with her little prank. It's then that I realise he's come out without a jacket or even a jumper. His shirt sleeves are rolled up to his elbows, and he looks utterly delicious, not to mention freezing cold.

'Let's go in there.' I point to a nearby pub, and he smiles. 'We can at least catch last orders.'

I dive into the ladies' while James orders the drinks. My make-up's a complete mess where I've been crying, and I quickly get to work. It could have been much worse, but I only put on a light covering after my swim. My mind reels while I wipe my face and touch up my mascara and lippy. I'm so relieved that James has seen for himself what a manipulative, conniving cow his ex-wife is. I knew she would try to split us up, and I'm glad he's realised it, too.

The lights in the bar are mercifully dim, and I find James waiting for me at a small table near the window. I take the chair opposite him, and we hold hands across the polished oak.

'I was afraid you'd think...' he starts.

'That you were kissing her?'

'Yep.'

'Nah. You've got better taste these days,' I say with a giggle.

He chuckles. 'True.'

He studies me, which always makes me nervous.

'How did you know it wasn't the way it looked? It would have been a natural assumption.' His gorgeous eyes are slightly narrowed.

I can't admit to him that for a fraction of a millisecond, I thought it was *exactly* how it looked.

'I couldn't believe it,' I say, remembering the thoughts that raced through my head as I ran away. 'It was just too unbelievable. You wouldn't do a thing like that. And I noticed her arms around you, but yours weren't around her. It was obviously one-sided. Besides, you'd already promised me a big kiss, remember?'

The smile he gives me turns me all gooey again. His eyes are large and dark, and his dimples show in his cheeks.

'Thank you,' he says. 'For believing in me.'

'I do.'

I lean forward for a kiss, my heart feeling so huge it might burst out of my body at any minute. His lips encase mine in the warmest, most sensual kiss I've had since we... no, never mind, you don't need to hear about that.

'I'm really sorry about tonight. I didn't mean to stand you up,' he says when we finally recover from our moment and get back to our drinks. 'I went straight to the solicitor's after work, and things took longer than I'd hoped.

'Did you get the right document in the end?'

'I think so, though it might not be complete. The solicitors are looking into it.' He purses his lips. 'It certainly looked like a genuine agreement, though.'

'So, what does that mean? Do you still have to pay for the repairs on the house? Is it still half yours?' I quickly take a sip of my drink, just to give him time to answer. I know I'm just firing questions at him, but it all has so many ramifications, and we don't have long to discuss it.

'The solicitor's going to let us know exactly what she's agreed to, and what she had the *right* to agree to. He just needs to check all the small print. In the meantime, I'm going to continue to get the place habitable. I just can't believe she can sign away the whole house because my name's on the deed as well as hers. The solicitor thinks it's highly unlikely, too.'

'That's good.'

'The papers weren't that hard to find,' he says with a knowing look. 'They were in a file in the office. Unfortunately, part of the ceiling had caved in, so it meant hunting through some rubble, but nothing too difficult.'

'So, Suzanne was stalling?'

'Yep.'

I bite my lip.

'What about you?' He swiftly changes the subject, eyeing me curiously. 'Are you okay? You said you wanted to talk to me. Is your new position going well?'

'Oh, yes,' I tell him. *I think*. 'But I came by tonight to tell you about something else.'

I explain about the guy at the sports centre, and his eyes widen. Just talking about it makes me feel all jittery again, and James strokes my arm reassuringly.

'His name was Johnson. Could it be the same man who took that boy earlier?' I ask, as the bell rings for last orders.

'Possibly. I'll give Alex a ring in a while, see if he knows anything. Good job you realised something was wrong.' He squeezes my hand. I think I've impressed him. It doesn't happen very often.

Alex is another detective sergeant who works opposite James a lot. He's a nice man, and I know James has a lot of faith in him.

'It was only because of the name on her top,' I say. 'I don't think I'd have suspected anything if she'd had her own name on it, and he'd used that.'

James nods, a grave expression crossing his face. 'It's so dangerous,' he says. 'And if it's becoming the latest fashion for everyone to wear their name, I'm afraid we'll have more of these incidents.'

My stomach clenches. I can just imagine Valerie's reaction if I told her the *Chronicle* should run a campaign to broaden awareness of the dangers of divulging your name in public—especially for children. It goes against the whole Fame ethos.

A few people leave the pub, and we get up to follow suit, James keeping an arm around me. It's only a short walk from there to the Tube station.

'Are you sure you're all right?' he asks, looking at me intently. 'I could come with you but...'

'It's okay. Maybe tomorrow night,' I say, smiling. There's nothing I'd like better than for him to be with me tonight, especially after the day we've had. He'd be such a comfort, and I hate the thought of him going anywhere near Suzanne. He doesn't have anything with him, though, and he's on the early shift tomorrow. He would have to get up at about four o'clock to get back here to change before work. It wouldn't be fair on him.

He smiles, too. 'As long as you're sure? Ring me as soon as you get in. I'll be waiting for your call,' he says, before leaning in for a goodnight kiss.

***

My mind's in a whirl as I stand on the Tube next morning. Seeing James last night has made me feel all bubbly inside. He's gorgeous, tall with dark hair, and a light, stubbly-type beard and moustache—not one of those thick, hairy styles, but just enough to graze against my face when we kiss. Which we do. A lot.

He's looking into that man, Johnson, who tried to kidnap Rebecca. My stomach goes all hot at the thought. I don't know what came over me when I confronted him—sheer adrenaline, I suppose. And fear. In droves. I still feel a bit shaky at the thought of what happened—and what *nearly* happened—so I'm trying not to dwell on it. It wasn't so easy last night, though. His evil face kept flashing through my mind, and I woke up screaming at one point. It was a good job Cassie hadn't come home. I couldn't help wishing James had been able to stay, though, but I understand why he couldn't. I honestly think the whole incident affected me more than I'd originally imagined, but I'm trying hard to think of other things. I'm not even telling Fran about it just yet—it'll only get me all upset again, and that's the last thing I need at work, especially now with everything else that's going on there.

There wasn't time to explain to James about Quinton Bellis and his phony company. I'm planning to fill him in tonight when he meets me after work. And talking of work, I'm dreading seeing Valerie today. She's bound to be in a foul mood after yesterday, and I can't blame her.

I'm wearing navy trousers from Jigsaw today, with a mustard-coloured blouse I got from Dorothy Perkins. I've also borrowed a navy jacket—perfect match, I couldn't believe it—and a pair of navy Jimmy Choo heels from Cassie. To top it all, I have a gorgeous, mustard Errotha bag from Aldo, which looks brilliant with the whole ensemble. I felt a bit fragile when I woke this morning and it gave me a massive confidence boost to put on such a great outfit. Nice clothes always make me feel better, somehow.

By the time I arrive at the office, most of the others are already there. Valerie's door is shut, and the blinds are down, so they're all speculating about whether she's in there or not.

'She went home ill yesterday, according to Siobhan,' Izzy says quietly with a very disbelieving look.

'Was she all right when you were in there?' Brianna asks me as I make my way to my desk.

'It's hard to say,' I tell them, searching my brain for the right answer. Well, not the *right* answer exactly that would be too cruel. But one that might stop them asking me any more awkward questions. 'I don't know her well enough. But she was a bit red in the face.'

'She's always like that when you're around,' Izzy quips with a laugh.

I smile back. I know it's true, but it's not like it's my fault or anything.

Tammy arrives, her hair coiled in a couple of buns on top of her head, making her look very cute. I, on the other hand, would look like a three-year-old with that style, but she really pulls it off, somehow. She's wearing a green jumpsuit that totally suits her, and taupe Kurt Geiger's. That reminds me of a pair of Louboutins I noticed on the web last night. They're new. Pointed toe courts in a black and nude ombre effect. Décolleté, they're called. I quickly bring them up on my screen.

The others are still murmuring about Valerie, but I've lost interest. These shoes are perfect. They're the right colours to go with just about everything. And they're only... oh... £545—which isn't bad for designer shoes, is it? Not really. And when you think about it, it's like having two pairs in one because of the versatility of the colours. I think they'd complement any wardrobe—especially mine.

I gaze at them for a bit, letting the world go by without me. Maybe I could get them at lunchtime? I'll put them on my... oh, no. I've just remembered my credit card bill. The card's totally maxed out, and they won't even let me increase my credit limit. It's preposterous. I mean, I've got a good job, haven't I? It's not like I'm about to leave the country or anything. And I *will* have enough to pay it all back just as soon as I get time to work everything out. And save up. A bit. Well, okay, *quite* a bit.

'Ooh, very nice.' Fran's just arrived and looks over my shoulder. 'Are you getting them?'

I want to say, 'Oh, yes, definitely,' but I stop myself just in time.

'I'm not sure,' I say, biting my lip. 'I'm going to think about it.'

'They'd suit you.' She smiles and goes to her own desk.

She's right. They'd look great with so many of my outfits. And Cassie's. She lends me her stuff quite often. In fact, now that I've lost a bit of weight, I'll be able to fit into even more of her clothes, making the shoes even more versatile. I have to get them. Somehow. In my head, I'm praying to the Goddess of Sales and Reductions. *Please find a way to make them more affordable for me. You only need to reduce the cost of one pair, size 7. I'm not greedy or anything. I just need those shoes.*

'Libby, can I have a word, please?'

Siobhan just appeared behind me. I hate it when people do that—especially when I'm shopping. Or hoping to be. I quickly bring up another window on my screen, but I think it's too late. She's seen. *Oh, shit!*

10

'Of course.' Can I get sacked for looking at shoes when I'm working in the fashion department? 'I was just... er... doing some research.'

She ushers me over to her desk, and I follow like a lost puppy. She's only just arrived, too, and is still taking off her coat as she walks.

'I just wanted to thank you for your discretion yesterday,' she says quietly.

I heave a sigh of relief. 'Oh. That's okay. Is Valerie all right?'

Siobhan grimaces. 'Time will tell. She should be in later.'

'Right... what about Fame? Are we still running the article?'

'It's on hold for now. I want you to help Brianna this morning. She's doing a piece on a new make-up brand that's recently been launched.'

'Great.' My heart swells. I didn't fancy wasting any more time on fruitless research today. I'm still full of adrenaline after last night. I don't mean James' kiss, although that was... never mind. Anyway, I can hardly praise the fashion style that nearly got that little girl kidnapped, can I?

Brianna is stunning. There's no denying it. She's tall and slim with short, curly hair that frames her face beautifully. She should be a model. I get the impression she's very independent and seems to have lots of different boyfriends, though she lives alone.

'I'm helping you today,' I tell her, clutching my notebook.

She beams at me, making her look even lovelier. 'Great. Can you open that box for me?'

I put my things on her desk and go over to where she's pointed. At the end of the central table, there are three boxes, one of which is already open. I feel like a kid at Christmas as I tear open one of the others and fish out several smaller boxes of eye shadow and lipsticks. The third box holds similar items, and I hold up a packet of blusher.

'Do we get to try these out?' I ask.

She giggles. 'You'd be disappointed if I said no, wouldn't you?'

'Yes.'

'Of course, we get to try them,' she says, still chuckling. 'I've made a checklist of all the things we're examining them for, but first, we need to tick them off against the delivery note.'

She hands me a piece of paper to sort out all the products and mark them off, in much the same way as I did with the Fame delivery. Then, after checking for breakages—luckily everything's perfect this time—I have to make notes on the qualities Brianna's listed. There are all sorts of details about the packaging and presentation that have to be considered before I can even open anything.

'Do you work with make-up a lot?' I ask. 'I mean, on the newspaper. You seem to know a lot about it, Brianna.' It's a very extensive checklist.

'Yeah, I trained as a make-up artist before I came here,' she says, frowning at an eye pencil. 'And you can call me Brie, by the way. I had that put in.' She points to a corner where there's a mirror over a small table, rather like at the hairdresser. 'The mirror lights up, which is great for showing the true colours of the products.'

I hadn't taken any notice of it before, assuming it was just a mirror where we could check our look, though it wouldn't get much use being tucked away in a dark corner, I suppose. The strips of light all around the mirror are quite subtle, and I can't wait to see it in action. It looks like it belongs in a star's dressing room. This is all so exciting.

'Did you ever make up anyone famous?' I ask, hoping for some juicy, showbiz gossip.

'There were a couple of people from a soap opera once,' she says, shaking her head. 'You wouldn't believe how self-obsessed they are. They get genuinely offended if you tell them you don't watch their programme.'

'Oh, no.' I'm a bit disappointed and don't want to ask exactly who she met in case I suddenly decide I don't like them anymore. Not that I'd have that problem, of course; my mum keeps up with all the soaps and fills me in on anything I've missed, so I'd definitely recognise one of the stars if I saw one.

'So, have you worked on the *Chronicle* for long?' I ask, marking off the product details on the checklist.

'A couple of years,' she says, sorting out some lipsticks. 'I started off in modelling, like Eva, then moved to Rimmel.'

'I knew you looked like a model.'

She's quite tall and stunningly beautiful. She and Eva carry themselves in a special, model-like way, walking as though they're always on a catwalk. I might get them to teach me one day. I love the way they move, so graceful and feminine.

'We're both getting a bit old for all that malarkey now,' Brie says with a chuckle. 'I'd already studied make-up, and Eva was into hair and fashion, so we both had something to fall back on.'

'You're not old.' My jaw drops at the thought. She and Eva are a bit older than some of the girls here, but nowhere near Izzy's age. They must be in their early thirties, I'd imagine.

'Thanks for that,' she says with a giggle. 'But modelling careers are very short-lived. And tiring. I'm much happier in a steady position like this, although I must admit, I miss some of the excitement at times. I've tried telling Valerie we need to get more famous faces in the supplement. I'm sure the readers would prefer seeing some of their favourite stars model the new collections instead of mannequins or members of staff. Eva agrees. She had a rough start in life but now half her address book's filled with contacts from the world of showbiz.'

'That's a great idea,' I say, my eyes widening. 'I'd be more likely to buy something if I saw a famous person wearing it.'

She nods. 'That's what we thought. We'll have to mount a three-pronged attack on the boss next time, see if we can persuade her.'

We both laugh, though it seems like a very good plan.

My smile drops as I notice Valerie coming into the room, her face hidden behind a scarf and dark glasses. I wonder if she's hoping we won't recognise her. We all try not to stare, though it's really hard when she looks like that. Siobhan glides across the room and greets her just as she gets to her office. She follows the boss in and closes the door.

'I wonder what's going on there?' Brie mutters.

Everyone else is whispering, too, and I suddenly feel like I'm being disloyal to them all for not telling them what I found out. Trouble is, if I did, then I'd be disloyal to Siobhan and Valerie instead, and they're the ones keeping me employed. I hope.

I don't see either of them again until we return from coffee break. I'm feeling surprisingly good, having texted James, who confirms Gerard Johnson *is* the guy who abducted the little boy yesterday morning. He's well-known to the cops, apparently, and was their prime suspect—especially when he went missing right after the little boy was recognised in the street by his uncle, who questioned Johnson before the bastard fled.

'We're going to try out some of these colours,' Brie says as we enter the office.

My stomach flutters with excitement. 'I can't wait.'

Then a massive lump catches in my throat, and I get a sinking feeling as I notice Valerie standing, arms folded, in her doorway.

'Liberty. In here, please.'

I swallow hard, my whole body glowing hot as everyone stares at me in silence.

'I trusted you,' she hisses as I catch up with her.

She stands back to let me enter her room before she slams the door shut. I stare at her, my heart hammering. I know I haven't betrayed her, but somehow, I feel like I must have.

She's still wearing the dark glasses as she struts over to her side of the desk. Siobhan sits next to an empty seat on my side, a disappointed expression on her face. I feel queasy all over again.

'Sit down,' Valerie barks her order at me, and I quickly do as she says. Not just because I wouldn't dare disobey her, but I don't think my wobbly legs would support me much longer.

'Well, you've certainly shown your true colours, haven't you?' Valerie leans forwards, and I'm glad I can't physically see her beady eyes that I feel burning into me.

'I-I don't understand.' I honestly think I might throw up at any moment.

Siobhan sighs. 'Libby, Valerie had a call from the police about ten minutes' ago. They're on their way.'

'What?' It doesn't make sense.

'They said they'd spoken to you last night.' Valerie's voice is clipped. 'They need to ask you a few more questions, apparently.'

'Oh.'

'There's no prizes for guessing what that's all about.' Valerie's lips are tight as she spits the words out.

My mind whirls. She's got it all wrong. 'No, I…'

'Save it,' Valerie snaps as there's a knock at the door.

Siobhan gets up to open it, and I recognise the two coppers who walk in.

As she closes the door again, I can hear gasps from the office. She pulls over a couple of chairs for them and sits down again.

'Detective Sergeant James Harper,' says the better looking of the two men, reaching over to shake Valerie's hand across the desk. 'And this is Police Constable Danny Warwick.' His voice is as smooth as chocolate, and his smile is utterly charming as he and PC Warwick shake hands with us all. My insides flutter and I feel my breathing become a little heavier.

'We met last night,' the constable says, smiling at me.

A weird noise that can only be described as a snort emanates from Valerie, and we all stare at her. Whether she notices or not, we'll never know, as those damned sunglasses still hide her eyes.

'Well, gentlemen, I'm a very busy person, so I'm sure you won't mind if we get on with this, will you?' Valerie sounds very officious, and the cops both look over in surprise.

'Of course,' James says. He still hasn't let on that he knows me, which can only be a good thing. 'We just wanted to know if Liberty had remembered anything else following last night's incident. And to make sure she's okay.' He gives me a smile, and I get the impression my welfare is probably the *only* reason he came. He sounded quite concerned on the phone, and I wonder if he was already on his way when he called.

'I take it this relates to the personalised clothing collection?' Valerie continues.

My heart sinks even lower. She's got completely the wrong end of the stick, but all I can do is sit back and watch the car crash.

'That's right.' James nods.

'You'll need this,' she says, handing over the information from Companies House. 'As you can see, the company in question, Rebel (London) Ltd was dissolved last month, unbeknownst to us, of course. We would never have taken on the contract if we'd had any inkling of all this. We'd met with their director, Quinton Bellis, on a number of occasions and ironed out the details of the publicity campaign. We were just at the stage of putting together some articles for them when Liberty came across this.' She nods at the sheet in James' hand.

'I see,' he says, slowly.

'I take full responsibility for the oversight, of course,' Valerie continues. 'I was stupid enough to be taken in by the man.'

'Valerie, you'd better tell them everything,' Siobhan says, softly.

I frown, my mind whirling as I wonder what on earth 'everything' could entail.

The boss sits back in her chair with a sigh and finally removes her glasses. Her face is pinched and her eyes red and swollen. I can't help gasping at the sight; she must have cried all night.

She nods. 'You're right.' She turns back to the cops. 'During our meetings, Mr Bellis and I became good friends.'

James and his colleague exchange glances.

'I was impressed by him and his company—or, at least, what he *told* me about himself and his company.'

'So, you didn't look them up?' PC Warwick frowns at her, and she looks taken aback.

'No.' Her voice is curt again. 'I believed everything he said. He showed me pictures on his phone of his company's headquarters, the products, him shaking hands with the directors of large American companies after they'd agreed deals—everything. He even showed me magazine articles in which his collection was praised—of course, now I realise they were false. Mock-ups.' She shakes her head and sighs. 'I was a fool. I know that now. And you know what they say about a fool and his money...'

'You gave him money?' James clarifies.

I gawp at him. It's like Suzanne and Oscar Reynolds all over again. He catches my eye, and I know he understands. I think he might be becoming a bit telepathic like Cassie and me.

'Yes. I invested in his company.' She turns to me defiantly. 'You see, Liberty, if that publicity campaign had been successful, *I* would have made money, too.'

I gulp. 'I'm sorry,' I murmur.

'Don't be,' she shakes her head. 'In fact, you did me a favour. I had no idea the clothing was of such a poor standard. What he'd shown me previously had been top quality, of course—very different to what arrived on that rail the other day. I would have been mortified to have my name associated with such rubbish.'

'Integrity and reputation,' I say quietly, remembering the conversation we had yesterday. I *knew* Valerie was better than that.

'Exactly.'

She heard. And just for a split second, our eyes meet, and I see a flicker of recognition there.

'So, do you have a contract with this company?' James frowns.

'I signed something,' she says. 'And gave him ten thousand pounds in cash. I don't think I kept a copy though. I know it was stupid of me, but I just trusted him.'

She looks like she might cry. I think I might, too. I feel so sorry for her. Not only because she was taken in by a con man, but she's just admitted it all when she needn't have. I'm sure James and his colleague will have come because of Gerard Johnson, not Quinton Bellis.

I take a deep breath.

'Quinton Bellis owns a 'company' called Rebel,' I tell James, using finger quotes. 'They make clothes with names on, like the one Rebecca was wearing last night.'

'I see,' he replies, though his expression suggests otherwise.

'Although the company doesn't even exist,' Valerie points out, a drop of acid in her tone.

'No, but the clothes do,' I say. 'Angela, Rebecca's mum, said they got theirs in Margate. It looked similar to the ones we had here, the ones from Bangladesh. Though the font may have been a bit different, come to think of it.'

James frowns.

'We were going to do a feature on them for the supplement, *Woman Matters*,' I explain, sensing his confusion. 'But Mr Bellis had said they were top quality and made in Britain. The ones we were given to write about weren't very good at all, and when questioned about it, he claimed we'd received the wrong delivery. He still wanted us to write the article, though.'

'Liberty didn't want to associate her good name with them,' Valerie says quietly. 'And quite right, too.'

I blush. Just for a millisecond, I think she actually smiled at me. But I can't be sure.

'While Fran wrote up a piece about the range, I looked into the company and its directors,' I go on. 'That's when I realised something was wrong. There's nothing about Mr Bellis or his company on the internet, despite the fact they're supposed to be big in the States. I checked out the company for their details, which is when I discovered that.' I point to the document in James' hand.

'It's a good job you did,' PC Warwick says, nodding. 'Or your boss might have lost a lot more than ten grand.'

'It was only a down payment,' Valerie says, biting her lip. 'I was going to invest ten times that amount.'

I stare at her in horror before quickly averting my eyes.

'Do you have any idea where Bellis is now?' James asks, pursing his lips.

I glance back up at her as she shakes her head. 'He won't answer my calls. I'm not sure where he was staying; he seems to move around a lot.' She shrugs.

'That makes sense,' PC Warwick says, pursing his lips.

'Did you give him your bank details or anything?' James asks, kindly.

'I had, but I closed that account yesterday,' Valerie says. 'As soon as I realised something was amiss.'

She looks over at me, and I suddenly want to give her a hug and tell her it'll be okay. But I know it won't. She won't miss the money so much, but I can see that she'll miss *him*. Or, at least the man she thought he was.

'That's good,' James says. 'Well, if you hear from him again, I'd be obliged if you could call the station.' He stands and hands her his card.

'Of course.' She takes it graciously. 'Can I just ask... um... is the newspaper in any trouble over this? Or me?' She looks quite vulnerable gazing up at him, and my stomach clenches.

'Of course not,' he says with a kind smile. 'You haven't done anything wrong.'

'Even though I didn't report it straight away?' She frowns.

'No.' He shakes his head.

'But I thought that...' She looks over at me.

'They weren't here for that, exactly,' I tell her slowly.

James frowns, glancing from me to Valerie and back again.

'Something happened last night,' I say and go on to explain about Johnson and his attempted abduction of little Rebecca at the pool.

Valerie gawps at me, and for a minute I think she's furious that I didn't say anything earlier.

'All because she had a named top on?' Her voice is just above a whisper, her eyes wide.

'That's how dangerous these things can be,' James says, nodding.

'And we were going to take part in a campaign to make them the latest fashion,' she says. 'We could have been responsible for...' She puts her head in her hands, and now I really think she might cry.

Siobhan sits forward. 'It's all right, Valerie. There's no harm done,' she assures her gently.

'Thanks to Libby,' PC Warwick points out, making me blush. James nods.

'I'm just glad I was there,' I say, feebly.

'It must have been terrifying,' Siobhan says, shaking her head. 'Well done for standing your ground.'

I want to shrug and say something like 'it's what anyone would have done,' but my stomach feels sick at the thought of what Gerard Johnson might have done to Rebecca and me if that other man hadn't stepped in. He was a desperate man on the run from the police—he could have been capable of anything.

'Are you okay, Liberty?' Valerie asks, removing her hands and looking over at me curiously.

'Yes... it's just...' I suddenly realise I'm shaking again.

'You don't look okay,' James points out, putting his hand on my arm.

For some reason, just the feel of him makes me want to cry. Probably delayed reaction.

'Take the rest of the week off,' Valerie says, quickly. 'You must be in shock after all that. Especially with... all this.' She waves her hand in the air.

'I'll run you home,' James offers.

I stare at him. 'No, honestly...'

'Your boss is right. You shouldn't be here.' He stands, quickly shakes hands with Valerie and Siobhan, and puts an arm around me, leading me to the door.

'We'll see she gets back safely,' PC Warwick assures them.

'And don't worry about a thing,' Valerie calls out as the door opens.

I nod, and Siobhan follows us into the larger office.

'Fran, can I have Libby's things please?' she calls up the office. 'She's not very well so she's going home now.'

'Is everything okay?' Brie asks, handing James my notebook.

'Yes. She's a bit of a heroine, you know,' he tells her proudly.

I'm a little embarrassed but also relieved. I'd hate for the girls to think I'm being carted off by the cops because I'd done something wrong. I know it's hard to believe, but it *could* be misconstrued. Especially as no one knows that James is my boyfriend. Which is a good thing. I think.

James takes me home while his colleague, PC Warwick, goes back to the station.

'Here you go.' James hands me a cup of tea. Ugh! He's put sugar in it.

'I'm not in *that* much shock,' I tell him, grimacing at the cup. I only took one mouthful and feel queasy already.

'You could be.' James looks at me gravely. 'I should've thought of it last night. What was I thinking, going home when you needed me here?' He rubs a hand through his dark, wavy hair and frowns. 'I'm so sorry, Libby.'

'Don't be.' I hate seeing him beat himself up— especially over me. 'I was fine last night. You helped take my mind off it, honestly.'

He stares at me, sitting by my side on the sofa. 'I suppose seeing me in the arms of my ex might have given you something else to think about,' he says incredulously. 'Though, I hardly think it helped, do you?'

I giggle. He looks so serious and worried, but he really doesn't need to.

'Yep, it gave me a totally new focus,' I say, putting my horrid drink on the coffee table in front of us. 'Don't forget to thank Suzanne for me, will you?'

I'm grinning as his eyes become wider, and he stares at me for a second, then we both burst out laughing.

'I'm so sorry about that,' he says, once we've recovered. 'It was a cruel thing to do, and I told her so.'

'Do you honestly think she'll move out in a week?' I ask, not daring to hope.

He nods. 'She will,' he says, firmly. I know he means it, too. When James has that look on his face, there's no relenting. He has quite a prominent jaw, even through his thin beard, and he juts it out defiantly. 'Even if she has to pay for a hotel or whatever, she'll be moving out.'

I snuggle into him.

'She'll be paying for her own removal van, as well,' he adds thoughtfully. 'Do you know she brings back more of her stuff every time she comes in? My poor little flat's starting to look more like a jumble sale than my home.'

'She thinks she lives there, now,' I mumble.

'Well, she doesn't. And she won't even be staying there after this.' James sounds very firm.

'What time's Cassie due home?' he asks, putting an arm around me.

'She's finishing at lunchtime for a dental appointment. I'm not sure if she's coming home after that or going back to work. It's only a filling so it shouldn't be too bad.'

'Will you be okay? I'm afraid I have to get back to work, but I don't like leaving you here on your own.'

'I *really am* fine,' I assure him. 'It's only when I think about what happened that I get a bit nervy.'

'You were very brave standing up to Gerard Johnson,' he says gravely. 'The guy can be pretty brutal, by all accounts.'

'He's done this before, then?' I ask, my heart beating faster.

James nods. 'We've suspected him on several occasions but never been able to prove it. He's slimy. Manages to wheedle his way out of it. Each time we've had a confirmed sighting of him being in the wrong place, he's had an alibi from several others, swearing he was somewhere else. This is the first time he's been caught red-handed.'

'Crikey.' I start to tremble again.

'Drink this.' James hands me the tea.

Reluctantly, I take a mouthful. He watches me until I take another. It really is gross, but it looks like I don't have any option but to drink it.

'I'd love to take some time off to be with you,' he says, tenderly, 'but I desperately want to make sure we get that scumbag behind bars this time.'

'Of course,' I tell him. 'I don't need a babysitter. And I'll be much happier knowing you've got him off the streets.'

He looks thoughtful. 'How about going to stay with your parents for a few days? A short break away from here would do you the world of good, I reckon.'

I balk. 'I hadn't thought of that. It has been a while since I saw Mum and Dad, and it'll be nice and quiet down there at this time of year.'

'I could come and join you at the weekend, if you like?' he offers, looking a little brighter. 'It's been years since I last went to Broadstairs.'

My heart leaps. 'Yeah, and you'll get to meet my folks. They'll love you. I know they will.' I can just see Mum fussing over him. I have a bit of a weird relationship with Mum, though I love her to bits, of course. I've always thought she was disappointed in me. She was amazed when I first got a job in London; she never thought I was capable. I was a manager at a hotel. I didn't tell her I was only a *junior* manager, of course, and I always wore designer shoes and clothes when I went to visit her—usually on loan from Cassie. It wasn't until I was mentioned in the newspaper for helping solve a couple of crimes that her attitude towards me changed. She was ever so chuffed when I told her I was seeing a police sergeant, too. I think even Dad was secretly impressed about that, though he wouldn't admit it in a million years.

'Relax for the rest of today and maybe think about getting the train tomorrow,' he says, studying my face. I honestly think he expects me to keel over at any minute.

'I'm fine, honestly.'

'I know. But just to be on the safe side.'

My phone buzzes, and I reach for my bag.

'It'll be Cassie,' I tell James, fishing it out.

I stare at the screen as my whole body turns hot. It's definitely not from my best friend.

You just love splitting up happy couples, don't you? Well, you won't get away with it this time!

James must notice the expression on my face as he immediately puts a hand on my arm.

'What is it? Bad news?'

Dumbly, I turn the screen to show him.

He frowns.

'Do you know who sent this?'

I shake my head as my entire body shivers.

'I don't know that number. I had one yesterday as well.'

I'd forgotten about what I'd assumed was a wrong number last night—there was too much else to think about—but I quickly scroll down my messages and show him.

'It's the same mobile,' he says, whipping a small notebook from his pocket to jot it down. 'The obvious person to send it is Suzanne, but that's not her number.'

I stare at him. It makes sense that she'd do something like this. I've no idea who else it could possibly be.

He tries to return the call.

'It's switched off,' he huffs. 'The oldest trick in the book. Buy a pay-as-you-go phone and keep it turned off when you're not using it so it can't be traced.'

It looks like Suzanne had taken some notice of his job, after all, to have picked up that idea.

'I'll check through her stuff tonight,' he promises. 'She might have stashed the phone somewhere at home.'

I nod. 'Thanks, James.'

'Don't worry,' he says, giving me a hug. 'She obviously has nothing better to do.'

'But I didn't even split you up,' I moan. 'You were divorced way before we got together.'

'I know. It's just her idea of a sick joke, I expect. Honestly, you've got nothing to worry about. I'm just sorry if she managed to get your number through me. She must have sneaked a look at my phone.'

It makes sense, but it's still not very nice. I used to feel sorry for Suzanne but now, I just wish she'd go away and leave us alone.

Just then, we hear a key in the lock, and I almost leap out of my skin as Cassie comes into the hall.

'Libby?'

'In here.'

'Thank God. I thought we'd been burgled when the door wasn't locked.' She throws her bag and coat on the sofa opposite and slumps down. Then she sits forward, looking at me, then James. 'Are you okay?'

'I'm fine,' I reply. 'What about you? How's the filling?'

She looks a little sheepish and sits back again. 'I didn't go,' she admits. 'Honestly, it feels so much better now, I thought it wasn't worth the hassle.'

I sigh. 'Well, it was hurting the other day. Surely, it's better to get it sorted now so it doesn't get to that stage again?' I know she hates the dentist, but really.

'Well... I thought about it.' She shrugs.

'So, why aren't you at work in that case?' I ask, curiously.

'Oh, I'd already booked the time off so I thought it would just confuse the issue if I stayed there. And besides, Perdita was in one of her moods, so I didn't fancy working with her any longer than I had to.'

'So, you're skiving?'

'Not exactly. I mean, I did have a genuine reason to take the afternoon off, didn't I?'

'For a filling? No. An hour at the most. Having a funny mouth doesn't stop you from doing your job, and it's not *that* painful.'

I eye her curiously. I know all about her aversion to dentists, but something tells me there's more to this.

'Well, I'd better get back to work,' James says, getting up.

I stand up, too, and throw my arms around his neck. Somehow, things always seem better when he's around. I've really fallen for the man in a big way. Huge. He gives me a lingering kiss that makes my stomach flip.

'Think about what I said,' he says softly when he releases my swollen lips. 'I'm sure your parents would be pleased to see you, and I think the sea air and a change of scenery will do you good.'

I smile. 'Okay.'

'You're going home?' Cassie's eyes widen as we hear the front door shut.

'I didn't get chance to talk to you last night,' I say, sitting back down and curling my legs up under me.

'Is everything all right?' Her brow furrows with concern, and she comes to sit next to me on the sofa.

'It is now,' I tell her. 'It's just... there was this incident.' I go on to tell her about Johnson and the little girl. I also explain about the named tops and the business with Valerie. She listens like the good friend she is, clutching my hand and letting me get it all out, even when I start shaking again.

'This always happens when I talk about it,' I admit. 'James thinks it's a delayed reaction. Adrenaline took over at the time but now, it's different.'

'You're a bloody hero.' She gives me a massive hug. 'Thank God you had your wits about you when that bastard called her by the wrong name.'

'Not so much a hero, just... *there*,' I say with a wry smile. 'Anyone else would have…'

'No, they wouldn't!' She sounds adamant. 'Most people wouldn't add two and two like that. They'd just get on with their own lives.'

I frown at her. 'Are you saying I'm nosey?'

'No, of course not,' she says, alarmed. 'It's good that you take notice of stuff. Most people in London go around with blinkers on.'

'Oh, and there's something else,' I tell her, scrolling through my phone and showing her the anonymous messages.

She frowns incredulously. 'It's got to be Suzanne.'

'That's what we thought. James is going to see if she has a second phone stashed away somewhere. That's not her usual number.'

'The cow. I hope he arrests her.' Cassie shakes her head furiously.

'Now that's something I'd love to see,' I agree.

I giggle, and she gives me another hug.

'So, do you fancy a cuppa? Or something stronger? Brandy's good for shock, you know?'

'No, thanks.' I chuckle, remembering the ghastly sweet tea that was also supposed to be good for the condition. I think it's the shock of the awful taste overpowering the original shock that makes it work.

She sits cross-legged, facing me. 'So, what's this about your folks? Are they all right?'

'Yep. Valerie's given me the rest of the week off, and James thought I could use a break. He's working hard on the case, but he said he'll come down at the weekend to join me. In the meantime, he thinks I should spend some time in Kent. It's been a while since I saw Mum and Dad, so I thought it might be nice.'

Her eyes light up. 'What a great idea. Can I come? We'll have a couple of days just relaxing by the sea. It'll be great. I love your dad, he's so funny, and your mum's chocolate cake's to die for!'

I roll my eyes. It's Mum's lovely cooking that's worrying me. It would be great to go with Cassie, though. She's met my parents a couple of times, and they adore her as much as she does them.

'What about your job?' I ask, frowning. 'Surely, you can't just take time off?'

Cassie rolls her lip. 'It'll be fine. I'll just tell Meredith I had some treatment at the dentist, and I can't come in for a few days. She'll understand.'

'Is everything okay with work?' I ask, narrowing my eyes at her. 'I thought you loved working at Crystal?'

'I do,' she says, slowly uncrossing her legs. 'Well, I *did*.'

'Has Perdita upset you?'

'No. Not really. It's just... everyone.' She waves her hand in the air as though encompassing the whole world. 'The atmosphere's changed. It's as though everyone's waiting for the hammer to fall but no one will admit it. They're all fighting to keep their jobs and they're not being as friendly to each other as they were.'

'Are they being horrid to you?'

She shrugs. 'Not especially. Everyone's just on edge, snapping at each other and not having a laugh anymore.'

'So, *is* Crystal in trouble, then?' I can hardly believe it. It's such a great company, and they produce some gorgeous clothes.

'It looks like it,' she says with a sigh. 'I even spoke to Rob and Ben last night, like you suggested. Asked if there might be a way of featuring them in the paper. Ben said there's usually a waiting list for promotional features, so we'd have to join the queue.'

I shake my head. 'There must be *something* we can do.'

'Yep, we can go on holiday and forget about it,' she says, resolutely. 'We'll take the car. It needs a good run.'

***

A couple of hours later, we've loaded up her boot as well as the backseat—a girl needs to be prepared, after all—and we're just getting a few last-minute things together for the journey.

Mum was thrilled when I'd told her we were coming down, though a little concerned that Cassie was driving. She immediately put Dad on the phone.

'You'll hit rush hour coming out of London,' he'd warned. 'The M25 will be nose to tail and the Dartford Crossing's always busy, it doesn't seem to matter what time you hit it.'

'I'm sure Cassie knows all that, Dad. We'll be fine, honestly.'

Dad wasn't so sure, but I got the feeling if we discussed it any longer, we'd hit rush hour before we got to the end of our street, so I quickly thanked him and hung up.

'I do *know* how to drive,' Cassie says, rolling her eyes. I knew I shouldn't have kept them on speakerphone.

'I know.' I shrug, hoping she wasn't offended. 'I grabbed all the fruit from the bowl for the journey down.' I hoped a change of subject might help. It did.

'You *are* being good.' She looks impressed. 'I was going to suggest stocking up on chocolate.'

'No way. I've lost nearly a stone, and I'm not going to pile it all back on now.'

'It must be love,' she says with a giggle, and I get a funny feeling in my now-slimmer-than-ever tummy.

***

We climb into the car, a cherry-red BMW called Mark Two, after an unfortunate incident with its predecessor, and Cassie hands me a pile of CDs. I pick one out, still in its wrapping.

'What's that?' She frowns.

'I bought it for Valerie, my boss,' I say with a shrug. 'It's Baroque music—quite stylish, apparently. I'd put it in the cupboard, and it must have got mixed up with these.'

'Really?' Cassie raises her eyebrows.

I grin. 'It's great, I heard some on YouTube. Sort of classical but fun at the same time. You know, vibrant and exciting. Valerie likes it, and the band had an appropriate name, REBEL, the same as the clothing brand we were working on, so I thought...' I break off, realising it's probably a good thing I hadn't given it to her yet, as it turns out.

'I'll have to check them out,' she says. 'Maybe stick with Rihanna for now, though?'

I giggle. 'Okay.'

I load up the music while she turns the key in the ignition. There's a click but nothing else.

'Damn!' she wails. 'It's got a flat battery. I knew I should've used it more.' She tries the key several more times before ringing Rob for advice.

'He reckons we need a mechanic,' she tells me, grimacing. 'It'll take ages to get anyone over here as it's hardly an emergency—and there's no telling how long it'll take to fix. Looks like we'll have to take the train.'

I know it'll make my parents happy, but it's a real pain unloading everything again and taking it back up to the flat.

'We'll need to condense it quite a bit to carry it all,' I say, slumping onto the sofa while we stare at all the cases and bags we'd squeezed into her car. 'I can't believe we had that much stuff.'

'Hmm. Perhaps we could do without all this food for a start.' She pulls out a couple of carrier bags. 'Your mum makes enough to feed an army.'

I curl my lip. 'That's the trouble. I just thought if I took a few cereal bars and fruit teas, it might be easier to keep track of my eating. I don't want to offend her, but I really don't want to put the weight back on.'

'Then *tell* her.' Cassie makes it all sound so simple. 'Just explain that you're being healthy and only need small portions of stuff. She'll understand.'

I wish I could be so sure. Mum's a great cook, and she loves having people to try out new recipes on, but they're not usually the most nutritious of meals. I'm beginning to wonder if it was such a good idea to visit them right now, after all. I've been so proud of my slimmer figure and it would be a shame to spoil it now. *I'd hate for my efforts to all go to waste—especially my waist.*

'Come on, it'll be fun.' Cassie's clearly read my mind again. She does that a lot. 'We'll just condense our clothes a bit and take a case each. It's a shame it's not summer though. Jumpers take up much more space than bikinis.'

We go through our things again, and I'm amazed how much stuff I thought I'd need for just a few days. I can easily fit into nearly all of Cassie's clothes now, so we pack stuff we can both share. We don't have to tell Mum who owns what. I always try to impress her by wearing designer outfits so she can see how well I'm doing with my exciting London job—even when it's not really that exciting. With one case and one large bag each, we eventually pile into a taxi headed for Victoria station.

We're travelling first class—Cassie insisted on buying the tickets—and it's a relief to get a comfy seat with a table to rest my book on. I look over at my best friend as we whizz out of the city. She looks a little more relaxed now, and I get the impression this break will be as good for her as I'm hoping it'll be for me.

12

Dad picks us up at Broadstairs station, clearly relieved we didn't drive down. He looks very pleased to see us, and I enjoy a big, manly hug from him, the type you can only get from your dad.

We get back home where the smell of cooking fills the air as soon as we open the door, and Mum's waiting for us anxiously. The house feels warm and inviting, and I can't stop myself from crying once I'm in Mum's arms.

'We had a call from James,' Mum says, holding me tight. 'He told us what happened. You're a very brave girl.'

I'm relieved but shocked. They've never even met my boyfriend.

'I gave him your mum's number,' Cassie admits. 'He thought they should be forewarned and didn't want you to have to repeat everything all over again.'

I sniff, pulling back from Mum's soft embrace.

'Thanks,' I manage. That was extremely considerate of him, and I'm surprised he'd even thought of it. I think I might have misjudged him a little. I miss him already.

'Now, how about a cup of tea? Dad's taking your things upstairs so you can sort them later. Dinner won't be long.' She's got her sing-song voice on, but her eyes are a little red, and I can see she's worried about me.

Cassie and I sit at the kitchen table while Mum pours out the drinks. 'Do you want a biscuit or a piece of cake?' she offers, placing two steaming hot mugs in front of us.

I shake my head. 'Not just yet, thanks. I don't want to spoil my dinner.'

Mum smiles. 'Very sensible.'

'We ate quite a bit on the way down, too,' Cassie pipes up, not mentioning it was only fruit.

'It's so lovely to see you both again,' Mum says, pulling up a chair. 'I want to know all about London and what you've been up to. You've both changed jobs since I last saw you. How's that working out?'

'Fine,' I say. 'I only moved to a new department this week, though, so it's early days.' I sip my tea, which tastes so much nicer than usual—especially without the sugar.

'Hmm, I thought you'd have been at the news desk longer than you were,' Mum muses.

'Everything works quicker in London, Mum,' I say. I haven't told her all the details of my 'sideways promotion.' Or the fact that it's only temporary. No point in worrying her even more.

'I suppose.' She pouts before taking another sip of her tea.

'Cassie's working for a fashion designer,' I point out.

'Yeah, it's a great firm,' Cassie adds. 'I even got to choose some fabrics for the new spring collection.'

'Ooh, now that *does* sound exciting.' Mum sits a little straighter while Cassie tells her all about her work.

That's one of the things I love about Cassie, she can read my thoughts. She must have known how awkward things were getting with Mum and stepped right on in. She's awesome at doing that.

We finish our drinks and go upstairs to unpack our things. It's great to be back in my own room again. It's still how I left it, although much tidier. I have lilac wallpaper with tiny white flowers, and white curtains with lilac flowers. My bedding matches the curtains and lampshades, and the carpet's a soft grey with a thick pile. I quickly kick off my Louboutins and sink my feet into the woollen luxury. It's blissful. Then I sit on the bed, closing my eyes and breathing in the memories and familiar scents of my old life.

A sudden thought makes me ping my eyes back open again. If I lose my job, I might have to come back here. I certainly won't be able to afford the flat in Chelsea—Cassie already pays the lion's share of the rent—and goodness knows how often I'd be able to visit her and James. Suddenly, my perfect little room doesn't seem quite so appealing. I mean, it's great to come home to occasionally, but no one in their twenties with a career and job in London wants to go back and live with their parents, do they?

'Hi.' Cassie pokes her head around the door. 'I love my room.'

She has the spare room, which is decorated in bright yellow and white. Mum reckons it's unisex, but my brothers were horrified with the transformation. It's been blue for years, as was the room next to it, which has now been knocked into an en-suite bathroom. Mum wanted guests to feel more comfortable with their own facilities, and it really is lovely. It even has a double bed, unlike mine.

'Are you okay?' Cassie comes in, frowning. 'You're not worrying about that man again, are you? You need to stop thinking about him. James is brilliant at his job, and he'll get him slung in prison for good. You'll never have to see him again.'

'I hope you're right.' I don't have the heart to tell her that what I am really concerned about is losing my job. Although, now that she's mentioned him, I do feel a bit jittery about Johnson.

'Come on, your mum said dinner will be ready in a minute. We should go down.' Cassie puts an arm around me. 'You grew up here, didn't you?' she asks, looking around my room.

'Yep.'

'You're so lucky.' She looks like she truly means it.

'So are you,' I point out, remembering all the foreign holidays she told me about, the riding lessons and private music tuition.

Her eyes are wide as she gawps at me. 'I never got to hear the seagulls or the sea,' she points out. 'Not unless we were on holiday. And my mum and dad are great, but they could never just drop everything every time I wanted to go home. I'd have to plan it months in advance to catch them both in the country, let alone at the house.'

I feel a lurch in my stomach. I've always envied Cassie being from such a rich family, but it seems I might have been wrong to.

'And my mum's cooking never smelled like that,' she goes on, as we make our way downstairs.

I smile. I know I'm lucky. I'm just beginning to appreciate *how* lucky.

'You've lost weight,' Mum says, narrowing her eyes at me as we enter the kitchen.

I swallow hard, waiting for a lecture on how I need fattening up.

'It suits you.' *Why do mums never cease to amaze us?*

'Thanks.' I beam, and she smiles back.

'I've made fish pie with plenty of vegetables,' she says, turning back to the oven.

'It smells lovely,' I tell her before giving her a big hug.

'What's that for?' She looks a bit taken aback as she turns to face me.

'Because I love you,' I tell her with a shrug.

She chuckles, then serves up the food. It's absolutely delicious, and I notice she hasn't given me such a huge portion as normal, though my plate's still full with all the broccoli and carrots.

We finish with apple pie and custard. I can't resist it, so I just have a small slice. It's worth every calorie.

Afterwards, we all go for a walk on the beach. It's not as cold as London, and the salty air feels so much cleaner.

Viking Bay is a horseshoe-shaped cove surrounded by rocks. To access it you go down some stone steps and onto the sandy beach, which feels soft and homely beneath my feet.

In the summertime, it's teaming with families who come to swim in the cool water. There are often fishermen on the rocks leading into the bay, and it's a favourite site for surfers. There are regular Punch and Judy shows for the children, as well as donkeys for riding over the sand. Ice cream vans always pitch up here in the peak season, and there are often funfairs to play on.

Along the back wall of the bay, there are rows of old-fashioned beach huts, mostly painted in bright colours, some with stripes. They even have competitions here for the best-decorated hut. I've always wanted to own one of those. Imagine having your own little hut where you can close the door and change in peace, or just sit outside in a deckchair, on your own reserved area of the beach. Dad has always said they were too expensive, on the rare occasions one ever came up for sale.

It's getting dark, and a couple of trawlers are silhouetted against the inky-blue sky on the horizon. The shushing of the waves is almost melodic, and I shiver at the thought of what might lie beneath them. The sea always looks quite ominous at night, to my mind.

I close my eyes and breathe in the sea air, which always comes accompanied by memories of my childhood. I can almost hear children giggling and kicking sand, building castles, and pouring buckets of water into their moats—and my shrieks when my brothers used to splash me when they'd just been swimming while I was sunbathing.

Being here is like being caught in a time warp. Not just because it's my home and the place I was brought up, but it looks like nothing's changed over the years. That's probably what I love most about it.

We saunter over the boardwalk, taking in the sights and smells almost in a reverential silence. I feel truly at peace. Even the events of the past few days can't affect me here. It's my safe haven, and always has been.

By the time we get home, we're too exhausted for anything other than a nice, hot cup of tea and bed. There's a knock at my door as I crawl between the sheets.

'Only me.' Cassie looks a little sheepish as she pops in. 'Just wondered if you've got any painkillers. My tooth's really hurting again—and before you say anything, yes, I know I should've gone to the dentist this afternoon.'

'We can try to get you an emergency appointment at my old place, if you like?' I try not to sound too judgemental. After all, she looks pretty miserable. I hand her a packet of Nurofen from the drawer of my bedside locker.

She nods, taking the tablets. 'Thanks, hon. I'll see you in the morning.'

After the best night's sleep I've had in ages, I'm woken by the sound of seagulls screeching outside my window the next morning. I can smell the salty air already and rush to get showered and dressed. I can just see the sea between a couple of houses farther down the hill from where we live.

***

Cassie doesn't look at all well when she strolls down to breakfast. Her face is pale, and she looks very sorry for herself.

'We need to call the dentist this morning,' I announce as soon as I see her.

Mum frowns. 'Oh, dear. I'll make you some warm tea, Cassie. Not too hot.'

'Thanks.' Cassie sits next to me with an apologetic expression.

Mum pours her drink, adding some cold water, and places it in front of her. 'Now, what would you like to eat? Something soft, I think. Yoghurt, perhaps, or porridge?'

I crunch my toast noisily, and Mum throws me a scowl.

'No, honestly. This is fine, thank you.' Cassie takes a sip of her tea and winces.

I whip out my phone.

'You finish your breakfast. I'll call Mr Pollock,' Mum insists and leaves the room.

Cassie stares at me incredulously. 'Is that really his name?'

I giggle. 'Yep.'

'I hope his secretary's a proficient typist.' She manages a smile, and I'm glad to see her looking a little more cheerful.

'All done. He'll see you at half past ten,' Mum says brightly, coming back into the room.

'That's good. I was afraid we might have to wait until two thirty,' I say with a grin. 'Tooth hurty, get it?' I giggle.

Mum rolls her eyes, and Cassie just shakes her head. Well, *I* thought it was funny.

Mum looks over at Cassie. 'You're looking a little better already, dear. Are you sure I can't get you something to eat?'

Cassie puts her hand up. 'No, thank you. Honestly, I'll be fine once this is sorted.'

'It's a filling,' I tell Mum, who looks surprised.

'Has it been hurting for long?' She sucks air through her teeth. 'Oh, dear, I'm afraid the cold air can't have helped last night.'

I give Cassie a knowing look but say nothing.

Just then, Dad arrives carrying a newspaper. 'Morning, all,' he says cheerfully. 'Brisk wind out there today. You'll need to wrap up if you're heading out.'

Mum gives him a cup of tea. 'They're going to the dentist. Cassie needs a filling.'

Dad gives a sympathetic frown. 'Oh, dear.' He pats Cassie gently on the back. 'Have you tried a saltwater rinse? That can help. Or whisky?'

'Malcolm! She can't go drinking alcohol at this time of the morning!' Mum admonishes.

Dad gapes at her. 'It's not drinking, it's medicinal.'

Mum gives him one of her looks, and he slumps into a chair and opens his paper. 'I was only trying to help,' he mumbles.

'Thank you, anyway,' Cassie says kindly, and Dad smiles with a wink.

I roll my eyes, and Cassie looks like she's trying not to laugh as we finish our cups of tea.

'Oh, look!' Dad points to something in his paper, as if the rest of us can see it. 'They're having a sale of Airfix kits at the Hornby Visitors Centre. I could do with another Spitfire Mk 2. I don't know what's gone wrong with the one I'm making. The construction was fine with the plastic cement but the glue's just not sticking properly to the aerial.'

'I told you not to get that cheap stuff from the corner shop,' Mum says with a sigh. 'Mr Patel tries his best, but when he says super glue, he doesn't actually mean superglue.'

'Just helping the local economy, dear,' Dad says. 'We can't let the big boys have all our cash.'

'No, but you need the right tools for the job,' Mum points out.

'They might have superglue in the Visitors Centre,' Dad says, pouting thoughtfully.

'You don't have time to go there today,' Mum says. 'You promised to look at the washing machine, remember?'

Dad looks crestfallen.

'We could go,' Cassie offers, peering over at the advert. 'I've never been to Margate.'

'Are you sure?' I ask with a frown.

She thinks for a moment. 'Yes, quite sure. I haven't been to Ramsgate, either.'

I shake my head. 'I mean, are you sure you want to go there with your tooth?'

'She can hardly leave her teeth behind,' Dad blurts out with a guffaw. 'Now, I, on the other hand could just...'

'No, you couldn't!' Mum looks panic-stricken as Dad reaches for his mouth.

Cassie and Dad laugh hysterically while Mum lets out a huge sigh of relief. I'm sure she expected him to remove his dentures right here at the breakfast table.

'Come on, we've got a bus to catch,' I say, standing up.

'I'll drive you,' Dad offers, folding his newspaper.

'No, you won't,' Mum cuts in. 'The girls are perfectly adept at going out on their own. This is their holiday, after all. Whereas you, Malcolm Lawrence, have work to do.'

'I just thought I could show them around the Visitors Centre,' he says, grumpily.

'It's fine, Dad, honest.' I spent enough hours trawling around plastic model displays and shops when I was young, I certainly don't want to do it now. We'll just pop into the shop at the centre without looking at a single aeroplane, pick up the kit and some glue and escape. I'm sure there's no limit to Dad's modelling capabilities, but there's definitely a limit to the number of bits of plastic I can bear to look at.

13

While Cassie's having her tooth filled, I flick through a magazine in the waiting room. It's eerily quiet, with just a couple of elderly women having a whispered conversation at one end of the room, and the occasional ring of the telephone behind the reception desk. The atmosphere is much calmer than in London, and most of the people are more casually dressed, too. Even the receptionist is wearing a T-shirt with her smart pencil skirt, and the two old dears waiting with me are in thick skirts with elasticated waists and hand-knitted pullovers that have seen better days.

Cassie returns after a while, looking much happier than she did when she arrived. I know how much she hates visiting the dentist, but even *she* had to admit it was the best course of action, given the pain she was in.

'It's all numb,' she tells me, although her actual words are more like 'It or um.'

'At least it doesn't hurt, then,' I say, putting an arm around her.

Once she's paid, we go outside into the winter sunshine. The breeze is cool as we head down the High Street and towards Pierremont Hall. We decide to head straight into Margate before Cassie's anaesthetic wears off.

She points out a lovely vintage clothing shop on the High Street, and we pass my favourite gift shop on Albion Street, which has pretty ornaments and lamps in the window, and fairies and mobiles hanging from the ceiling. We agree to come back this way later if she still feels up to it.

We're on a route called The Loop, which travels from Margate through Broadstairs and then on to Ramsgate before returning to Margate. The buses are quite regular, and we're soon trundling northwards. I feel quite nostalgic as we pass familiar territory, and Cassie looks enthralled by it all. I had a happy childhood here, although a lot has changed since I was small.

Several housing estates have sprouted up since I last visited, many blocking the view of the sea, but one thing we're both thrilled with is the big shopping centre that's expanded at Westwood Cross.

'We're definitely coming back here,' Cassie says in her funny voice as we gaze out the window at signs for Debenhams, Monsoon, Accessorize, River Island and Outfit, among others.

We arrive shortly afterwards outside the Hornby Visitors Centre and clamber off the bus.

'Looks like we're in the middle of nowhere,' Cassie says, looking around.

'Come on, we'll get what we need and catch the next bus back,' I assure her. She's not used to large expanses of countryside.

We go inside and head straight for the shop. It's busier than I expected, and most people are buying tickets to look around the centre.

'Are we going in there?' Cassie asks me.

I gawp at her. 'No. We'll just get Dad's stuff and go.'

She shrugs, and I know she has no idea what it's like to spend hours staring at plastic aeroplanes, tanks, and railways until you're blue in the face. To be honest, they're very impressive if they're your thing, and the people who make them are obviously incredibly skilled. When you're a young girl, however, you don't quite see the appeal.

I pull out the voucher Dad clipped from the paper and hand it over in exchange for a red box with a Spitfire on the front. But unfortunately, he can't get the glue he needs.

Then we go back outside and shiver while we wait for the bus to come and take us back to civilisation. There are a couple of other people at the bus stop, too, including two teenagers, evidently called

Tyrone and Jason if their hoodies are to be believed. I shudder, biting my tongue hard. How can I point out the dangers of wearing your name on your clothing to a couple of complete strangers?

The bus finally arrives, and I notice there are several others on board sporting the same style of hoodie. Kylie and Tegan sit near the front, and we pass Kevin farther back, too. Angela was right about everyone wearing them around here.

It's a relief when the bus pulls in at the busy shopping centre at Westwood Cross, and we joyfully climb off. Our first port of call is Costa's for a skinny latte. Cassie also has a glass of water to cool her drink a little, then uses the rest to take a couple of painkillers as the feeling slowly returns to her mouth, although her voice is still funny. Then it's a whistle-stop tour of the shops to take her mind off her tooth. Outfit has a sale on, and Cassie's clearly tempted with some new black trousers.

'This means you have to buy something, too,' she tells me.

I can almost feel my credit card quaking in my bag as I check out some T-shirts. Finally, I decide on a plain white one with pretty, fluted sleeves.

'I'm trying to curb my spending,' I remind her as we leave the shop with our goodies. 'James is so worried about how much the house is costing to repair, and I don't know what he'll do if it turns out he doesn't even own it.'

Cassie frowns. 'Is that really likely?'

It's a good job I can interpret her words.

'He seems to think so.' I shrug. 'The solicitors are looking into it now.'

'So, why do *you* have to stop spending?' She looks puzzled.

'I don't know. I just feel that it's like rubbing his nose in it if I keep buying stuff knowing he can't.'

James is naturally quite frugal and drives around in a battered, old car. He insists on taking his own lunch to work—and thinks I should do the same, which I tried, by the way. It's so much hassle *and* your sandwiches get squashed. He also rarely buys takeaways.

Cassie purses her lips. 'That's a shame.'

I can see her eyeing up River Island.

'*You* can still get new things,' I remind her.

Her eyes light up. 'Then you can help me choose. After all, you will be borrowing them, won't you? So, we have to have stuff we both like.'

I follow her into the store. She really is the best friend a girl can have. We look through the jeans, but there's nothing we particularly like. Then we notice the blouses and tops. There's a lovely cold shoulder T-shirt in bright red that catches my eye. Cassie pounces on it at the same time.

'Ooh, we have to have this!'

'It's lovely and soft,' I say, feeling the fabric.

'They've got it in blue as well,' she notices. 'And black.'

She pulls out a couple from the rack. 'What d'you think?'

'Beautiful. What colour are you getting?'

She peers at the tops, putting first the red in front, then the blue, and finally the black. Tilting her head from side to side, she frowns. 'I'll have to take them all,' she decides.

I shake my head, following her to the till.

'The blue one will look lovely with your hair,' she says, as the cashier bags up the items.

'You're not supposed to be buying for me,' I remind her.

She rolls her eyes. She does that a lot when she's with me. 'Then we'll share.'

I give her arm a squeeze.

The cashier's looking at Cassie a little strangely, and I remember she probably can't understand what she's saying. I giggle as we leave the shop.

Two skirts, three pairs of luxury tights, a jumper, and a host of make-up later—Boots also had a sale on—we decide it's time to head for home. I'm actually quite peckish but don't want to eat knowing Cassie can't, so I'll wait until we get back and sneak something when she's not looking.

We take the bus back to Broadstairs, then pop into the local pub, The Dolphin Inn, on our way towards home. We're both dying for the loo by now, so we go there first before getting a drink. It's quite olde-worlde with wooden beams and a low ceiling and feels all homely and welcoming.

'This is lovely,' Cassie says, sitting back in her chair and looking around.

'You should see it at the height of summer,' I say with a smile. 'You wouldn't get a seat for love nor money.'

'I'm not surprised.' She takes a sip of her Coke and winces.

'Too cold?' I ask, guessing her teeth must be throbbing by now.

'Just a bit. And that's even without any ice in it.' She moves the glass away from her with a sigh.

I quickly finish mine while we chat about how peaceful it is in this part of the world. I do love it here, but I don't think I'd like to live here again. I am too used to the bustle and noise of the city now.

'Let's go,' I say, standing up.

'I'll just nip to the loo again,' she says. 'Meet me outside, if you like.'

As soon as the cold wind whips around me, I wish I'd opted to stay in the bar. I breathe in the salty air while the doorman gives me an odd look. It doesn't feel too comfortable waiting here for Cassie, so I take a short stroll down the road, in front of the inn and then up a little side street. That's when I see it. My heart thumps, and I shiver, not with cold this time, but with dread.

Footsteps click behind me, and I swing around nervously.

'There you are. I thought you'd gone home without me.' Cassie looks quite indignant and then studies my face. 'What's wrong, hon?'

We're standing in front of a dilapidated building, and I point up at the sign above the door. 'BaROQ Printing Services.' My mind immediately replays some of the Baroque music I listened to by that group REBEL. *That reminds me, I must decide about giving Valerie that CD.*

'That's Bellis' company,' I say, almost in a whisper. 'I remember Fran telling me, though I assumed it was spelt like the music.'

Cassie frowns at it. 'Nice to know it actually exists, then.' It's a good job we're so well-tuned into each other, or I wouldn't have understood a word of what she said. The numbness must be wearing off slightly, but she still sounds completely foreign.

'It looks like it's still in business, too.' I frown. That means Bellis *does* have a bona fide company after all—or does it? 'Pity I can't go in and see if he's in there,' I mutter. 'He'd recognise me right away and know I was on to him.'

'He doesn't know *me*,' Cassie says, a glint of mischief in her eyes. 'I'll go in.'

'Hang on.' I feel panicked. 'We don't know what he might do.'

She grins. 'From what I've heard, the guy's more likely to *chat* me up than beat me up. Besides, I have a plan.'

She shows me her mobile phone. 'I'll just have a little conversation with him and record it. What harm can that do?'

I sigh. It's a good idea, and at least it'll give us some evidence of whatever he's up to. I learned from James that you need evidence for everything, no matter how small or trivial.

'What are you going to talk about? Why he's selling fake goods and conning middle-aged women out of their money?'

'Something like that.' She presses a few buttons on her phone and puts it into her bag. Gucci. At least he'll see she has money. 'So, I'm looking for George Clooney, right?'

I nod. 'Be careful.'

She gives me a quick hug as well as her bags of shopping. 'Don't worry.'

I watch her strut confidently up the little stone steps and fling open the door. Reluctantly, I walk away from the building and down the street a short way. I busy myself gazing into the window of Owler's Nook, the lovely gift shop we passed on the way here. They always have such pretty and quirky items in there, but I'm finding it hard to concentrate on them today. *Focus, Libby.* I force myself to scrutinise a pretty, ornamental fairy in bright-red shoes that's placed in the middle of the window display. *I wonder how much it costs. Would it make a nice gift for someone? Or could I fit it on the little side table in the flat? The longer I stare at it, the more I want it. I can picture it on my bedroom windowsill now. It'd look fabulous. You don't see many fairies in London.*

***

I hear Cassie's Manolos clicking down the street before I see her. She's beaming. 'Meet me round the corner,' she says as she passes me. 'He might be watching.'

I turn back to the shop window I've been staring into, moving slightly as though I'm trying to see something more closely. The fairy's even prettier from this angle, I notice. Cassie struts on past me, and I wait a short while after she's disappeared into the next street before I follow her. To be honest, I find it hard to drag myself away from the beautiful fairy and promise myself I'll come back tomorrow and buy it.

'I think I have something,' she says, her face glowing. 'Let's get back, and I'll show you.'

My heart's almost pumping out of my chest as we make our way towards home.

'He's a dead ringer for George,' she mutters.

'I told you.'

'He's had a lot of work done to look like that.' Cassie notices these things. 'I saw a scar behind his ear. And that nose certainly isn't natural.'

'Makes sense. Nothing about that guy's real.'

'Except the trouble he's in,' she whispers. 'He wasn't working there. He was gathering his things. The place was empty. When I arrived, he was emptying drawers of papers into bin bags.'

It takes less effort to understand her, as the numbness is obviously wearing off a little. A thought occurs to me.

'Did you manage to speak to him okay? With your mouth, I mean?'

She shakes her head. 'No. I used my toes.'

'Ha, ha, very funny. You know what I mean.' Her humour's worse than mine. Yes, honestly, it *is* possible.

'He thought I was foreign,' she mutters. 'I said I was from a small island off the coast of Dubrovnik. He sounded impressed—especially when I told him my family owned the island.' She sniggers.

My eyes feel like they're about to bulge out of my head.

'I told him I was just after a T-shirt with my nephew's name printed on it, but he said the equipment was all shut down. The large room behind him looked empty from what I could see through the open door, and the whole building echoed. I reckon he's sold everything off—or had it repossessed.'

'I already had my purse out, and you should've seen his eyes light up when I 'accidentally' dropped it and a wad of notes fell out.' She giggles. 'His attitude changed completely.'

'Oh, no. Don't tell me he made a pass at you?'

'Almost.' She laughs. 'He was absolutely charming and offered me a cup of coffee.'

I roll my eyes. Cassie clearly enjoyed herself in there, while I was worried to death outside.

'As long as that's all he was offering,' I say.

'It wasn't, as a matter of fact. He also suggested I buy shares in his company. Said his business partner had gone to live abroad so he was looking to replace him. Apparently, I'd make the perfect 'partner.' She uses finger quotes, and I gasp.

'He was propositioning you?'

'Don't look so surprised.' She mocks offence.

I giggle. 'I don't mean it like that. It's just...'

'I know. He was complimenting me the whole time and told me how profitable his company was, and that they were just clearing out this building as they were moving to new premises nearer London.'

I start. 'Really?'

'And that's not all.' She looks around us surreptitiously. There are a few people walking along the street, but none taking any notice of us. 'I asked if he had any stats to back up his claims about the business. He had to go into a little office at the back, and that's when I grabbed these.' She pulls a handful of papers from her bag.

I stare at them.

'I think they're bills, but I didn't have time to check.'

'We'll go through them later.' My mouth feels dry with excitement as she quickly tucks them back in her bag.

'I've recorded all the rubbish he told me about his company and even about the contract he wants me to sign. I asked who his solicitor was, as I said I didn't know any in England. He wrote down all the details for me.' She taps her bag.

'That's fantastic!' I shout excitedly.

'Shh.' She puts a finger to her mouth, and I notice several people looking our way from the other side of the road.

I feel my face heat up. I've completely forgotten where we are for a moment, it is such brilliant news.

'Sorry,' I whisper, but she just rolls her eyes, smiling.

'I'll tell you the rest when we get home,' she says, looking at the couple walking behind us who seem to have taken quite an interest in our conversation, all of a sudden.

We walk quickly towards the house in silence. My mind's occupied on what's on those papers inside Cassie's Gucci, and the tape I'm hoping might send Bellis to prison.

14

We burst into the kitchen where Mum's just taking a cake from the oven.

'Wow! That smells delicious,' Cassie tells her.

Mum beams. 'Thank you, dear. How's your mouth?'

'The numbness has worn off, and it doesn't feel too bad,' Cassie tells her with a smile. 'I just have to take more Nurofen if it hurts.'

'That's good. Did you manage to eat any lunch?' Mum puts the kettle on while Cassie and I sit at the table.

'We didn't even notice the time,' I admit, looking up at the clock. It's after three. *No wonder I'm starving!*

'You should eat something. I'll make some sandwiches. Ham and cheese okay?'

Mum's already got a hand in the breadbin as she asks, and I'm surprised when she pulls out a wholemeal loaf. 'I'll pop some salad in them, too,' she says, smiling.

'Thanks, Mum.'

She gives me a knowing smile, and I suddenly jump up to hug her. I didn't expect her to understand my need to keep the weight off. But here she is, offering healthy food and reasonable-sized portions. Totally different from what I'm used to.

'Mum, is everything okay with you and Dad? Healthwise, I mean?' I release her from my hold as it suddenly occurs to me there might be another reason for the dietary changes.

'Yes, of course, love.' She looks surprised. 'Why do you ask?'

I shrug, not wanting to tell her. 'No reason.'

I give her another squeeze, and that's when it hits me. 'You've lost weight,' I tell her, accusingly.

She smiles. 'Just a little. Don't want to be getting fat in my old age.'

I stand back and look at her properly. She removes her apron, and it's clear to see that her dress skims her body beautifully. 'You look great,' I tell her.

'I knew there was something different about you, Mrs L,' Cassie pipes up. 'Well done. It really suits you.'

'Thank you, dear.' Mum blushes and pours the tea.

I take the cups over to the table while Mum slices some cheese.

'So, what have you been up to?' she asks, placing the sandwiches on the table a few minutes later. 'Apart from the dreaded dentist, of course.'

'Actually, he wasn't that bad,' Cassie says, pulling the papers from her bag.

We both stare at her. Suddenly, she stops what she's doing and turns bright red.

'I mean, *it* wasn't that bad,' she corrects.

Mum and I exchange glances. Mr Pollock, the dentist, is a grey-haired man in his late sixties. He has a long nose and tiny glasses, which he looks over in an old-mannish sort of manner. He's always quite pleasant—well, as pleasant as a dentist can be, I suppose, but I honestly didn't think he'd be Cassie's type. Cassie's *grandad*, maybe.

She gives us a look of horror, presumably reading my mind. She's good at that.

'I didn't see *your* dentist,' she points out, 'I saw a locum. His name was David Daniels. He was in his twenties and very good at what he was doing.'

I raise my eyebrows.

'In my *mouth*,' she adds quickly. 'He managed to do the filling without hardly hurting me at all. He was very... competent.'

'Hmm. Competent,' Mum echoes, giving me a sideways grin.

'That's just want you want. Competent,' I say, trying to keep a straight face.

Mum giggles, and suddenly, we all burst out laughing.

'You two are awful!' Cassie accuses, shaking her head. She takes a delicate bite of her sandwich.

'Yep,' Mum agrees, smiling.

Cassie chortles.

'Well, I'll leave you girls to it,' Mum says after washing her hands. 'Dad's finally mended the machine, so I'll get a load of laundry on.'

'Oh, I almost forgot,' I say, delving into one of my bags for the model. 'He wanted this. Sorry, they didn't have the superglue.'

'Thanks, love. That'll please him.'

She disappears out of the room, and Cassie passes me half the pile of papers from her bag.

'Looks like they're massively in debt,' she says, holding up a bill for just over three thousand pounds. 'And this one's from the bank, threatening a foreclosure of their account.' She shows me another.

'No wonder he was so keen to get his hands on Valerie's savings,' I mutter.

We enjoy our lunch while studying the papers. After sifting through a bunch of threatening letters and overdue bills, I pounce on a form. It looks like some sort of legal agreement written in a very small typeface.

'Cass, who was that solicitor Bellis recommended to you? The one he uses?'

She hands over a small piece of paper.

Brey & Co. It's the same name on the form I'm scanning, which seems to be some sort of investment agreement. It's very hard to read.

'Do you want to hear the conversation?' she offers, pressing a few buttons on her phone.

It starts with Bellis sounding very disinterested in Cassie. Then she drops her money, grabbing his attention. From there on in, he's a charming, gushing lump of jelly, hanging onto her every word and weaving innuendo into the conversation at every given opportunity. To give her her due, Cassie does a great job of fobbing him off by 'not understanding' him.

'Call me Quinn,' he says, and my stomach roils. Slimy bastard. I can easily see how someone could be taken in by him. That's the trouble.

He waxes lyrical about his brilliant company and plans for expansion. He's getting new, state-of-the-art equipment, apparently, and has headhunted the guy he wants to run the printing side of things for him. Listening to him talk and looking at the pile of bills in front of me just makes me sick.

I feel so sorry for Valerie. And I wonder how many other women have been taken in by him and parted with their hard-earned cash on the promise of a great return—among other things.

He probably put the cost of his plastic surgery through as business expenses. After all, it's what it was for. His face literally is his fortune. *And that's probably what it cost, too.*

'I can see why his partner buggered off abroad,' I mutter, as we hear about him suddenly being left without his 'right-hand man' and needing a replacement as soon as possible. 'Did he say where he went?'

'Nope. Outer Mongolia I expect. Getting as far away from the creep as he could.'

'He might have been just as bad for all we know—it was a man, wasn't it?'

Cassie frowns. 'I think so. That's certainly the impression I got, and I'm pretty sure he said 'he'.'

She rewinds the conversation a little as my heart beats so heavily it feels like a lead weight. I don't know why, but I'm consumed by a feeling of dread.

'My business partner was brilliant with the paperwork and all the accounts and stuff,' Bellis says, in an almost crooning tone. 'I do all the legwork and get the orders while he sits around making phone calls and telling people what to do—and taking a huge whack of the profit, of course.' He chuckles. 'Poor Ol' had to go abroad because of some family matters, though. I don't blame him, of course, family comes first, and all that. I'd always put my woman and any kids before work.' His voice has become even smoother, and I can just imagine the look on his smarmy face.

'Poor Ol' who?' Cassie shouts at the phone.

'Definitely a man. Does he mention him again?' I ask.

'I'm not sure.'

She sets it playing again while I doodle idly on the back of one of the bills. 'BaROQ, Bellis, money, women, Rebel, Fame, name, Quinn, Quinton, Kent, Margate, printing.' I turn my head, hoping that seeing the words from different angles might somehow put them in some sort of order that makes sense. It doesn't.

Cassie switches off the recording once she's reached the end. It's mostly Bellis fawning over her, trying to persuade her to invest in his company, and in his unctuous words, 'invest in *him*'.

'Gosh, I was glad to get away from him,' she says with a shudder. She looks over to my doodles. 'Any thoughts?'

'It's this word, BaROQ,' I say. 'It's shouting at me.'

'That'll be the capitals,' she says with a nod.

I purse my lips. 'I get that Bellis is into Baroque music and his favourite group is called Rebel,' I say slowly. 'And BaROQ looks a bit more stylish than the correct spelling, which might not make the company sound as contemporary as he's hoping.'

'It's never going to sound contemporary while it's called Baroque, no matter how you spell it.' Cassie rolls her eyes. 'So what if he likes that kind of thing?

Why would you want to name your company after it, anyway?'

She has a good point.

'I know the group REBEL use capital letters so that might be behind the way it's written. The company Rebel uses lowercase, so they've just swapped them—apart from the 'R,' of course.'

'Okay.'

'And BaROQ's got his initials in it, so that might be a reason for capitalising that particular word,' I say slowly. 'So maybe 'R' and 'O' are his partner's initials? The other half of the company.'

As soon as the words leave my mouth, it hits me. 'Shit!' I thump the table. ''O' 'R'.' Oliver Reynolds. He's the partner who's suddenly disappeared!'

'Of course!' Cassie jumps up from the table, and we high-five each other.

My eyes are wide, and my whole body turns hot. I stare at the piece of paper, with the sound of blood pumping through my ears.

'So, what's the 'a' for, Sherlock?' Cassie asks, looking to where I'm studying the words. ''And' perhaps?'

'Arseholes!' I reply without thinking.

'Liberty!' Mum just walked in, a horrified expression on her face.

'Sorry, Mum. It's just...'

'Libby just solved a mystery,' Cassie explains.

Mum raises her eyebrows in a dumbfounded sort of manner.

I add a couple more words to my list of doodles: Oliver Reynolds.

'Now it makes sense,' I say, my heart sagging a little. 'Rebel is an amalgamation of **Re**ynolds and **Bel**lis. And didn't you say their solicitors were called Brey & Co?'

'**B**ellis and **Rey**nolds!' Cassie blurts out the names.

'We need to tell James,' I say quickly. 'If Bellis is packing up the place, he might be getting ready to run.'

I hurriedly text him. There's no time for niceties or kisses or anything this time, but I just know he'll understand.

Need to Face Time you urgently. Are you free?

His reply's almost immediate, thankfully.

Go ahead.

I can hear Mum gasping behind me as I explain all about the events of the morning—missing out the bit about the dentist, of course. I also show him some of the bills. My heart's thumping like a steam engine, not just with the excitement from what we've just discovered, but also because James looks so delicious in his white Ralph Lauren shirt, rolled up to his elbows as usual. I have a big thing about his arms. And his eyes. His voice. Well, everything about him really.

'You need to be quick. He was emptying the place while we were there. He might disappear,' I urge him when I've explained it all.

'Don't worry. I'll contact Kent Police now. Their Thanet division can keep an eye on him while we gather some evidence. Can you send me what you have?'

'Of course.'

He's already reaching for his desk phone.

'I'll talk to you later. Well done, sweetheart.' He winks and switches off.

The room's suddenly in silence. My mind's whirling. Sweetheart. He called me sweetheart. James has never been into PDAs and he knows Mum and Cassie are here, but he still said it. I suddenly feel much calmer and lighter.

'Such a nice young man,' Mum says at last.

I realise there's a stupid grin right across my face, but I can't stop it.

'Great at his job, too,' I say, nodding.

'I'm sure that's not the only thing he's great at,' Cassie jibes, waggling her eyebrows.

I blush while she giggles like a naughty schoolgirl. Mum clearly doesn't know where to look.

'Well, I think this calls for a celebration,' Mum says, quickly composing herself. 'We've got some

Prosecco in the fridge. Why don't you call your dad, Libby, and I'll fetch the glasses?'

We all go through to the lounge and enjoy some bubbles, while Cassie explains to Dad what's been going on.

'Well done, you two,' he says, astonished. He turns to Mum. 'We've got a regular *Cagney and Lacey* here, Wendy,' he says proudly.

I've no idea who he's on about, but I assume it's a compliment. Mum nods, happily so that's a good sign, anyway.

I haven't seen Mum and Dad so relaxed in ages as we sit and talk, laugh, and sip wine for longer than anyone would care—or be able—to remember.

'Look at the time,' Mum says, squinting at the clock.

It's already getting dark outside.

'I haven't put the dinner on or anything!' She stands, swaying slightly.

That bottle of Prosecco turned into a couple, then a little white wine followed by some of Dad's homemade elderflower concoction.

'Don't bother cooking now, love,' Dad says. 'Why don't we all get fish and chips?'

Dad has the best ideas, and we gasp at the fresh air as we walk towards the beach to get our supper. One or two seagulls are still crying out overhead, seemingly piercing my brain in its fragile state. The salty smell of the sea welcomes us as we look out over Viking Bay. The dark shadow of a tanker on the horizon looks ominous, and red lights flash from a wind farm way out at sea.

Just outside The Seafarer, our favourite chippy in the area, stands a life-size statue of a sailor, dressed in a bright yellow sou'wester. He looks a little more dishevelled than I remember, and I can only imagine how many tourists will have hugged him in a selfie.

Dad opens the door to the shop, and we all moan our appreciation. The smell is to die for, as the fish and chips are all cooked fresh to order. We sit down, and Dad orders cod and chips for all of us, including mushy peas for himself. I never did see the appeal, but he likes them.

It doesn't take long for our meal to arrive, and we all stare open-mouthed at the size of the portions. I know I won't eat all of mine, but I'm determined to enjoy what I have. I'm not disappointed. The taste is out of this world.

'You can't beat real fish and chips by the sea,' Dad proclaims, as we enjoy our meal.

'Of course, you can beat fish,' I say. 'That's why it's called *battered*.'

Dad rolls his eyes, but I can tell by the twitch on his lips that he's trying not to laugh.

My head's not half as bad as I'd feared it might be when I wake on Saturday morning. The gulls are already screeching outside my window, and the winter sun tries to poke through the dull clouds. I've already got a smile on my face as I jump out of bed and get ready. James is hoping to come down later with Rob. I can't wait to see them—James, especially, of course.

Dad's humming away as Mum brings a fresh pot of tea over to the breakfast table. I'm surprised Cassie doesn't look happier, though.

'Is your mouth still sore?' I ask, as she sits down.

'No, it's fine,' she says with a weak smile.

'What about your head?' Dad asks, looking over from his paper.

'Much better than I deserve,' she says with a chuckle. 'Your elderflower wine's pretty lethal stuff, you know. It should carry a government health warning.'

'It would if the government knew anything about it,' Mum says with a smile.

'They could use it as rocket fuel,' I jest.

Dad chuckles. 'I could be sitting on a goldmine out there.'

The phone rings in the hall, and he gets up to answer it.

'Wow! You've got a landline?' Cassie marvels.

Mum giggles. 'I know it's a bit old-fashioned in this day and age, but it's force of habit, really. We're just used to it.'

'How's Dad getting on with his mobile?' I ask, warily.

She sighs. 'He can answer calls okay, but texting takes him forever. Honestly, he'd be quicker writing a letter and sending it by post.'

'That was Zachary,' Dad says, returning with a smile. 'He's hoping to pop over later.'

'Fantastic!' I yell. 'What about Ewan and Natalie?'

Zachary and Ewan are my older brothers, Zak being the eldest. Natalie's been Ewan's girlfriend for years and just feels like part of the family, though they've never mentioned marriage or anything.

'They can't make it this week,' Dad says with a grimace. 'Something to do with getting the new shop ready.'

I nod, though I can't hide my disappointment. 'That'll be the hairdressers,' I say. 'I read something about it on Facebook.'

'Oh, that's old news, Libby,' Mum says, finishing her toast. 'Natalie was going to go into business with her sister to run that, but they decided it's safer not to mix family with work. She's looking into a little boutique now.'

I gape at her. 'How did I not know this?'

'They only saw it last week,' Dad explains. 'And they've put in an offer already. It was accepted right away, so she and Ewan are already making plans. They're off to Rochester today to take another look at the property and check measurements.'

'That's great,' Cassie says, smiling. 'We'll have to go visit once it's up and running.'

'Definitely.' It's good to see Cassie looking a bit more cheerful. I am, too. It's just occurred to me that I might be able to get a job with Natalie if things don't work out at the paper—though I'm sure it'll all be okay. 'Hey, maybe we could help with some advertising for her?' I suggest.

'Great idea. I'll mention it to Ewan next time he gets in touch,' Mum says.

'Well, we'd best get moving. There are a couple of little boutiques we thought we'd check out here in town today,' I say, standing up. 'And I have to take Cassie to Morelli's, of course.'

'Of course,' Dad echoes.

'They do nice coffee in there,' Mum says, clearing away the dishes. 'And paninis and sausage rolls—all sorts of things.'

Dad catches my eye and grins. 'Oh, no, Wendy. You can't possibly go to Morelli's and not have ice cream.'

'Absolutely,' I say, as Cassie and I leave the table. 'It's the law.' I know I'll have to eat nothing but lettuce leaves for the next month to make up for all the calories, but Morelli's ice cream is *so* worth it.

***

Cassie and I spend a lovely morning mooching around the shops of Broadstairs, culminating in a stroll along the promenade before arriving at Morelli's. I can tell there's something wrong when Cassie doesn't buy anything, so I intend to quiz her over a chocolate sundae.

Outside, there's a row of small, white, plastic tables and chairs and inside is awash with pink and white. There's a small, tiled pattern on the floor and the tables are inlaid with a pretty, pink geometric design. The chairs are white wicker with pink cushions, and soft pink sofas line a couple of the walls. Pink and white striped Venetian blinds cover the far wall, which is on a little, raised area, approached by a couple of shallow steps.

The black and white photographs on the wall depict Morelli's in days gone by, showing that the layout hasn't changed much over the years. There are also some round, brightly-lit pictures of ice cream sundaes that stand out like portholes in the wall.

Although the front of the shop overlooks Viking Bay, the gurgling of water comes from inside, where a large fountain bubbles over a selection of beautiful shells.

Despite the bitterness of early November, several people buy ice cream from the array at the counter, and I can't wait to join them.

We peruse the menu and marvel at the pictures with titles like 'Choc-oh-lah!' and 'Tutti Frutti!' Then Cassie turns the cover, and we gasp at 'Tipsy Treats' and 'Bubbles by the Beach.'

'They've got cocktail sundaes!' She pounces on one made with Irish cream. 'I have to have one of those.'

Luckily, we picked up a couple of sausage rolls earlier, which we ate while window shopping, so I'm sure our stomachs are lined enough for a little more booze—not that I'd expect much in an ice cream, anyway. And we had a good breakfast, so that should help, right?

They taste delicious, and we savour every mouthful, sitting back in our chairs and moaning with delight.

'You're so lucky to have been brought up with all this,' Cassie says, gesturing to the beach outside the large window.

I know she's right, but when it's the norm for you, you don't seem to appreciate it as much as you should.

'How are things with you?' I ask, narrowing my eyes slightly. 'We don't seem to get so much time to talk these days.'

'I know.' She swallows another mouthful. 'There's just so much other stuff going on.'

'Rob's coming down later, so that'll be fun, won't it?'

She smiles. 'Yeah, he's great. We're really close, you know?'

I nod. I do know. James and I are getting that way, too.

'Are you still worried about work?'

She sits forward, nodding. 'Yeah. I really like this job, Lib, and I'm good at it. I don't want to lose it now.'

'You seriously think Crystal will close down?' I frown. It's unusual for Cassie to be so passionate about work. We met while we both worked at the same hotel, but while I was trying to carve out some kind of career, Cassie was only there to win a bet with her father.

She shrugs. 'It looks that way. Everyone's worried, I can tell. There's lots of whispering going on, but no one's admitting anything. Allegra messaged me today, though, to see if I was feeling any better.'

'That's good. You like her, don't you?'

'Yeah. She's absolutely great to work for; doesn't lord it over you like some people might.'

Allegra Cohen-Haugh is one of the supervisors at Crystal and seems to have taken Cassie under her wing. She's one of those rare people who don't mind teaching and helping other members of her team, and genuinely wants Cassie to do well there.

'I think you should talk to her. Tell her you're worried about the future of the company and your job. She might be able to help.'

'Or she might say I'm absolutely right and send me off to HR for my P45,' Cassie says, gloomily.

'Time for another, I think.' I swipe the glass dishes off the table and return to the counter. I hate seeing Cassie like this. I'm hoping another sundae will do her good, though I'll just have a Diet Coke this time.

I place the order and idly admire the photos of all the different desserts on the wall behind the counter when someone wraps their arms around me from behind. I yelp, checking in the mirrored wall opposite to see who it is.

'Zak!' My eldest brother looks more handsome than ever with his blond, tousled waves and a little fair stubble around his chin.

I reach up and kiss him on the cheek before he lets me go and comes to stand next to me at the counter.

'How's it going, titch?' His pale-blue eyes twinkle, and dimples appear on his cheeks as he grins at me.

I can't resist throwing my arms around him again and giving him a tight squeeze.

'Fine. It's so good to see you!'

The familiar scent of his after-shave and feel of his long arms around me take me back to my childhood. Zak was always great at giving hugs.

'Here you go,' the woman behind the counter says, placing my order on a tray.

'I'll get these,' Zak says, releasing me while he reaches for his wallet.

'Are you sure?'

'Of course.'

Zak always treated me when we were younger. I smile up at him, fondly. Then I glance back to the counter and notice a familiar figure in the mirror behind it. James stands near the door watching me. My entire body fills with a mixture of delight and dread. I'd been so looking forward to seeing him again, but I can tell by his confused expression that he's just caught me in the arms of another man. He doesn't know Zak's my brother, and he'll naturally think...

'Hi,' he says, walking towards us with a smile.

'James.' I gasp. 'It's not... I mean... I don't want you to think...'

He's still smiling, though he looks a little bemused by my reaction. I want to throw my arms around him, but I can't. I need to explain first.

'Hi, I'm James Harper.' He holds his hand out to Zak who shakes it with a grin. 'Zak Lawrence,' my brother says. 'I've heard a lot about you. You're the cop, aren't you?'

'That's right. And you must be Libby's brother. Good to meet you.'

I gawp at them as a woman behind me clears her throat.

'Where are we sitting?' Zak asks me, lifting the tray out of the woman's way.

I point over to Cassie, and he makes his way over.

'Lovely to see you, too, Libby,' James says, his eyes shining down at me.

It's then that I throw my arms around him, unable to speak. It's wonderful to have him here, and I'm so relieved he didn't jump to the wrong conclusion about Zak. I'm enveloped in his strength and almost want to cry, I'm just so happy.

We follow Zak over to the table where he's already introduced himself to Cassie. He turns as we join them.

'James, I thought I'd get a coffee. Can I get you the same or something else?'

'Coffee would be lovely, thanks.'

Zak goes back to the counter and we settle down. Cassie gives James a quick hug as he sits between us.

'Rob's been delayed a while,' James explains. 'He's coming by train, and there's been a holdup, apparently.'

'I thought you were travelling down together?' I query before sipping my drink.

'We were, but I had to work an hour or two this morning and didn't want to detain him, so he said he'd come by train.' James chuckles at the irony.

'Typical.' Cassie rolls her eyes.

'Is that okay with your sore tooth?' James nods at the ice cream in front of her.

I should've thought of that myself. She must be in agony!

'The first mouthful was a bit tense,' she says, nodding, 'but once the alcohol kicked in, it numbed the pain completely.'

'Alcohol?' Zak's just returned and put the coffees on the table in front of James and himself.

'For medicinal purposes,' I interject.

He shakes his head. 'You sound like Dad.'

'Funny you should say that,' Cassie says with a smile. 'He did say something about whisky.'

'Nothing new there then.' Zak grins and takes a sip of his very sensible—but boring, in my opinion—coffee. 'How are the old fogies?'

'I'll tell them you called them that,' I threaten him with a laugh.

'Not if you want another of those, you won't,' Zak retorts, grinning.

'I think he's got you there, Libby,' Cassie says with a giggle.

She's right.

'They're fine. I take it this means you haven't been home yet?'

'Nope.' He shakes his head. 'I was on my way, when I thought I'd just pop in here for a decent coffee before I get subjected to the oldies' instant rubbish.'

'Snob.' I pull a face at him.

'Yeah.' He nods with a smile.

'Any news about you-know-who?' I ask James.

'We'll discuss it later,' he says.

Good point. We're not far from BaROQ, though we've avoided going there again this morning. Not only because James warned us not to go near the place, but I wanted to stay relaxed today with him coming down and all. Oddly enough, I feel very calm now that he's here. I didn't realise just how much I miss him.

Cassie's mobile lights up, and she checks her messages. 'It's Rob,' she says. 'He took a taxi over to your parents' place. Apparently, your Mum's plying him with tea and chocolate cake.' She grins.

'You'd better eat that up so we can go and rescue him,' Zak says with a grimace. He turns to me. 'You know what the mothership's like. He'll be too fat to get out of the house again once she gets her claws into him.'

Zak's always referred to our mum as that ever since I was tiny. He managed to convince me once that she was a real alien. Dad wouldn't let me watch *Star Wars* again after that.

'She's a lovely lady,' James says with a giggle. 'We had a good chat when I arrived. She told me I'd probably find you in here.'

I gawp at him. 'You've met my mother?'

'Of course. It was the address you gave me, remember?'

He's right. I didn't expect him to arrive so early.

'Yes, but...'

'And you didn't answer your phone,' he adds.

I quickly pull it from my Radley. Damn. I must've switched off the ringer last night when I'd had too much to drink and forgotten to check it this morning.

'Sorry,' I say, quickly turning it back on again.

'That's okay. Your mum offered to put me up tonight, as a matter of fact.'

I blush. 'What?'

'Yeah, she said there's a large sofa-bed in the lounge I'm welcome to use.' His eyes twinkle.

'I've only got a single bed,' I tell him.

'We couldn't sleep together at your parents' place,' he says firmly. 'Not when I've only just met them. It's disrespectful. I was planning on finding a B&B.'

'I hadn't thought of that,' Cassie says, chewing her lip. 'I just thought, as I have a double bed and all...'

'You'll be fine,' Zak assures her. 'Rob can stay with you tonight. That's just one of the countless advantages of not being part of the family.'

We all giggle, and I'm surprised to notice a very thoughtful expression cross James' handsome face.

We stroll back towards home, James with an arm around me, and Zak and Cassie chatting like old friends. They're both very easy people to get along with and I'm really glad they like each other.

A slightly familiar-looking woman passes us, quickly placing sunglasses on when she sees me watching her. I'm sure I recognise her from somewhere, but I can't place her, and she doesn't acknowledge me as she struts past. Probably one of my old teachers, I suppose. It's safer not to acknowledge her; I can't remember liking any of them much. She's obviously in a hurry too, as she strides ahead of us.

I point up the road towards The Dolphin Inn as we pause in our tracks.

'That's where BaROQ is,' I whisper to James. 'It's just behind the pub.'

He immediately holds me a little tighter.

'We're sticking to Albion Street,' he says, glancing at the street name. 'And you're sticking to me, okay?'

My stomach flip-flops at his deep voice. He sounds very firm, and I know he means it. Unfortunately, we can't avoid going this way unless we double-back and then take a much more protracted route home.

'Thank you,' I whisper, glad of his protection.

We walk past the little alley leading to the printers, and I notice a couple of police cars parked outside. I glance up at James, who looks in the same direction.

'It's not our problem,' he mutters and hurries me past.

I look back at Cassie, who mutters something to Zak, probably telling him all about the place and what we discovered there. She gives me the thumbs up, and I assume she's spotted the police presence, too. Then she whips out her iPhone and takes a few snaps.

I'm surprised how much calmer I feel about the whole incident, now that James is here. He seems to have that effect on me.

Once we're on Stone Road, Zak points out some of the houses and regales us with useless but very funny facts about the people who used to live there. I'd totally forgotten what an odd bunch of neighbours we had while growing up.

'Remember Mr Finch from that bungalow?' Zak asks, turning to me. 'He used to leave his milk on the doorstep for days until it went off and then bake scones with it. He reckoned it was the only way to make them.'

I'd forgotten all about him.

'And Mrs Crackett who lived down there?' He points. 'She was accused of putting down rat poison and killing all the cats in the street, as well as loads of birds,' he says, his eyes wide. 'I heard they took her to court, but she was let off. Turns out it wasn't rat poison she'd scattered about the place, it was some crumbled-up scones she'd received from Mr Finch!'

We all burst out laughing.

'That's not true,' I protest, still giggling. 'We always used to think she was a witch. That was how she never got caught.'

'No, I think that was the mothership's role,' Zak says, as we reach home where Mum's on the doorstep.

'I heard that, Zachary Lawrence!' She points at him in mock anger before throwing her arms around him.

'Oh, hi, Mum. I didn't see you there,' he claims, giving her a big hug.

'Come on in, everyone. The kettle's on,' Mum says as we all pile into the hallway. 'And look who's here.'

Rob's waiting for us in the kitchen doorway, and Cassie rushes over to throw herself into his embrace.

Soon, we're all sitting in the conservatory drinking tea and eating the remains of Mum's chocolate cake—though I only have a small slither.

The phone rings while we're all chatting, and Mum gets up to answer it.

'Oh, dear,' she says, 'that's awful. What will you do?'

She grimaces, clearly listening. 'Libby's here. Maybe she'll have an idea?' She perks up, nodding at me and then comes over with the handset. 'Ewan said they love the new shop, and it's going to be ready much sooner than they'd anticipated,' she says. 'Trouble is, Natalie can't find a supplier of quality clothes.'

I take the phone from her, pleased to speak to my other brother. 'Hi Ewan.'

'Hey, sis. We can have the shop ready in four weeks' time,' he tells me. 'Any idea where we can get some nice clothing to fill it?'

My mind reels with ideas.

'Here, I'll put Natalie on.'

'Libby?' She sounds concerned. 'I was hoping to source some locally made stock, but I can't find anything I like.'

'What're you looking for?' I ask.

'Something classy,' she says. 'There's plenty of places selling run of the mill stuff, but I want this to be really special. All the wholesalers seem to be selling the same style that's in every other shop, and the only handmade items I can find aren't classy enough for the image I'm hoping for.'

I pout, glancing over at Cassie, who's snuggled up to Rob over by the window.

'Cass, is Crystal supplying independent retailers?' I ask.

She shrugs. 'I think they only have their own shops,' she says.

'Perhaps that's the problem,' I say, pouting.

Cassie stares at me. 'You're right!'

'Do you think they'd be interested in a high-class boutique in Rochester?'

'What a great idea! They need to diversify if they want to succeed. I'll speak to Meredith about it when we get back, if you like? See what she says.'

'Great.'

'I heard that,' Natalie enthuses down the phone. 'I love Crystal clothing! And there's certainly a niche down here for that sort of style.'

I nod at Cassie, who beams at me.

'Okay, Cassie'll make enquiries and get back to you asap, okay?'

Natalie whoops for joy at the other end of the line, and Ewan comes back on to thank me before hanging up.

'Well, I'd better be getting back,' Zak says, after another good natter.

It's sad to see him go, and I decide to make more of an effort to see the family in future. Things seem much easier with Mum now, and I'd look forward to coming down to the sea more often.

***

'What are your plans for this afternoon?' Mum asks, refilling our drinks. 'It looks like it's going to stay dry.'

'I thought perhaps a walk on the beach,' James suggests, smiling at me. His eyes twinkle, and there's a promise behind them I can't resist.

'I'd love that.'

'What about a tour of the town?' Mum suggests, smiling at Cassie and Rob. 'I have a leaflet somewhere.'

She pops into the lounge and opens a drawer.

'Here you go.' She quickly returns and hands over a little brochure. 'You can learn a bit about the history of Broadstairs.'

'Thanks, Mrs L,' Rob says, taking it from her. 'We might do that.'

We go back out into the winter sunshine and head towards town.

Rob opens out the leaflet.

'Right. *Town Trail*,' he reads. 'Looks like we start off at Dickens House Museum, *the home of Mary*

Pearson Strong, upon whom Dickens based his character Betsy Trotwood in David Copperfield.' He looks up and down the road. 'This way, I think. Looks like it's near the bottom of the High Street.'

'Ooh, the High Street? There are some nice shops up there,' Cassie says, suddenly looking interested. 'In fact... look.' She points to a map on the back of the leaflet. 'This map shows you a trail of them all. We could follow this one.'

James and I get closer and peer at the colourful town map. Instead of having all the historic places of interest numbered as on the side Rob was studying, this one has all the shops numbered with adverts for each one.

I burst out laughing. 'Trust you!' I say, playfully.

'It was so nice of your mum to suggest the trail,' Cassie says with a grin. 'It would be rude not to take her up on her idea.'

Rob and James shake their heads and exchange an exasperated look.

'I suppose you want to go with them?' James asks me.

My stomach flutters. I'd love to go around all the shops—who wouldn't? Just for once though, I'd rather spend some time with James doing what he wants.

'We don't want to intrude,' I say. 'Why don't we let the lovebirds do their tour, and we'll have a quiet walk on the beach?'

James looks slightly taken aback, and his mouth twitches into a smile. 'Are you sure?' He frowns.

I nod. '*Quite* sure.'

'Are you feeling okay?' Cassie quickly puts a hand to my forehead. 'You're not coming down with something, are you?'

'Hey, don't knock it,' Rob interjects. 'I'll get you all to myself for a while.'

Cassie giggles. 'Okay.'

We leave them turning the map this way and that and pointing in all directions. Goodness knows where they'll end up, but with an English-speaking tongue in their heads, they won't stay lost for long. People here are so friendly, and they're well used to tourists.

James leads me towards the Promenade and then down Harbour Street to Viking Bay. The seaweed piled up on the shore gives off a strong stench, and we slip off our shoes to feel the soft sand under our toes as we slowly walk past a row of brightly painted beach huts.

'This is lovely,' I say, snuggling into his embrace.

He stops and faces me, tilts up my head and takes my lips in a memorable kiss that starts off soft and sweet and becomes more crushing and urgent as it goes on. My stomach flips. I can feel his need as he holds me tighter, and I'm filled with warmth.

'I've missed you,' he whispers.

I know.

'I couldn't wait for you to get here,' I admit. 'And I'm sorry if you thought Zak was my...'

'I didn't think anything,' he assures me. 'I just assessed the situation, knowing you wouldn't go off with someone else and accepted that there was a reasonable explanation. Just like you did when you saw me with Suzanne.'

I stare into his handsome face. He's right. Except that he didn't run off first. I don't think that would be his style. Running off. He's not the running off type. He's too cool for that. I wish I was cool.

He gives me another kiss, one that doesn't leave me gasping for breath this time, and we wander through the sand. The tide's out so there's just a gentle lulling of waves, while the seagulls screech overhead. We're the only ones on the beach, and it feels like the only ones in the world right now. I've missed him so much and hated the thought of him being so far away from me, especially as he was with Suzanne.

'I'm planning to spend much more time with you when we get back,' James announces. 'Once Suzanne's out of the flat, we can come and go as we please.'

I'm stunned for a second—it's as though he was reading my mind.

'Is she really leaving?' I don't dare believe it. Suzanne has a nasty way of getting out of things, and I know how much she wants to stay there.

'She doesn't seem to think so, but she is,' he assures me. And I know he means it. He has that stubborn look about him. His jaw's tense, and his back's straight.

'Did you find out if she made the phone calls?' I ask.

He pouts and shakes his head. 'I went through her things, but I can't find another phone anywhere.'

'Oh. Well, thanks for looking, anyway.' I can't hide my disappointment.

'It must be someone else,' he says. 'That message about splitting up happy couples. It was plural.' He picks up a pebble and throws it towards the water. 'It must be referring to her and me, and her and Reynolds, right?'

'I don't make a habit of splitting up couples, you know.' I feel a bit offended, to be honest.

'No, I don't mean it like that. I mean from *her* point of view, that's what she meant in the message, don't you think? I'm trying to get into the head of the sender, and I'm damned if I can think of anyone but her.'

Thank God for that!

'Well, it came right after I'd made the discovery about Quinton Bellis, and I know Valerie had a bit of a thing about him,' I say slowly.

He turns and stares at me. 'That's it! I was trying to work out why it's happened *now*.'

'But Valerie wouldn't send a message like that. She was truly grateful I'd found out before she invested even more money into his business. And, besides, she wouldn't know about Oliver Reynolds, would she? And it's only Suzanne who's trying to accuse me of splitting you two up. Valerie doesn't even *know* you.'

He narrows his eyes. 'But does she know Suzanne?'

I balk. 'You tell me. I've never seen her at the *Chronicle*.'

He shakes his head. 'I didn't recognise Valerie when I saw her the other day. Mind you, Suzanne wouldn't bring any friends back to my place, would she?'

'What about before that? When you were living in Richmond?' My heart's pounding.

'I don't recall seeing her,' he says, shaking his head.

James is incredibly astute, and I'm sure he'd remember if he'd seen Valerie somewhere before. It just doesn't make sense.

'But it has to be someone connected with Bellis,' I say, thinking aloud. 'Otherwise they wouldn't have sent the message *now*.'

'That's right. If it had been purely about Reynolds, they would surely have sent those horrid messages sooner. Not that I'd want them to, of course.'

He squeezes me a little tighter as we both stare out to sea, trying to make sense of it all.

'If Bellis is as much of a gigolo as Reynolds, it could be someone who's been fooled by both of them,' James says.

'So, it might have nothing to do with Suzanne?'

'Maybe. I'm sure I'd know by now if she were involved with Bellis.'

'But it could be anyone.' This sounds hopeless.

'Not necessarily,' James says, turning to face me again. 'It has to be someone who also knows you and can get hold of your mobile number.'

I suddenly feel a bit panicked. This is a bit too personal for comfort.

'So, one of my friends?' I say, my voice trembling. The thought of someone I care about betraying me is just horrid beyond words. I trust my friends—but is one of them taking me for a fool?

'Not necessarily,' he says, squeezing me a little tighter. 'I said someone who knows *you*—that doesn't necessarily mean you know *them*. There are lots of people who work in the same place as you, live in the same block of flats as you—even shop in the same places as you. Even people who work in shops you often go to, or restaurants you use, or whatever. They might have an interest in you even though you wouldn't give them a second thought.'

He must see the horror in my face as he takes me in a full embrace. It's good to feel his warm, hard body next to mine. I snuggle in close. I feel protected, assured. Even though I'm still a bit nervous. You don't expect people to even think about you if you don't think about them, do you? This is all a bit too creepy for my liking. In fact, it's a *lot* too creepy.

'What do we do?' I ask, looking up at him.

'We don't panic,' he says, gazing into my eyes. 'We play the waiting game. Bellis will be locked up by now so we know he's out of the way. Whoever's doing this is bound to show their hand soon enough.'

'But what do they want? They're just saying horrid things about me. That could go on forever. Surely, there has to be a way to make them stop?' Hot tears prick the back of my eyes. I refuse to believe I'll have to just put up with this shit.

'It sounds like some woman's been hurt by Bellis and is just venting. She's blaming you because you're the one who discovered he was a rat. She'll be mad at herself for not realising it sooner.'

'So, I just have to wait until she gets fed up of abusing me and gets herself a life?' I practically spit the words out at him.

He raises his eyebrows in surprise.

'No, of course not. What she's doing is against the law. We'll find her, believe me.'

'It's against the law to text someone?' Now, it's my turn to be surprised.

'She's harassing you. And you have the proof. We can use a text message as written evidence in a court of law, you know? So, don't delete any of them, okay?'

I nod, finally realising there's some hope, after all.

Mum makes us a lovely cottage pie for dinner, and we sit around the kitchen table devouring it. Something about the sea air makes me feel hungrier than ever, and I'm glad to note that she piled loads of vegetables onto my plate, as well as hers.

Everyone seems very chatty except me. I feel a bit quiet tonight—though I know you'll find it hard to believe. James and I were so relaxed this afternoon, and it was lovely just spending quality time together. After we finished talking about the phone calls and Bellis and all that stuff, he changed the subject and just talked about 'things.' Simple things. Like what movies I wanted to see when we got back, and how often I could spend the night at his—at least four nights a week if he's not too tired. It's good, actually, as Cassie seems to be spending more and more time over at Rob's so I get a bit lonely in the flat all by myself.

'Did you see all the sights?' Mum asks Cassie and Rob. 'Broadstairs is such an interesting place, isn't it?'

'Oh, yes.' Cassie eyes the shopping bags she'd left on the chair by the door. 'It has some amazing... er... buildings.'

I giggle. *Shops. She means shops.*

'Yes, Cassie was quite taken with some of the *buildings*,' Rob says with a grin. 'Especially the ones up the High Street. A couple of boutiques in particular.'

Mum laughs. She knows Cassie quite well and doesn't look at all surprised.

'Did you go into the vintage one?' she asks. 'I saw some lovely dresses in there the other day.'

'Ooh, yes.' Cassie's eyes light up. They often do that when she's talking about clothes. 'That mint-green one with the lace.'

'Oh, that one's gorgeous!' Mum croons before they go off into a dreamy conversation about the latest merchandise in our local stores.

'Time for a beer, I think,' Dad says, rolling his eyes. He gets up and stacks some of the empty plates. 'Are you in, boys?'

'Yes, please,' Rob says, chuckling.

James nods and helps with the dishes. He's rolled his sleeves up again, and I can't help gawping at his arms. I have a bit of a thing about them, in case you hadn't noticed. You would, too, if you saw them.

'I'll wash up,' I offer, as Dad hands around the beers. 'You go and relax.'

James looks surprised, though not quite as shocked as Dad.

'Are you sure you're all right?' Dad asks, frowning.

I narrow my eyes at him, and he takes it as a yes. The men all adjourn to the conservatory, leaving Mum and Cassie still sitting at the table talking about clothes. I've never known Mum to be so interested in fashion; she honestly has changed since losing a bit of weight. I'm glad. Now she can see things the way Cassie and I do. I'm not so sure Mum would appreciate the price tag on a pair of Louboutins, though, no matter how fashion conscious she becomes.

It's a long night, and I toss and turn, wishing James was with me. Today was so romantic, and it seems a pity to have had to sleep separately tonight. I understand, though. It would be a bit odd to sleep with my boyfriend in my old bed, especially with Mum and Dad just down the hall. James gave me a lovely goodnight kiss before going back downstairs to sleep on the sofa. My tummy goes all fuzzy at the memory. Then other parts of me start to go a bit fuzzy too, and I decide it's time I was asleep.

I'm woken by seagulls screaming ferociously outside my window. I almost jump out of my skin. I can't believe I was ever used to that sound. In a way, I'll be glad to get back to the sound of traffic on the

London roads, though I'll miss the whooshing of the sea.

We're all travelling back in James' car later, but there's still time for a walk on the beach first.

'Let's *all* go,' Dad suggests, folding his newspaper. We've finished breakfast and are just sitting around chatting. It feels so relaxed I don't want to move, but it would be a shame not to take one last look at the sea before we head off.

'I'll have to change my shoes,' I say, getting up.

'Oh, yeah, you can't wear Loubes on the beach.' Cassie giggles, glancing up.

I'd put on my heels to impress James but planned to take them off once we were in the car. They look great with my skinny jeans, too.

'How about these?' Mum hands me the New Look pair I'd worn yesterday. They have a little kitten heel and look quite expensive, although they weren't at all. 'You left them in the hall,' she tells me, rolling her eyes.

I remember now... I just kicked them off when I got home. They'll be fine for the beach, especially as I know I'll take them off once we reach the sand anyway.

'Thanks, Mum.'

James takes my Louboutins and puts them tidily next to his suitcase while I slip on the lower heels. Then, we all pull on our coats and head down the hill towards the sea.

'Smell that fresh air,' Dad says, inhaling loudly. 'I bet you don't get this in London, do you?'

I wrinkle my nose. 'No, Dad. We can't smell stinky seaweed up there.'

'Oh, I hadn't noticed that,' he replies with a grimace.

We've just reached the Promenade, and the stench is even worse than yesterday. I'm not so sure this walk was a good idea, after all.

James' mobile rings and he pulls it from his pocket with a frown. Then he puts it back without answering it.

'Is that the station needing you back?' Mum asks. 'I don't know how they're managing without you.'

'There are plenty of other people to do the job,' James assures her, with a hint of a smile.

'Yes, but not as well as you can, I'm sure, dear.' Mum sounds quite adamant.

The phone rings again, and he huffs as he checks it one more time. He shakes his head and tucks it back into his pocket. I secretly wish he'd put it on silent, but he's probably concerned not to miss anything about work.

'Are we going to brave the sand today?' he asks.

'I'm not sure that's such a good idea,' Mum says, eyeing the pocket where he replaced the phone. 'It all looks a bit muddy down there.'

I peer over the edge of the wall. She's right. The sand looks damp and the tide's still on its way out. The washed-up seaweed is straggled all over place, and I can see myself getting tangled up in it and tripping over. That would really impress James. *Not.*

We decide to stroll along the path instead, still trying to ignore the smell of soggy seaweed. James also seems to be trying to ignore his phone as it goes off another couple of times before he actually deigns to answer it.

'I'm going to have to take this,' he says, apologetically and walks a little way in front of us. His shoulders slump, and he shakes his head as he speaks to the caller. He's quite animated, clenching his fist and running his hand through his hair. Then he stands still.

'What is it?' I ask when we catch him up.

He has a face like thunder, though I can tell he's trying to smile and pretend everything's okay. He purses his lips as though deciding whether to tell us. This doesn't look good.

He sighs. 'It's Suzanne.'

I might have guessed. In fact, I *did* guess. I just didn't want to say anything.

Mum and Dad walk on, obviously feeling it's none of their business.

'She's broken her ankle,' James goes on, his jaw tense. 'That was one of her friends, apparently. She's really pissed off that I wouldn't answer when she rang so she got someone else to do her dirty work. I wouldn't have picked up otherwise. It was only because the number came up without a name, but it looked vaguely familiar.'

'How's she done that?' Cassie asks, wide-eyed.

James snorts. 'Well, according to the friend, Davinia, she was moving her stuff out of the flat when she fell down the stairs. She's at the hospital now, getting it plastered up.'

My heart pounds, and I can see the answer to my next question written all over James' miserable face.

'Does this mean she can't move out?'

He looks at the ground and nods. 'I'm sorry.'

I put my arms around him. I know he's not to blame, and I was half-expecting Suzanne to come up with some kind of excuse not to go.

'Why? She'll have a crutch or something, surely?' Cassie points out, defensively. 'It doesn't stop her moving.'

'Her friend says it was a pretty bad break,' James says, on a sigh. 'She's in a lot of pain, apparently, so she'll be on some strong meds. Davinia reckons she won't be able to look after herself properly for a few days. She'll need help.'

'Can't Davinia help her?' I ask. *Trust Suzanne to have a friend called Davinia, of all things!*

'I don't even know the woman,' James says, 'She might have a family or something. Anyway, according to her, Suzanne won't be able to manage on her own for a while.' He looks down at me. 'I'm so sorry, Libby.'

'It's not your fault. And it won't be forever,' I say. I'm trying to sound cheerful, though right now I could cheerfully throttle the woman. I'm trying hard to hide my disappointment—James *promised* she'd be leaving.

Then James' lips graze mine, and I somehow know everything's going to be okay. *Eventually.*

***

It's a long, quiet drive back to London, with Cassie and Rob snoozing in the back of the car and me admiring James in the front. I do that a lot. He's gorgeous. Unfortunately, he doesn't look too happy, and I can tell he's dreading getting home.

'Why don't I come back to yours for a bit?' I suggest.

He looks over at me, surprised. 'You can if you like, but I expect Suzanne to be back by the time we get there.

'That's okay.' I secretly hope to see for myself that broken ankle of hers. Even though I know it'd be a hard thing to fake, I still need to witness it with my own eyes. 'She's not going to stop us from seeing each other.'

He grins. 'Too true.'

I haven't forgotten his promise to spend more time with me when we get home, and I'll be blowed if I'll let that bitch spoil all our plans.

'Are you going to be okay going back to work tomorrow?' he asks, softly.

I nod. 'Yeah. I'm fine now. It feels much better knowing that Bellis is behind bars. I wonder how Valerie's feeling about it all now.'

'I'll give Alex a ring later to see how the arrest went,' James says.

Rob's awake when we reach his place, but he has to rouse Cassie. Poor thing has a crick in her neck from sleeping awkwardly, so she's not too happy at being disturbed.

'I'll be home later,' she tells me once we've unloaded their stuff, and I've given them both a hug.

'Great.'

'Let's go and see the invalid, then,' James says, rolling his eyes as he gets back behind the wheel.

'Where's she moving to?' I ask as we set off for Fulham.

'I'm not sure. She's been quite secretive about it all, to be honest. I'm beginning to wonder if she had anything lined up at all.'

I'd been thinking the same thing, though I didn't like to say.

***

We draw up alongside Suzanne's shiny black Merc a short while later, and James lifts his case from the boot.

I have a funny feeling of dread as we make our way up to his flat, and he opens the door.

'I wondered where you'd got to,' Suzanne calls from the living room. 'I notice you're not answering my calls.' She sounds thoroughly pissed off.

'Hello,' I say, poking my head around the doorway.

Now she *looks* thoroughly pissed off.

'What're you doing here?' She's sitting on the sofa with a soft blanket over her with her leg, in plaster to her calf, placed on a footstool.

I want to say, 'I'm his bloody girlfriend. What's more to the point is what the hell are *you* doing here?' Instead, I take a deep breath, compose myself and plaster on my sickliest smile.

'I came to see how you are,' I reply, delighting in her furious expression. 'I heard you'd had an accident.'

'Not that it's any of your business,' she scorns.

'As a matter of fact, it's very much Libby's business,' James says, coming in from the kitchen carrying a bottle of wine. 'Being as it's ruined all of our plans, you still being here.'

Suzanne looks taken aback. 'Where else would I go? You know I can't manage on my own like this. Surely, you didn't expect me to still move out, did you?'

'Yes, actually,' James says, looking around the room. 'I thought you'd have your friend helping you out. What's her name? Davinia, isn't it? The one who rang me.'

'*I* rang you,' she points out, angrily. 'Several times. But you didn't even bother to take my calls, even when I was in the ambulance on my way to hospital.' She waves her hand in the air to make her point.

'That's right. I was away, taking a break.' James sounds very matter-of-fact as he pours out two glasses of Cabernet Sauvignon.

'But I was in hospital!' She's shouting now.

'Yes, your friend told me. What was I supposed to do about it?'

He hands me a glass of wine and takes a sip of the other.

'Care. *That's* what you were supposed to do. I was your *wife*, after all!' Her face has turned red, and she's gritting her teeth.

'Not this morning, you weren't,' he says, smacking his lips and admiring his glass. 'In fact, you haven't been for over a year now. Which is why it's most inappropriate for you to be living here.'

I gape at James in admiration. I never expected him to be so blunt with Suzanne, but it's all true.

'Oh, kick a woman while she's down, won't you?' She looks pointedly at the wine bottle that James has placed on the coffee table. He and I sit on the chairs opposite the little sofa. 'And where's mine?'

James feigns surprise. 'I didn't think you'd be able to drink alcohol with all the strong medication your friend said you'd be on. It would be totally irresponsible.' Suzanne tightens her lips and screws up her eyes in frustration. She can't argue with that.

James winks at me, and his lips twitch as he adds, 'And besides, I think you've had enough for one day. I heard you got plastered earlier.'

He and I burst out laughing but Suzanne doesn't see the joke. *Big surprise there!*

'That's not funny,' she snaps.

'*I* thought it was,' I say before taking another swig of my wine.

James' phone rings, and he frowns at the screen.

'It's Alex,' he says, 'I'll take it in the other room.'

Suzanne glares at me as he heads for the kitchen.

'I don't know what you're looking so smug about,' she spits out. 'Anyone would think I'd done this on purpose. I know James doesn't believe it was a genuine accident. You'd think I was a liar as well as a fool to hear him go on.'

I stand to refill my drink.

'Well, if the cap fits, wear it,' I say, feeling surprisingly brave. *It must be the wine.*

Just then, James returns, holding my Louboutins. He must have slipped them in his case so I wouldn't leave them behind this morning. I giggle, turning back to Suzanne.

'Or, should that be, if the *shoe* fits...' I look pointedly at the thick plaster on her foot. 'Hmm, maybe not.'

Suzanne narrows her eyes furiously.

I tuck the shoes next to my bag so I can't forget them, and watch James refill his glass. He doesn't look as relaxed as he did when he left the room, and I get the impression he's in need of his drink.

'Is everything okay?' I ask as he sits down.

'I'll get you a lift home tonight,' he says, gesturing to his glass.

'Don't worry, I was planning to take the Tube anyway.'

'No, I insist.'

I narrow my eyes at him, the determination in his voice taking me by surprise.

'Okay.'

'Bellis got away,' he tells me quietly.

I stare at him, my mind whirling.

'Oh, dear,' Suzanne pipes up in a condescending manner. 'What a shame.'

James is still looking at me.

'It looks like he had a tip-off,' he goes on. 'Alex said the police were watching his hotel, as well. Somehow, he'd managed to sneak out without them knowing. They found lots of papers in the shop, though, which they're examining for clues.'

'But he's free. And he'll know I dobbed him in.' I feel sick and suddenly wish I hadn't touched the wine.

'He doesn't know anything about your involvement,' James assures me. 'The only people who knew you'd found out about him were Valerie and Siobhan, and they're not about to tell anyone. Valerie confirmed she hasn't heard from Bellis all week, and he's not answering his phone.'

I take a deep breath. 'But who could have told him you were onto him?'

James shakes his head. 'We don't know yet, but we'll find out. Alex is coming over in about an hour to drive you home. He might know a bit more by then. We'll catch him, don't worry about that.'

But I *am* worried. *Very* worried.

18

I feel quite jittery as I get ready for work the next morning. It's bad enough that it's Monday, but Alex didn't have any good news for us last night, so I still feel like a sitting duck. He said there would be a strong police presence in the area for a while until Bellis was caught, and that would include keeping an eye on the *Daily Chronicle* offices, but somehow, I don't feel that it's enough.

I'm power-dressing today to try to make myself feel a bit more confident: red suit by Stella McCartney—bargain from eBay, white vest top—H&M, black, shiny Louboutins that I wore last week but don't think anyone will notice that. I've tied my hair up in a messy bun and even used waterproof mascara, so it won't smudge.

'Go get 'em, girl,' Cassie says with an approving look.

I smile, stick my chin up as I grab my Radley and head out the door. All the way to the Tube station I imagine people are looking at me, following me, watching me. I tell myself they're probably staring because I look so great this morning, but it doesn't help. I half-wish I'd hidden in a black dress with large, matching coat.

I arrive at the office a little earlier than usual. Kiki and Eva are already there, and they both come over to give me a hug as soon as I get through the door.

'Are you okay?' Kiki asks. 'We've all been really worried about you. Valerie and Siobhan won't tell us anything, and none of us had your number to check on you.'

'I'm fine,' I reply, my mind in a whirl. I wasn't sure if the Bellis business would be common knowledge around the office or not, but it looks like no one has a clue. That makes it a bit awkward for me, to be honest, as I know they'll all be burning with curiosity. I hate not being able to come clean, especially around my friends.

'We heard all about how you saved that little girl from being abducted at the pool last week,' Eva says, her arm still around me. 'There was a piece in the paper about it, warning people not to dress their kids in clothes with their names on. But we got the impression from Valerie's reaction that there was more to it than that.'

'No one's been working on the Bellis contract, either,' Kiki says. 'We assume it's because of the names-on-shirts thing, but it seems a bit odd that he hasn't been around to defend the collection.'

Just then, the door to Valerie's office opens, and a familiar-looking lady steps out.

'Who's she?' I whisper to Eva.

'That's Ms Urquhart,' she murmurs. 'Sort of Agony Aunt for the supplement.'

'Right.' I suppose it's a better name than Miss Tut, which was how I was thinking of her since our previous encounters. I smile at the woman, but she narrows her eyes at me, scowling. Talk about rude!

'Good morning,' I offer, checking out yet another pair of Santonis. This time they're grey suede with a low block heel and the same square toe she seems to favour. She's wearing them with a royal-blue dress and grey jacket. Her outfit looks much nicer than her face right now.

She looks like she's about to speak, but then Valerie follows her out the door. Her face lights up when she sees me.

'Liberty. You're back. How nice to see you.' She smiles at me as Ms Urquhart scurries out of the department. 'Come in,' Valerie urges me, and I follow her into her office.

'Did you have a nice break?' She seems genuinely concerned, and I relax a little. To be honest, I'd been a bit worried about what sort of reception I might get from her on my return, but I needn't have been. She seems genuinely pleased to have me here.

The blinds are down, and she's playing some Baroque music quietly in the background. It really is pleasant, and I make a mental note to bring the REBEL CD in for her tomorrow.

'I heard you found Mr Bellis' printing offices,' she says in a low voice.

I nod. 'Only by accident.'

'The police came to see me,' she goes on. 'They've retrieved lots of paperwork from there, quite a few contracts and so forth. Apparently, there's some doubt as to the actual legality of the agreements made. I'm trying not to get my hopes up, but there's a slim chance I might get some of my money back.'

'That's great news,' I say, forgetting to keep my voice down. 'When will you know?'

She pouts. 'I'm not sure. These things can take ages, can't they? But it's not so much the money I'm excited about, it's the fact that he'll be proven to be the crook that he is. Justice will prevail.'

'Absolutely,' I say it a little more quietly this time.

'Once they catch up with him, of course,' she says with a sigh. 'Did you hear that they had him cornered in his hotel, but somehow he managed to give them the slip? Dreadful business.'

'I know. You don't think he'll come here, do you? To see you, or anything?'

She shakes her head. 'No. The police asked me the same thing. I doubt he'll want anything to do with me now that he knows he won't be getting his hands on any more of my money.'

'I'm sorry.' I feel so bad for her. She seems like a very nice person once you get to know her, and it's sad she's been treated so badly by that con man.

'Don't be,' she says, jutting out her chin. 'I was foolish to be taken in by him. I'm just glad you outed him before I gave him any more cash. Because I would have, you know? I'd have given him everything at one time.'

She looks a little dreamy, and I realise she must have thought much more of him than I'd imagined.

'I didn't know,' I admit.

She shakes her head as though ridding herself of the thought. 'No one did. It's against the rules to mix business with pleasure in this company. Unfortunately, I was on the cusp of doing just that. Though I would've had to explain the situation to Mr Peerless before it went much further, of course. Fortunately, Mr Bellis was being charged the full amount for his features with us so there was no harm done morally. But it did weigh heavily on my mind.'

'What's happening about the features now?' I ask.

She sighs. 'They won't be going ahead. A couple of men from the news desk want to talk to you about a follow-up article they're working on about the dangers of named clothing—without admitting we were about to advocate the whole collection, of course, and *promote* it.' She shakes her head. 'But unfortunately, after that, we're left with a month's worth of blank pages to fill in the fashion supplement.'

She puts her head in her hands. 'I have a meeting with Mr Peerless today to discuss a way forward. I've no idea how we'll come up with something at such short notice.'

'I might have an idea,' I say slowly, my brain running like a steam train.

She removes her hands from the sides of her head and frowns at me in astonishment.

'Really?'

'We'll need to make some calls. What time's your meeting?'

'I have two hours,' she says, glancing at her Cartier. 'I need to be up there for eleven o' clock sharp.'

'Right. Do you have any connections at Crystal?' I ask.

She looks taken aback. 'Of course.'

'Great. Who do we need to speak to regarding a possible franchise deal?'

She frowns. 'They don't do anything like that.'

'Not yet,' I say. 'But I wonder if they might like to consider a proposition about it? It'd be a good way to inject more money into the company, spread their name even further—and, of course, it would make a great story for the fashion supplement.'

Valerie stares at me. 'Well, actually,' she says quietly, 'I do happen to know that Crystal's in a bit of financial trouble at the moment. Maybe this is just what they need.'

'There's a niche boutique opening in Rochester in four weeks' time that would love to stock their range,' I tell her. 'And, of course, they'll need some publicity for the opening.'

Valerie beams at me. 'Write down the details. We'll skype Henrietta Winfield now, so you can speak to her, too.'

My stomach lurches. I've heard Cassie mention Henrietta before. She's the owner of Crystal, I think, and she sounds quite scary. Valerie sets up the call and invites me to her side of the desk with her so we can both see and be seen by the monitor.

An elderly-looking lady with perfect skin and a bright-yellow dress comes into view, and Valerie introduces us. She tells Henrietta all about my idea and at first, I think she's going to reject it.

'We've never done anything like that before.' Henrietta frowns.

'Maybe that's why you're in such a mess, dear,' Valerie replies bluntly.

I gape at them both, expecting Henrietta to take umbrage and shut down the call straight away, but she doesn't. In fact, she looks quite thoughtful for a few moments.

'You might be right, darling,' she says at last.

'It's a great way to spread the word about the brand,' I chip in, not sure whether I'm actually permitted to speak or not. 'And the shop in Rochester's in a lovely area where they don't have anything as classy as Crystal. The lady who wants to partake is a massive fan of your company and will do a wonderful job of promoting it.'

'Can you set up a conference call with her?' Henrietta asks. 'I'd love to talk this over. It might be just what the company needs. A breath of fresh air.'

'Of course. And I'm sure other shops will be interested in a franchise, too, once word gets out,' I throw in for good measure.

'And we'll negotiate a favourable rate for the advertising here at the *Chronicle*,' Valerie adds. 'Providing we get exclusivity, of course.'

'Of course.' Henrietta smiles, then winks at me. 'Well done, Liberty. You might have just got us out of a hole.'

'I know the feeling, dear,' Valerie says, giving me a smirk.

***

Natalie's over the moon when I tell her the news.

'That's brilliant! How soon does she want to speak to me?' I can hear the excitement in her voice.

'No time like the present,' I say, glancing at the clock. We have less than an hour before Valerie's meeting, and I know she'll need some answers to give to Phil Peerless.

Valerie calls Crystal again and soon we're all chatting together. Natalie's certainly done her homework and knows exactly how much she can afford and what kind of stock will sell in Rochester. Henrietta looks very impressed, and the two get on really well together.

'Well, I think we should dip out at this stage, dear,' Valerie cuts in as they go on about the legal side of things. 'Can we assume it's a yes?'

Henrietta nods. 'Darling, was there ever any doubt?' She smiles, and her financial director, who joined us for the call, chuckles.

'Good, I'll tell Philip we're expecting something soon, shall I?'

'Of course. I'll get my marketing department to send you lots of background information to be going on with. Then we'll have more when we've finalised the contracts. I'm hoping to move quickly with this so be prepared.'

'Me too,' Natalie replies before we say our goodbyes.

'Well, I think that's what you call a result,' I say to Valerie as she sits back with a sigh.

'It certainly is.' She smiles at me. 'Thank you.'

'Leave that until it's all signed and sealed,' I warn her. 'You know how things can be in the business world.'

'Not just in business, dear,' she says, a little more seriously.

'Are you okay?' I ask, not sure if I'm being a little impertinent or not. I'm genuinely concerned about her. The poor woman's been through a lot, and it can't help having to go upstairs and face Phil Peerless on a Monday morning.

'I will be,' she says, thoughtfully. She gives me a little smile. 'And so, will you. I won't forget this, Liberty. And I'll be telling Mr Peerless whose brainwave this Crystal business is, too.'

A thud hits my stomach. 'It might be better to leave me out of it, actually,' I tell her, frowning. 'Mr Peerless doesn't seem to like me much, and he'll only think I've stuck my nose into something I shouldn't.'

She raises her eyebrows in surprise. 'Then Mr Peerless doesn't know you very well, does he?'

I want to reply that I think he might know me a little *too* well, but I keep quiet. I think she's paying me a compliment, and I don't get many of those so I'm not going to ruin it. Instead, I just smile.

'Right, well, I have a meeting to attend, and you're due a coffee break,' she says, straightening up.

'Good luck,' I say, returning my chair to the other side of the desk.

'Thank you, dear. Though I don't think I'll need it.'

I wish I had her confidence.

19

I quickly call Cassie on my way to the canteen. She sounds quite miserable.

'Meredith didn't want to know about your idea about franchising,' she says. 'She reckoned the boss would never go for it.'

'Would that be Henrietta Winfield?' I ask, grinning.

'Yes. She's the owner.'

'She's chatting with Natalie about it as we speak,' I tell her.

'What?'

I go on to explain briefly about my morning, and Cassie gets more excited as I go on.

'That's incredible!' she says. 'I honestly thought it was a lost cause when Meredith vetoed the idea.'

'I think Henrietta could see that it made sense— she had her financial director with her and everything.'

'Well, she's obviously serious, then.'

'She'd better be. Valerie's talking to Phil Peerless about it right now. I think this might just save all our jobs.'

'Hang on, Meredith's just come in the office. I have to go.'

She clicks off her phone, and I can't help wishing I was a fly on their wall right now. Still, Cassie'll fill me in later and in the meantime, there's a skinny latte waiting with my name on it.

I join the rest of the girls at the large table in the refectory. They're all pleased to see me, which is lovely.

'I don't suppose there's much point in asking what you've been up to all morning, is there?' Tammy asks, smiling. 'We heard you were keeping Valerie occupied—for which we're all eternally grateful, I might add.'

We all giggle.

'She's been like a bear with a sore head since you left last week,' Brie explains. 'No one will tell us what's going on, but we can all guess it's something to do with Quinton Bellis—who's been very conspicuous by his absence, by the way.'

'We're not at liberty to divulge private business,' Siobhan cuts in. 'I've told you this before, ladies. I'm sure Valerie will inform us all when there's something we need to know. Isn't that right, Libby?'

I nod, taking another sip of my coffee. I feel awful not being able to tell the girls everything I know, but there's no point in getting their hopes up in case this all falls through. And, besides, it's Valerie's business, not mine. I'm glad I have Siobhan on my side, though.

'Who was that hunky copper you left with?' Kiki asks, her eyes wide. 'He was gorgeous!'

I feel a flutter of pride in my stomach. I'm glad in a way that James' handsome looks haven't gone unnoticed, but not sure if I should mention he's actually spoken for—by me.

'Oh, my God, he can take me home anytime,' Izzy says, fanning herself with a napkin.

'Hey, join the queue,' Eva says, chuckling.

'Time to get back, everyone,' Siobhan says, giving me a wink. She hasn't met James, but she knows I'm seeing a copper, so it doesn't take a genius to figure it out. I love that she manages to keep a confidence without alienating the girls in the office.

My phone pings as I make my way down the corridor, and I eagerly pull it from my Radley, expecting it's Cassie with some news.

Why can't you keep your big nose out of everyone else's business, Bitch? Do you realise how many lives you're wrecking?

I stand still, staring at the screen while my whole body trembles. Goose pimples stab at my flesh, and I feel sort of hot on the inside and cold on the outside. My hair feels like it's standing on end, and my skin feels too tight for my frame.

It's not Cassie, it's that unknown number again. Quickly, I try to call it back, without a clue what to say to the caller if I get through. It's not a problem, though, as the phone's already been switched off. Clever.

'I'll catch you up,' I tell Alice, who's walking past me with a quizzical expression.

'Okay.'

I forward the message to James with a note explaining that it just came through. My phone rings straight away.

'Are you okay?' he asks.

'I think so.' I feel pretty crappy to be honest, but there's no point in worrying him. 'I've just spent the morning with Valerie, and things are going great, but then this came right out of the blue.'

'I have people trying to trace the mobile, but it's never on long enough to actually track it. We're also looking into whether the number was already allocated to the phone before it was sold. If we can track down where it was bought, there might be security cameras at the shop that we could check.'

'Thanks, James. I do appreciate it.' I feel quite relieved knowing something is physically being done to find the caller. She sounds like a really hateful person, and I feel edgy to think it's someone who knows me.

'Are you sure you're going to be all right?' James sounds concerned.

'Yes, honestly, I'll be fine. In fact, I'd best get back. I'm late as it is.'

'Speak to you later, then.' He hangs up.

I smile. I know he cares about me, but he can hardly get soppy in an office full of his colleagues.

My phone pings again, and I glance down at the message.

Missing you! Xx ;)

He's even put a winking emoji! James never does things like that. In fact, I'm amazed he knows how to. But he has. I giggle and can't stop my smile spreading even wider as I tuck the phone into my bag and head for the office.

I'm working with Brie for the rest of the day, testing out make-up and reviewing it for the beauty page. She's great fun and very knowledgeable about skin and chemicals and stuff. And she even shows me how to contour properly. I thought my face looked good when I came out this morning, but it looks even better now—all slim and radiant.

As I admire my new look in the mirror, I notice Siobhan whizz across the room to Valerie's office. Ms Urquhart has her hand on the door, but Siobhan stops her from going in.

'Valerie isn't back yet,' Siobhan explains politely. 'Can I ask her to call you when she returns?'

'Where is she?' Ms Urquhart demands, scowling.

'She's in a meeting,' Siobhan replies. 'I don't know how long she'll be, but I'll ask her to give you call when she gets back to the office, okay?'

Ms Urquhart eyes the door and then purses her lips angrily. 'Or I could just wait for her.'

'There's no point. It would only waste your time as she could be up there all afternoon for all I know.' Siobhan sounds very firm but still polite.

'Up where? Is she with Philip Peerless?' Ms Urquhart snaps.

'I'm not sure.' Siobhan looks a little uneasy but is still holding her ground.

'Right.' Ms Urquhart scowls furiously as she turns and leaves the department.

'What was that all about?' I ask Brie, who's applying some mascara to my left eye. It's supposed to be extra-long length, but it doesn't look any different to me.

'Dunno,' she says with a shrug. 'Auntie Annie's a good friend of Valerie's, but she doesn't look too happy, does she?'

I roll my eyes, careful not to smudge the mascara.

'I can't imagine going to her with my problems, can you? I mean, she hardly looks like an Auntie

Annie, and she certainly isn't helpful when people write in.'

'It's not her real name,' Brie says, 'and she hates the job. It's just as well, in fact, because most of the readers hate her, too. We're always getting complaints that she gives the wrong advice, and she's too blunt with her suggestions. Valerie thinks it makes for good reader interaction, though.'

'I suppose she has a point. At least if people write in to disagree, it proves they've read the paper.'

'Exactly,' Brie tells me. She frowns. 'I think it's a no for this 'Long and Lovely' Mascara, then?'

''Fraid so.'

She hands me a wet wipe.

***

James is working late tonight, but I'm secretly hoping he might pop over when he's finished. It's been ages since we... you know... and I'm badly missing him. Especially after that message today with the emoji. It's so unlike him, but I feel that we're closer than ever right now. I just wish we could spend a few more nights together.

Anyway, Cassie's in tonight as well, as Rob's out watching football with some mates from work. We've had a nice meal and now we're lounging around in front of the telly. *EastEnders* is on and there seems to be lots of shouting, but neither of us is taking any notice. We're scrolling through our phones, as usual.

'I forgot to say, I took a picture of the outside of BaROQ yesterday,' Cassie pipes up from the opposite sofa. 'I'll send it over to you now. It's really quite funny.'

'Okay.' I'm only half-listening as I gaze at the message from James again. It's great having stuff on texts as you can always look at them whenever you want. The only trouble is they're also there as a constant reminder when they say things you'd rather not read again. Like that horrid one I got this morning.

'I had another nasty text today,' I tell Cassie, looking up.

'Oh, no! Are you okay, hon?' She's frowning.

'Yeah. I think James is onto them. They have all sorts of ways to track down mobile phones, apparently, even pay-as-you-go ones.

'It's definitely not Suzanne, then?'

'No. We think it's someone connected with Bellis because it started just after we cottoned on to him. I don't think it's Valerie, though, as she's being too nice to me.'

'Meredith was in a good mood this afternoon, so it looks like something's happening with the franchise idea,' Cassie says, smiling. 'Although, I'm sure she'll never admit it was anything to do with me suggesting it.'

'Valerie didn't come back to the office all day, so she must have been setting the ball rolling,' I say.

My phone pings, and I look down to see the photo of the little side street just outside BaROQ.

'See that woman?' Cassie says, with a giggle.

There's a woman with a pushchair going up the hill and someone in a black trench coat and sunglasses walking down it.

'With the sunglasses?' I snigger. 'Didn't anyone tell her it's winter?'

'That's what I thought. I was going to put it on Facebook with a caption about the British weather but thought better of it. Not when it's so close to the printers.'

I use my fingers to enlarge the picture a little. The woman has a scarf around her head so I can't see her hair, and she has a very slight frame. I'm sure it's the woman who overtook us in the street. I zoom in on her shoes—it's a habit of mine—and gape.

'Santonis.'

Cassie enlarges her image and nods. 'Looks like it. I was thinking of getting some of those myself, with the squared-off toe. They look great, don't they?'

'A woman at our place wears them,' I say, frowning. 'Ms Urquhart. She's Auntie Annie, the Agony Aunt for the paper.'

'Oh, God, she's horrid!' Cassie blurts out. 'Someone wrote in the other day to say she thought her fella was cheating on her, and that bitch just told her to go and find someone else, then. What sort of advice is that?'

'I know, she's hopeless. Always getting complaints, apparently.'

'Complaints? She should get the sack.'

'Exactly.'

We settle down to watch *Pretty Woman* for the umpteenth time, and I try not to keep checking my watch. I've left my make-up on in case James pops in tonight, but as time goes on, I lose hope. I also lose my wine all over my pyjamas when I nod off towards the end of the film.

'Damn.' They're from Victoria's Secret, and the liquid goes straight through the silky material to my skin in seconds. 'I think I'll just go to bed.'

'Okay, hon. I won't be far behind you.' Cassie looks tired, too.

I can't help being a bit fed up as I change into clean pyjamas and hop into bed. Alone. *Again.*

***

I feel a lot more positive when I get up next morning—and even more so when I read a text from James.

Hi, sweetheart. Sorry I couldn't get there last night. We've made some headway in the case. Think

I'm so thrilled. James rarely uses terms of endearment, and *three* kisses? This is going to be a fantastic day. I can just feel it. I'm wearing a smart skirt from Oasis. It's in a grey check and includes a flattering, wide belt. I've teamed it with a soft, red, merino-wool jumper with a round neck from Hobbs, which I bought with some birthday money. Add to that my black patent Louboutins, and you can see why I'm so excited. There's nothing like a brilliant outfit to lighten your spirits.

I remembered the CD for Valerie, so I pop into her office as soon as I arrive. She smiles up at me.

'Morning, Liberty. We had a very successful meeting yesterday. I can't say too much right now, but it all seems to be going through smoothly.'

'I'm so glad.' And, frankly, surprised. My plans don't normally go this well, but I won't mention that. I take the CD from my bag and hand it to her. 'I thought you might like this.'

Her eyes light up and she beams. 'REBEL? I love their music. And this is their latest release. Thank you so much.' She looks like she might cry, which was certainly not my intention. I hope it's not because of the name bringing back horrid memories. 'That really is thoughtful of you,' she says.

'I heard the Baroque music you had on in here,' I explain.

'Don't you just love it?' She holds the CD to her chest. 'Such beautiful sounds. In fact, there's a REBEL concert on tonight. I was going to go with...'

'Oh, no, I'm so sorry.' I notice how her face falls, but she tries to smile anyway.

'No, it's all right. I'm better off without a certain person, and I know it.'

'Well, I hope you like the CD.' I smile at her and leave the room, not quite sure what else to say. I hadn't expected it all to get so awkward.

I go back to my desk and grab my phone.

'Just going to the loo,' I tell Fran as she arrives.

'Okay.'

I rush to the ladies' and call James.

'There's a REBEL concert on tonight,' I tell him quickly. 'I'm not sure where, but there's a chance Bellis might go. He'd already planned to take Valerie, but...' I break off as I hear someone coming in.

Quickly, I dive into a cubicle, whispering to James that I'll text him.

Sorry, can't speak. Someone just came in. xxx

That's okay. I'll look into it. Well done. See you later xxx

Can't wait xxx

I'm amazed—and delighted—we've progressed to three kisses. And *he* instigated it! I'm such a lucky girl.

I leave the cubicle to wash my hands, and my smile instantly falls from my face. In fact, it's a good job I'm not nearer the sink yet, as I'm sure it would fall right down the plughole.

'Good morning, Ms Urquhart,' I manage through my suddenly dry throat.

She quickly stuffs a mobile phone in her pocket. I'm surprised it's not a more state-of-the-art one, to be honest, but she's entitled to her taste. She frowns at me. *I suppose she's entitled to do that too, but I do wish she wouldn't.*

'Good morning,' she says abruptly and leaves the room.

It's not just me who sneaks off to the loo to make private calls, then.

I wash my hands, out of habit, and return to the office.

'You're with Eva and Izzy today,' Siobhan says, looking a little puzzled. 'Is everything all right?'

Just then, my phone pings. I flinch, desperately wanting to check it in case it's good news from James, but not daring to in case I get into trouble for taking personal calls.

Siobhan nods at my bag. 'Under the circumstances, I think it might be better if you take that first,' she says quietly.

'Thank you.'

I whip the phone out of my bag and stare at the screen.

You just can't stop interfering, can you? Well, you'll pay for this, you'll see!

'Oh, no.' I look up at Siobhan who's frowning. 'I just need to... um...' I gesture towards the door with my thumb.

'Go. It's fine.'

I rush back to the ladies' and forward the message to James.

Immediately, he calls back.

'Are you okay?'

'Yes, it's just...'

'It's a threat,' he says through gritted teeth. 'But they won't get away with it.'

'I don't get what I've done.' I'm trying hard to hold back the tears. Today was supposed to be such a good day, and it's gone to pot already. Crikey, I haven't even been here an hour yet.

'They're the ones who've done wrong,' he says calmly. 'As soon as we pick Bellis up tonight, it'll put an end to it.'

'I hope so.'

'I'll probably have to work a bit late to get all this sorted, but I promise I'll be over later. Suzanne's going out with Davinia again, so at least she won't be making any demands on me.'

'How is she?'

'Hobbling about the place, but she doesn't seem to be in much pain.'

'Good.' *I just wish she'd hurry up and hobble out the bloody door!*

'Well, if you're sure you're okay, I'll get back to work.'

'Yep, I have to get going. Thanks for ringing.'

'Take care.'

My heart pounds, and I jump when the door swings open and Fran comes in.

'Just making sure you're okay,' she says, frowning at me. 'You look like you've seen a ghost.'

'I *am* a bit jumpy,' I tell her. 'Someone's threatening me.'

20

Fran immediately throws her arms around me, making me want to cry even more. I hold it back, though.

'I thought it was my boyfriend's ex,' I whisper, 'But now, I'm not so sure.'

'What do they want?' Her big eyes are wide as she faces me.

'I wish I knew. They just say horrid things that's all.'

It suddenly occurs to me that I shouldn't be talking about this here. Not that I'd suspect Fran of being involved, of course, but walls tend to have ears in places like this.

'Does Valerie know?' Fran asks.

'No. And it might be better not to mention it. To anyone, I mean. We don't know who it is, so there's a chance it could be someone from here. We don't want them to get wind that we're onto them.'

She nods, a grave expression on her face.

'I won't say anything,' she promises.

'Thanks, Fran.'

We go back to the office, and I try to act like nothing's wrong. It's not easy. I hang my bag on the back of a chair, praying my phone doesn't ring again and try to concentrate on the job in hand. Izzy and Eva are working with some new perfumes that need reviewing, but there are only so many words you can use to describe a scent.

'Fruity, spicy, musky, or flowery?' Izzy asks, spraying some perfume onto my arm.

'Urgh! Stinky.' I feel sick. How can they call this fragrance?

'Hmm, that's what we thought,' Eva says glumly. 'It's called 'Morning'.' We can't pretend it's nice when it's not, but how do we put that in a review?'

Morning *breath*, more like. 'We have to be honest with our readers,' I agree. 'Our personal integrity's at stake here. Can't we just say something like 'it's an acquired taste'?'

'That's good.' Izzy nods. 'It's an acquired taste for those with no taste.'

'Or sense of smell,' Eva adds, chuckling.

'Or friends,' I joke.

We all giggle, and Siobhan looks over. I thought she'd be cross, but she just smiles.

Luckily, not all the perfumes are as horrid as 'Morning',' and I keep spraying myself with a lovely floral one called 'Dewey Days' to try to mask the smell of the first one.

'Liberty, do you have a minute?' Valerie pops her head out of her room just as we're clearing up, ready for lunch.

'Of course.'

I follow her into her office, and we sit down.

'It's good news,' she tells me. 'Henrietta's just rung to confirm the franchise is going ahead with that shop you told us about, and she's planning to have Crystal in a couple of other high-end boutiques as well.'

'That's great!' I want to jump up and hug her, but I don't. Valerie doesn't seem like the hugging kind.

She stands up and opens a window. 'They're also planning to bring forward their next collection now that they have more outlets for it, so that'll keep their staff happy. 'And Mr Peerless agreed to us handling the publicity for the venture, so we've got lots of work coming up, too.'

She smiles, and I can't help thinking how much prettier she looks when she's happy.

Just then, the door bursts open, and Ms Urquhart walks in with an odd expression on her face.

'Davinia? Is everything all right?' Valerie asks, frowning.

That name rings a bell.

'Of course. I have something to show you that's all. Come with me. You, too, Liberty.' Her voice is a little higher than usual.

We follow her out the door and through our empty department to the lift. The girls have all gone to lunch, and I'm hoping this won't take long as I'd really like to join them. My stomach gurgles in agreement.

'This is all very intriguing,' Valerie says, as we head for the ground floor.

'We're taking my car,' Davinia announces, leading us towards a blue Audi.

'I haven't seen this one before,' Valerie comments. 'What happened to your little Citroën?'

'I changed it.'

Valerie jumps into the passenger seat, and I strap into the back. Immediately, the locks are activated and Davinia drives us off the car park and down the road.

'I must say, this is all very mysterious,' Valerie says, peering out the window. 'Is it work related?'

'Sort of.' Davinia's not giving much away.

'Do you know Suzanne Harper?' I ask, trying to work out where we are. I don't recognise the roads at all. But I certainly recognise her name.

She smirks at me through her rear-view mirror.

'Well deduced, Miss Marple. You're quite good at solving mysteries, aren't you, Liberty?'

I don't like the way she said that.

'I heard you helped her when she broke her ankle,' I say, trying to divert the course of the conversation.

She sniggers. 'Oh, yes. *That.*'

She curls her lip.

'Is it just me or is there a funny smell in here?' Valerie asks, sniffing. 'Perhaps you could open a window or something?'

I sink back in my chair, afraid it's *me* that smells odd. I tried to mask that awful fragrance, but the mixture of scents may have just made it worse. I decide to say nothing and just breathe a sigh of relief when Davinia opens her window a crack. I wish I'd had time to grab my coat though, as it's freezing in here.

'Where on earth are we going?' Valerie's craning her neck to see a signpost, but we're overtaking a lorry so we can't read it.

'You'll see.'

'I have an appointment this afternoon,' Valerie explains, checking her watch. 'I can't afford to be late.'

'Really?' Davinia sounds most disinterested, which makes me feel a bit nervous.

Valerie gawps at her. 'Is everything all right, Davinia?'

'Well, now. That's a very good question.'

My stomach churns, and I don't think it's just hunger. This woman's acting very strangely, and Valerie's looking a little unnerved too.

The car speeds up as we whizz through a tunnel, and she veers sharply to the left, taking us out onto some open land.

'Are you sure this is the right way? We're miles from town.' Valerie eyes her curiously now.

'We're nearly there,' Davinia says with a sneer.

'But where?' Valerie stares out the windscreen.

The area is quite desolate with just a few large, wooden huts dotted around.

Davinia pulls to a halt outside one of the buildings.

'Come on. This'll be fun.' Davinia perks up as she unlocks the car, and we all climb out.

'Here?' Valerie frowns at the hut. It looks old but sturdy enough.

'Yes. Come inside, it's warmer in here,' she urges us, 'And it'll soon be even hotter.'

We follow Davinia inside, my heart pounding. It's like a large warehouse with absolutely nothing but the four walls surrounding us and one tiny window. The skylight is way up in the roof, and the room smells damp.

'What's this?' Valerie asks.

Suddenly panicking, I turn back towards the door, but Davinia's too fast. She quickly locks it and turns back to face us.

'This,' she begins, waving her arm around, 'is a time of reckoning.'

Valerie shakes her head in confusion.

Davinia pulls some rope from her bag. 'Get on the floor, both of you!' Suddenly, her voice is loud and demanding.

'W-what?' I take a step back, but she draws back her fist and thumps me on the cheek, knocking me to the floor. *Why didn't I see that coming?*

Stunned, I try to stand up but my head feels like mush. She grabs my hands and ties them behind my back.

'Whatever's going on?' Valerie objects, but Davinia has already got hold of her arms and twists them behind her.

I'm forced to sit on the hard, wooden floor while Davinia positions Valerie next to me, back to back.

'Has Suzanne p-put you up to this?' I ask, my voice trembling while my head throbs.

Davinia lets out a loud 'Ha!'

'Just what is all this about?' Valerie demands. 'Untie us this minute!'

'Or what? Haven't you noticed, Valerie, you're not in charge here. *I* am.' Davinia struts back and forth in front of us, clearly relishing her moment of glory. I feel sick and groggy, closing my eyes for a few minutes while leaning against Valerie's stiff, upright frame. I haven't got the energy to make conversation right now.

'Is it some kind of joke? You do realise you'll lose your job for this?' Valerie points out.

'My job? What the hell do I care about that? You know I can't stand that dreadful position you've allocated me. Besides, *you're* about to lose a lot more than your stupid jobs.'

'What's that supposed to mean?' Valerie demands.

'You'll see. I'll teach you to appoint me the most menial job you could find, you bitch,' Davinia sneers.

'But I thought you liked helping people? And it's a very well-paid position. Most people would give their eyeteeth for a post like that.' She sounds most indignant, and it's clear she honestly isn't aware that Davinia doesn't enjoy her job.

'Oh, yeah, like who?' Davinia snaps.

'I'd do it,' I chip in, opening my eyes as my mind clears a little.

'*You?* You can't even sort out your *own* problems.' Davinia sounds disbelieving, which I find quite offensive, frankly. 'Suzanne's told me all about how you're still trying to steal her husband even though they're back living together. And she's damn sure you can't afford to live in Chelsea, which means some other mug is funding your living expenses. How can *you* possibly help anyone else?'

'That's not true,' I say, indignantly. Although I know Cassie's paying a bigger portion of the rent than me, but she does have the larger bedroom. I'm not sure it's entirely fair, but that's what she points out every time I mention feeling guilty for not paying my way.

'*Are* you struggling financially, Liberty?' Valerie asks, bewildered.

'Well...' I shrug, not wanting to admit the mess I'm in—especially as I received yet *another* nasty letter from my credit card provider yesterday. *I'm also struggling physically with this damn rope, which is tied far too tightly around my wrists.*

'See? Useless,' Davinia scorns.

'I am *not* useless,' I point out, momentarily feeling more angry than worried about our predicament. 'I'd be very helpful to people as an agony aunt, I'll have you know. I could advise them on... on...' I suddenly lose my train of thought.

'We're waiting.' Davinia taps her foot on the wooden floor.

I glance down at her shoe. It's one of those square-toed ones she likes, as usual.

'Like *shoes*,' I say quickly. 'And clothes. Yes. That's it. People could write in and say things like 'Dear Libby, I need something to wear to my cousin's wedding that's stylish but affordable,' and I'd reply with all sorts of suggestions for outfits that don't cost the earth. We could tie them in with other fashion features that we have in the supplement, and our readership will rocket.' It's only an idea off the top of my head, but I have to admit to being quite proud of it.

Both women stare at me. Or at least, I *think* Valerie's staring. It's hard to tell when you can only see half of someone's face—and that's only because I've finally squidged myself around a bit—but I'm sure her left eye's staring anyway.

'What a fabulous idea,' Valerie says at last. 'That would be a wonderful addition to the supplement. We'll talk about it more when we get back.'

I smile, glad that she's impressed. It would be a fun column to write, too—of course, I'd have to do lots of research into the latest fashions and who's stocking what, so it would involve lots of shopping and online browsing. A tedious job, I know, but someone would have to do it—*ha!*

'You really think you're going to get back, don't you?' Davinia says in an icy tone.

I stop smiling and suddenly feel stone cold. It's like she's an iceberg, passing her frostiness onto me. The rope feels even tighter around my wrists.

'Of course, we'll get back,' Valerie says calmly. 'Now, how about untying us, and we can talk about whatever the problem is over a nice glass of Merlot? There must be a wine bar or something near here. It would certainly be much more comfortable than this.'

'How about you get it into your thick head that *I'm* calling the shots here?' Davinia shouts. For such a petite person, she has a very loud voice. 'You've always been the one in charge and now, I'm putting an end to it. You're the one who always gets what I want—the job, the man—'

'You never wanted to do my job,' Valerie interrupts. 'You said yourself that the long hours wouldn't suit you, and you hated Phil Peerless and could never work with him. That's why I gave you the easy job.'

'Easy? I haven't got a clue what those people are moaning about when they write in, and no one ever agrees with my solutions. I get nothing but backlash for all my hard effort, and you know it!'

'But it's an asset to the supplement. People like having something to complain about, and it encourages reader interaction. I've told you before, it's all good.' Valerie shakes her head, clearly oblivious as to how riled Davinia is about the whole thing.

'And you know Quinton doesn't like you, don't you?' Davinia goes on, as though she hasn't heard Valerie's reply. 'He was only ever after your money. You made a complete fool of yourself over him, and everyone knows it.'

Valerie slumps against me. 'Yes, I know.' Her voice is quiet now. 'I was taken in by the attention of a handsome man and I fell for his tricks, hook, line, and sinker. I was such an idiot.'

'But *I* wasn't.' Davinia suddenly sounds quite smug. 'In fact, he's meeting me this evening, and we're going away together. For good.'

Valerie cranes her neck to look at her, and I feel my jaw drop.

'You and Quinton?'

'Don't look so surprised. You were right about him only being after your money. I, on the other hand, had more than that to offer.'

'Did you invest in his company?' I ask.

'Only a grand. We're not all on the same kind of wages as Valerie.'

'You're on much more than most of the staff,' Valerie points out indignantly. 'And a lot more than you should be on for your position. Phil and I have had countless disagreements on that fact.'

'Well, it won't be a problem for any of us soon,' Davinia says, with an evil glint in her eye. 'I'll be leaving the country tonight with Quinton and all his money, and no one will bother about the two of you. Apart from your boyfriend, of course, Liberty, but then it'll give him a flavour of how it feels to be forcibly parted from his lover, won't it?'

'Suzanne's put you up to this, hasn't she?' I knew it.

'No, actually. Although I'm doing her a great favour getting you out of the way so she can have her husband back. That's what friends do.'

'I thought *we* were friends.' Valerie points out. 'We've known each other for years. Why are you being like this now?'

'We've never been friends,' Davinia sneers. 'You've always thought you were better than me. Well, Quinton didn't think so. He only pretended to like you, so you'd part with all that money.'

'He didn't get half of it,' Valerie snaps.

Davinia scowls at me. 'Only because of this interfering little bitch.'

'It's a good job Liberty did her homework. I have to admit to being too besotted by the man to look into everything properly, but luckily, she discovered the truth before I'd given him any more money. I can't believe you still like him after what he's done.'

'Like him? I *love* him. And he loves me.' Davinia sounds very sure of herself. 'That's why he rang me.' She pulls out her phone and holds it up. I can't read the message from this distance, but she's clearly making her point. 'We're meeting in just over an hour at Victoria station. Then we fly out from Gatwick tonight. He's surprising me with the destination, but he says it's somewhere hot and romantic.'

She's surprised *me* by having the latest model iPhone. My stomach roils with realisation.

'That's not the mobile you had earlier,' I say, narrowing my eyes. 'Why do you have two phones?' *As if I didn't know.*

'Think you're smart, don't you?' She curls her top lip. 'This is the one I use for calling you.' She pulls out the basic one I saw her with in the toilets earlier. 'Quinton was very knowledgeable about how to make anonymous phone calls.'

'I'll bet he was.' I roll my eyes.

'And you're sure he's going to be there tonight?' Valerie asks, wriggling a little as she tries to free her hands. *Davinia must have been a Girl Guide to tie knots this well. Even Christian Grey would be impressed!*

'Oh, yes. Because he was never planning to take you to the concert.' Davinia sounds vicious. 'Though, I'm sure you'll have told Liberty about that, who will no doubt have tipped off the police, haven't you?'

Her eyes burn as she stares at me accusingly. I don't bother to answer.

'Won't they be pleased when they find you've led them up the garden path?' Davinia's clearly enjoying this. 'All their resources wasted while they wait for him at the concert hall, only to find that *you* got it wrong.'

Damn! It's a good job I'm tied up, or I'd happily slap that smirk right off her face.

'I can't believe you'd want a man like that,' Valerie says. 'You must see that he's nothing but a con man, a gigolo. You could do much better for yourself.'

'But I know him,' Davinia replies. 'I'm the one he wants. He told me. He had to flirt with you and those other women just to get you to part with your cash.

That's what he does. And all that lovely cash is just waiting for us in an off-shore account that he's going to access as soon as we land.'

'You really believe that, don't you?' I ask, incredulously.

'Just like you believed your boyfriend would actually leave his wife for you?' Davinia sneers.

'He didn't leave her for me,' I protest. 'They'd split up a year before we even met. They're divorced. Suzanne just can't seem to accept that.'

'Of course, she accepts it. She was in love with Oliver Reynolds, you know?'

'You know Reynolds?'

'Of course. He was Quinton's business partner. Suzanne introduced me to Quinton, and I set him up with Valerie.'

I bloody knew it!

'Some friend you are.' I shake my head. 'So, when Reynolds was caught, didn't it occur to you that Bellis would be next? That he was nothing but a con artist who was only after you for your money and connections? They're both users, Davinia, surely you can see that?'

She tightens her jaw. 'I was a little perturbed at first, of course, but then Quinton explained it all to me. He'd fallen in love with me and was only trying to make some money so we could run away together.'

'And you believed him?' Valerie asks scornfully.

Yes,' Davinia says, straightening up a little. 'Just like you believed you'd both get out of here alive.'

21

Valerie's body tenses against mine, and I suddenly want to throw up. Davinia's mad. Mental. Delusional. And downright bloody dangerous.

'What *are* you talking about?' Valerie asks, clearly trying to keep the tremble from her voice.

'You'll see.' Davinia has the evilest grin I've ever seen. And I've seen a few, believe me.

'I need to get back to the office. People will be missing me,' Valerie says abruptly.

'Like who? It's not unusual for you to disappear for a few hours,' Davinia jeers. 'And no one's going to bother about Liberty. I'm sure it's not unusual for *her* to skive off for hours at a time.'

I suddenly feel angry again. 'How dare you suggest that?' I demand. 'For your information, I never skive off work—and I'll be missed by lots of people.'

'You honestly think that?' Davinia turns up her nose. 'No one likes you at the *Chronicle*. They're only putting up with you, so you don't—how did Phil put it?

—attract adverse publicity to the paper. Isn't that what he said, Valerie?'

'I don't know what you mean.' I can hear how gritted Valerie's teeth are as she replies.

I feel sick. This is exactly what I was afraid of. They don't really want me there at all.

'Is it true?' I ask, doing my best to look at Valerie's expression—or, at least, half of it. 'Have you only given me a job to stop me from opening my mouth?'

Her body sags. 'Not exactly,' she says. 'It's quite a complicated situation, but it doesn't matter now.'

'No, it doesn't.' Davinia sounds quite gleeful all of a sudden.

'Because she's no longer on probation,' Valerie interjects sharply. 'Liberty has already proven to me that she's an asset to the company, and she'll be kept on in my department for as long as she likes. *And* for your information, Siobhan tells me she's *very* popular with the staff, so don't you try to make out otherwise. If anyone's not liked by them, it's you, Davinia Urquhart. In fact, once we get out of here, you can kiss goodbye to any kind of future in journalism. I'll make sure everyone knows what an ungrateful, lazy, conniving little scam-artist you are.' She spits the words out, her body becoming straighter as she speaks.

'Oh, is that right?' Davinia sneers, her face looking uglier than ever.

'You'd better believe it. You're finished, Davinia. Do you hear me? Finished!'

'As a matter of fact, Valerie, I think you'll find it's *you* who's finished. And your pathetic little sidekick there, of course.'

'What's that supposed to mean?' My elation at hearing Valerie's words was short-lived, as Davinia seems to be strutting even more determinedly now, and she sounds far too confident for my comfort.

'You'll see.' She glances at her watch. 'Well, I have a train to catch. And a new life to start—unlike you two losers.'

She swaggers towards the door, and I feel panicked again.

'Wait! Why are you doing this?' I'm praying she'll come back and keep talking, but she doesn't.

The grating sound of the key in the lock makes me shiver, and she slams the door behind her, locking it again.

'I can't untie these damn knots,' I moan. 'We need to get out of here.'

'Don't panic,' Valerie says. 'Someone's bound to come looking for us soon. We'll be all right.'

'How on earth will they find us out here? *We* don't even know where we are?' I keep struggling with the rope, but it's no good. I've already scanned the area for any bits of stone or other sharp object, but there's nothing here.

'Wait a minute. What's that smell?' Valerie sits up straight, sniffing the air.

'I'm sorry,' I admit. 'It's me. We were trying out some perfumes in the office, and I got sprayed with this awful…'

'No. It's not that,' she says. 'Listen.'

There's a sort of sloshing sound, and a familiar stench fills my nostrils.

'Petrol!'

'My thoughts exactly.' For the first time, Valerie actually sounds scared. I, on the other hand, am petrified! 'That can only mean one thing.'

'Yep.' I scour the room—or as much of it as I can see from this angle. 'She's even more insane than we took her for.'

***

'It's only wood. Let's see if we can kick it through. Valerie suddenly springs into action. 'Over there, come on.'

We bum-shuffle to one side of the wall, and she kicks hard against the wood.

'It's a proper building, not like a large, garden shed, as I'd hoped,' she moans, 'My feet feel like they're hitting concrete. It must be just the inner walls that are wooden.'

'I wish I'd worn hob-nailed boots instead of Louboutins today,' I grumble. 'It'll have to be the window.'

'It's too small,' Valerie snaps, 'And too high.'

'Use the wall to stand up,' I say quickly as my mind spins. 'We can do this.'

We have to work together to get to our feet, using the wall as a support as well as each other, but we finally manage it.

It gets hotter as we become upright, and we check the building for flames.

'Down there.' I nod to a corner at the front of the building where a couple of small flames lick at the base of the wall.

'We'll make it,' I shout. 'We just need to smash the window.'

'I hope you're right.' Valerie doesn't sound convinced. I'm used to people doubting me but it just makes me even more determined to prove them wrong.

'Remember the smell of damp when we came in?' I say, trying to stay positive. 'The wood's not dry enough to burn right away. It should buy us some time, if nothing else.' All those episodes of Bear Grylls I've watched haven't gone to waste.

It feels odd to be walking again, and I lead the way over to the filthy window.

'We'll smash it and use the glass to cut the rope,' I say, between coughs. The smoke's much worse when you're off the floor. It's getting thicker by the second.

I lift one foot up and grab the heel with the tips of my fingers.

'The fire will spread once it's smashed,' Valerie warns me, 'We'll have to be quick.'

'We will be,' I assure her.

She's coughing quite badly.

'Try to stay against the wall,' I urge her, concerned for her chest as well as flying glass.

We hastily position ourselves so I'm standing mostly with my back towards the window and Valerie's by the wall. It's much harder to smash glass with your hands tied than I'd hoped, but after a couple of attempts, I jerk my wrist, flicking the shoe out of my hand, and it hurtles through the window. I duck, as glass shatters across the tiny ledge and onto the floor.

I grab a couple of shards and pass one to Valerie before we both hack at the ropes. The fire crackles all around us, and we instinctively leap away from the window as more glass crashes to the floor, and the walls become engulfed with flame.

'Get down,' Valerie yells, and we both head for the floor, where the air is only marginally less smoky.

I keep my breathing shallow, determined not to pass out as I finally feel my wrists part. I tug at

Valerie's ropes and pull her hands free, noticing how limp she's become.

'Stay with me,' I tell her, throwing my arms around her, as she lies on the floor.

Even her coughing is weak as I shake her, trying to keep her conscious. The heat's unbelievable, and I feel myself flagging with the effort to keep alive. I can't see anything but flames through the thick smoke, and I know there's no way out. But this isn't it. It just can't be...

A moment later, I feel a splash of cold water on my hand. Is it raining again? Will it be enough to put out the fire? Of course not. Now, who's delusional?

Then there's more water, drenching my leg. It feels like it's burning it, as the skin is so hot. I scream out, using practically all the breath in my body. I'm trying to see what's happening, but the smoke's so thick. There are flashes of yellow, and I can't be sure whether they're flames or something else.

'Here.' I try to shout, but the smoke smothers my voice.

Something yellow moves nearer to me, and I can just make out the shape of an arm as it reaches for me. Someone's here...

***

I can breathe. I open my eyes and then shut them again. The lights seem so bright, and yet, they're probably only dim. My chest feels tight, but if I inhale, I know the air's there. Fresh. Clean. Not thick and suffocating anymore.

'She's awake, but only just.' A man's voice. Familiar and comforting.

I open my eyes again, slowly.

'James.' I thought I whispered his name, but all I could hear was an echoey hiss.

'It's all right, sweetheart. You've got an oxygen mask on.'

That explains it.

'Just keep breathing. You're going to be okay.'

He's blurry, but I can see the shape of his face as he leans over me. The light shines like a halo around him, and I wonder for a moment if I'm in heaven. If I am, quite frankly, I'm disappointed. It's not very comfy, I'm being jostled around all over the place, and it's much noisier than I imagined. Someone's moving nearby, and machines are beeping all around me. And it seems cramped. Too many people are up here. But at least it's much cooler than where I was before.

'Shh.'

I close my eyes again. It's the easier option. I breathe deeply, listening to the soothing tone, which I know is James. He's here. It doesn't matter where we are, as long as he's with me.

***

The next time I open my eyes, I'm in a room. The light's dim, and it's quiet. Or it would be if it wasn't for that incessant beeping noise in my ear. The mask on my face feels uncomfortable, but the air's much easier to breathe with it on.

There's a horrid tickle building up in my chest and I have to cough. Then I can't stop.

James is suddenly there, in front of me.

'Sit up, sweetheart.'

His voice is low and calming. He puts an arm around me, and a nurse plumps up the pillows behind my back as I slowly sit. James carefully removes the mask and passes me a cup of water.

My hands tremble as they cover his, grateful he doesn't let go of the cup, and take a drink. Cold water slides down my throat. At first, I just cough even more, but after a couple of sips, it subsides. It's more of an effort to breathe without the mask, but much more comfortable on my sore face.

A man with a stethoscope around his neck suddenly enters the room and peers at me.

'You're a very lucky girl.'

'I know.' I look up at James. My voice is a rasping whisper, but James gets the message. He

309

squeezes my hand and smiles before stepping back to allow the doctor to get closer.

I'm not sure exactly what the doctor's doing, but he pokes and prods me a bit, hums a lot and frowns at some notes. He's quite odd-looking, with an extremely large nose and frizzy hair—on his head, of course, not coming out of his nose. That would be too gross. His finger is indented from a wedding ring, and I can't help wondering what his wife looks like. How big is her nose? Do they have lots of frizzy-haired children running around?

'How do you feel?'

His question throws me for a loop. I don't know. I mentally assess my body. My head aches and my chest hurts like hell. My skin feels tight and fragile, and my brain's gone to mush. My entire body feels sore, but I can't quite say what's wrong.

'I think I'm okay,' I tell him in a half-croak, half-whisper. My throat feels like it's full of razor blades, but I can't possibly not speak, can I?

'Well, you have no broken bones,' he informs me. 'Though you cut your hand quite badly.'

I hadn't even thought about my hand. I look down at it and notice it's all bandaged up. It's my right hand, the one I used to smash the window. My heart lurches as I recall the sight of my precious shoe flying through the pane.

'My Loube,' I whisper, looking up at James.

'That's the least of my worries,' he assures me, grinning.

The doctor looks shocked, his face colouring up. 'I think it's best that you refrain from anything that... er... requires... er...'

'Her *shoe*,' James clarifies firmly. 'Christian Louboutins.'

'Oh... right... well...' The doctor looks relieved. 'I'll just um...'

Totally flustered, he leaves the room, and James and I burst out laughing.

'Did he really think…?' I whisper.

'Looks like it.' James shakes his head, bewildered.

The nurse didn't seem to get the joke and just goes to leave the room.

'What about Valerie?' I whisper loudly, causing myself to cough again.

'Your friend is going to be fine,' the nurse says, turning back. 'She's in the next room. You were both very lucky.'

'Thank you,' I whisper to James once she's gone.

'You had me worried,' he says softly.

'Me, too.'

'Valerie's faring a bit better than you, though she's in the same condition; no broken bones, just smoke inhalation.'

I sigh with relief, leaning back a little farther into my pillows. 'How did you find us? We were sure no one would think to look all the way out there. We thought we'd just smash the window, cut our ropes, and then climb out of it.'

'That window was tiny, if my memory serves me correctly,' he says with a frown. 'Which is actually a good job as it would have made the place burn down even quicker had it been any bigger.'

He looks tired, his brow furrowed with concern. I suppose it shows how much he cares about me, but I just wish I hadn't put him to so much worry.

'You didn't answer my question,' I whisper, my voice hurting even more. 'How did you know where to look?'

He sits up straight and stretches. 'It's a long story, and it's very late,' he says. His eyes twinkle. 'Though a Christian Louboutin flying out the window certainly helped to pinpoint you once we got there. It probably saved your lives.'

I'm glad it did some good. I would hate for it to have been wasted.

'There'll be enough time for all the details later.' He leans over and kisses me on the nose. 'You need to get some rest.'

'So, do you,' I reply.

He nods. 'Yep. Close your eyes and get some sleep. We'll talk again tomorrow, okay?'

I nod slowly, and he helps me to snuggle back down into the bed. His lips meet mine in the gentlest kiss I've ever had, and my stomach goes all gooey.

'Night, night, sweetheart,' he whispers.

I love it when he calls me that.

I'm delighted to see James sitting in the chair opposite me when I wake the next morning. He looks rested and refreshed, wearing jeans and a white Hugo Boss polo shirt, which gives me a lovely view of his muscular arms. He's smiling.

'Morning, sleepyhead,' he says softly.

Someone must have inserted oxygen nasal tubes while I slept as I can feel them irritating my nostrils. As if he already knows, he leans forward and carefully removes them for me, making me cough.

'Up you get,' he says gently, as he helps me up into a sitting position, aided by lots of firm pillows.

My mind's filled with questions as the events of yesterday flood my brain, but right now, I just want to admire the gorgeous man in front of me. Butterflies are having a ball in my stomach, and I savour the moment before opening my mouth.

'What happened?' I whisper. 'I mean, how did you…?'

He holds up a finger to stop me.

'We'll talk about it soon,' he promises. 'Right now, you need something to eat, and the nurse needs to run some checks on you.'

'Oh.' I can't hide my disappointment, but he just grins.

'It won't take long,' a plump nurse with a beaming smile promises me.

'Okay.'

'I'll just step out and make a few calls,' James says. 'I'll only be in the waiting room.' He stands up and gives me a tender kiss on the cheek before leaving the side room.

My insides fill with warmth.

'He seems very nice,' the nurse says, placing a tray on my little table. It's one of those wheeled ones that fits over the bed.

'He is,' I tell her, smiling.

'He's hardly left your side since you got here,' she goes on, helping me sit up even straighter. 'He insisted on staying until you woke up and he could see for himself that you were okay.'

My stomach flutters again.

'There's some porridge for you,' she goes on, gesturing to the bowl.

I'm so glad she clarified what it was. It just looks like a dollop of greyish mush. She seems to read my mind.

'I know it doesn't look all that appetising,' she says with a chuckle, 'but anything else would be too rough on your throat.'

She's right. The porridge slides down beautifully. It's not too hot and seems to smother my ragged throat in a protective coating, soothing all the way down.

'Would you like anything else?' she asks. 'Perhaps some yoghurt?'

'Maybe later.'

'Okay. Let's get you cleaned up then.'

She takes my blood pressure and checks my temperature before I have a refreshing wash and clean my teeth, then I comb my hair. James had even bought me some body spray and perfume, as well as all the essentials, and I feel much brighter by the time he returns to the room.

'You look lovely,' he says, leaning over to kiss me.

'Thanks to you,' I say, smiling. My voice is still hoarse, but it's not quite so sore to speak now, thank goodness.

'And talking of thanking people, Valerie's desperate to see you, but they won't let her out of bed just yet.'

'Is she okay?' I frown.

He nods. 'Yes, she's fine. Can't wait to get up and moving, truth be told. They just want to make sure before they discharge her that's all. She sends her love, though, and says she'll be in here as soon as they set her free.'

I giggle. Somehow, I can just imagine Valerie saying something like that. I've certainly seen a completely different side to her in the past few days.

'Someone else is here, though,' James goes on.

The door bursts open and Cassie and Rob appear, with Ben just behind them. Ben, Rob's best mate, is another reporter and a lovely guy. They beam as soon as they see me. Cassie's holding the string of a large balloon with 'Get Well Soon' written on it, and Rob's carrying chocolates. Ben's got me a bowl of fruit.

'You scared us all to death!' Cassie tells me, coming over to give me a big hug. The guys squeeze me gently, too, before plonking themselves on the bed.

'I'm sorry,' I say. 'I didn't mean to.'

'Well, the good news is we managed to get Bellis and Davinia Urquhart,' James says. 'Alex is with them right now.'

'How?' I gasp.

'You'll never believe it,' Cassie says, her eyes wide with excitement. She's tied the balloon to the railings of the bed, and Rob's already opened the chocolates, passing them round. Ben's started on the grapes.

'I knew something was wrong when you didn't answer your phone,' James says. 'Apparently, you'd left your bag and coat in the office, and the girls heard your phone ringing. Francesca became concerned and confided to Siobhan that you'd been threatened. They thought it was odd that you'd suddenly disappeared. They're used to Valerie leaving the office, but not you. And you'd never leave your phone behind.'

'So, Siobhan rang me,' Cassie explains. 'She said you'd gone, and someone was trying to call you. I knew it'd be James, so I rang him. Everyone was worried sick.'

'At first, we didn't have a clue what could've happened to you,' James says, pursing his lips.

'We just talked about what was going on for a bit, then I had a brainwave,' Cassie says. 'That picture from Broadstairs had been bugging me, so I sent it to James. He had it blown up, but I still didn't recognise the woman. I noticed the square-toed shoes, though, and told James you knew someone from work who always wore that style. Then I sent the picture to Siobhan, and she recognised it as Davinia Urquhart.'

'Suzanne's friend,' I say with a nod.

'Yes, but that's not all,' James adds. 'When I heard the name, I remembered the call I received while we were in Broadstairs. The one from Davinia saying that Suzanne had broken her ankle and needed me to come home. I knew the number was vaguely familiar when she rang. She'd made the call from a mobile, which I checked, and it was the same number you'd been getting those calls from. We were able to ascertain it was definitely the same Davinia.'

I remember James making a note of the number when I'd had one of those nasty messages. He hadn't been able to trace it because the phone was always switched off.

'Suzanne was already at the police station,' James continues. 'The officers had gone through the papers they picked up from Bellis' printers, and she helped identify the names on them that were familiar to her. It turns out the solicitor Bellis used was a complete fake, just some letterhead he and Reynolds had made up on a computer,' he says, with a grin. 'So, the house is still ours.'

'That's brilliant!' I'm so pleased; he's been worried sick about all that business, and I really hadn't meant to add to his concerns. I'm so relieved something good's come out of all this.

'But that's not it,' James goes on. 'I demanded she tell me what she knew about Davinia. At first, she wasn't very helpful, so I told her about the threat you'd received. When Suzanne saw how worried I was about you, she decided to come clean about her friend.'

He swallows hard, and I can imagine it must have been a horrendous time for him. I feel so sad to have put him through all this.

'Suzanne had previously told me that she was going out with Davinia last night, but it turned out it was just to provide her friend with an alibi. I'm afraid you're not going to like the next bit.' He takes my hand, and my stomach lurches at the grave expression on his face.

'Go on,' I urge.

'Davinia had been seeing Bellis and believed they were romantically involved.'

'I know.'

He raises his eyebrows. 'So, did you realise she held a grudge against you for discovering what a fake he was?'

I nod. 'She also hated Valerie for getting the top job and giving her one that she thought was beneath her.'

'Well, she was totally crap at it,' Cassie cuts in.

'We gained lots of readers because of that,' Rob says, and Ben nods. 'People were buying the paper just to see what rotten advice she churned out so they could complain about it.'

'Well, it's one way to sell newspapers, I suppose,' James says incredulously.

'Give people what they want, something to moan about,' Ben says with a chuckle.

'So, Suzanne knew all along that Davinia worked at the same place as me?' I say, thoughts racing through my head.

'Yes,' James says. 'When Davinia mentioned you were going to be working with Valerie, Suzanne took the opportunity to inject a bit of poison about you, I'm afraid. Through Davinia, she'd already turned your boss against you before she'd even met you.'

That explains a lot.

'She wants to apologise,' James says slowly. 'Can Suzanne come in to say sorry?'

My stomach churns. This is unbelievable. I nod dumbly.

'Hang on a minute.' James stands up and goes to the door. He calls Suzanne, who must have been waiting just outside. He takes something from her and follows her back into the room.

'Hi, Libby.' Suzanne enters, looking gorgeous. Of course, her hair and make-up are immaculate, as always, and she's in a beautiful, white satin dress by Joseph. It has long sleeves and is buttoned to the neck. The belt shows off her incredible figure, and she looks a bit like an angel. Innocent. Totally blameless.

'Hello, Suzanne.'

She doesn't look in the least sheepish or sorry, which is a major disappointment, and I wonder if she really has come to apologise, after all.

James places a large bag on the floor and offers her the chair he was sitting on. The others just gape at us in silence. The atmosphere is as thick as yesterday's smoke, and I suddenly find it hard to breathe. As if reading my mind—which he's been doing a lot lately—James reaches for my water and helps me take a drink.

'I was just telling Libby that you managed to turn Valerie against her before she'd even started the job,' James says, matter-of-factly.

Suzanne swallows hard. 'Yes. I shouldn't have done that, it was wrong of me,' she says, nodding. She sounds more like she's just pointing it out rather than saying sorry.

'But when you heard that Libby had gone missing, you actually helped,' James prompts.

She sits a little straighter. 'I'm sorry,' she says, quietly.

Hallelujah!

'Are you?' I didn't mean to say it. It just sort of slipped out. I was just so stunned by her admission.

She gives me a weak smile. 'Yes. I told Davinia all sorts of things about you that weren't true. You see, she was already angry with Valerie for not giving her a more managerial role. Also, Quinton had been flirting with Valerie to get her to part with her money. Davinia knew what he was up to, as she'd introduced them for just that reason, but found it hurtful that she had to pretend not to know him while watching him make advances towards Valerie.'

I'd already got that impression from hearing Davinia yesterday. But I'm still amazed she would still think Bellis wanted to be with her, knowing he's a con artist. She must have known deep down that she was just being used.

'I was annoyed with you for finding out that Oliver was a con man, a crook. I blamed you, but, in fact, it was my fault for falling for his lies. I was grateful to you in a way, but at the same time, I resented you for being the one to discover what I should have known from the start. Anyway, I took my revenge by lying to Davinia in the hope that Valerie would sack you from your job. I'm so sorry.'

She means it. She's truly sorry for what she did. In a way, I can understand her motives, but she didn't need to try to ruin my career. I nod, not sure what to say.

'I knew Davinia planned to meet Bellis last night,' Suzanne goes on. 'And of course, she hated you for discovering the truth about him as well as Oliver Reynolds, his business partner. You totally ruined all their future schemes.'

'Did you know what she had planned to do to me?' I ask, warily.

Her face clouds over, and she looks down into her lap. Then she takes a deep breath and looks up at me again.

'She told me she wanted you and Valerie out of the way so there was no chance of you interfering with her meeting Quinton and them catching that plane. We know how smart you are, so you could easily have discovered something else that could scupper their plans. Quinton had invited Valerie to a concert, but now that she knew what he was like, it was just possible Valerie might do something to get in their way. Davinia knew Valerie or you would tell the police to expect Quinton at the theatre, which had been her hope to divert their attention.

'She'd found that place, miles away, and had taken me to see it. I agreed with her that no one would ever think to look for you there, so you'd be gone a good while until you got out.' Her eyes get wider as she stares at me. 'I swear to you, she'd said nothing about setting fire to the place. She told me she was just planning to detain you long enough so she and Quinton could make their escape.'

Are those tears in her eyes?

I stare back at her. I believe her. Even though Suzanne seems to hate my guts at times, I just know she wouldn't want me dead—and certainly wouldn't contribute to my attempted murder. I nod.

'When James told me you'd gone missing, I was surprised at just how worried he was. At first, I didn't think much of it. I knew you would just be locked up for a while, and that you'd be fine. But then, James said you'd been threatened. I hadn't expected that. He was beside himself. We're no longer a couple, but I do care about him, and I couldn't bear to see him like that. So, I told him what I knew.' Suzanne trembles.

James pours her some water, which she takes with a grateful nod.

'I called the fire brigade, as Suzanne had said there was no escape except for the skylight or perhaps that tiny window. I thought we could use their help. I also had a really bad feeling about the whole thing,' James explains, crouching at the side of the bed and placing a hand on my arm. His eyes are wide, too.

'I'm so glad you did,' I whisper, suddenly reliving the moment I realised we couldn't get out.

'They started to put out the fire right away and were just checking the window when suddenly this shoe came flying out of it,' he says with a weak grin. 'It's a good job those firemen wear helmets.'

We all giggle.

'I can just see the headline now,' Ben says with a beam. 'Death by Louboutin.' He waves a hand in the air to make his point. 'The *Chronicle* would get the exclusive, of course, putting us squarely on the map.'

'I think we have enough of a scoop here without adding that to it, thank you,' Rob says.

Just then, the door opens.

'Did someone mention the *Chronicle*?' Valerie asks, poking her head around.

'Valerie!' I squeal.

'So, this is where the party is,' she says, smiling as she comes towards me.

She's wearing a hospital gown, the same as mine, and her hair is all ruffled up. Without any make-up, she looks much younger. We share a very gentle embrace, and I realise I was wrong about her—she really *is* the hugging type.

'Here, sit down,' Suzanne says kindly, standing up to vacate her seat for Valerie.

'Thank you.' She sits with more of a slump than normal.

Luckily, the nurse left a whole stack of disposable cups, so James pours some water for her.

'Does your throat feel like a bramble bush?' I ask her before taking another swig of my own drink.

'Without a single blackberry,' she confirms with a giggle.

'It's nice to see you up and about,' James says smiling kindly.

'Does this mean I can get up too?' I ask hopefully.

'You just wait,' James replies. 'You'll be on your feet soon enough.'

'They're keeping us in for observation,' Valerie says. 'It's quite normal, apparently.'

'But there's so much going on at work. I just want to get back,' I tell her, surprising myself at how eager I am to return to my job. It's true, though. With

Natalie getting the franchise with Crystal, it'll be all hands to the pump getting features together, and I know the boys will be reporting on it, too, from a different angle.

'It's all going through. Let's just give it time for the dust to settle,' Valerie says, raising her eyebrows. 'There's all the legal wrangle to wade through and then the actual logistics of it all. We've got plenty of time to sort it all out.'

I'm a bit disappointed to be honest, but I know she's right. It always takes longer for these things to go ahead than we expect. I'm just raring to go.

'We're rolling with the story about Bellis at the moment,' Rob says. 'There's so much involved with it, I think the story will run and run for a while.'

'And Siobhan and the girls are tying it in with some features about Rebel clothing, and why it should be avoided,' Valerie adds. 'They're getting publicity, but not quite the sort they were hoping for.'

Her eyes twinkle, and I chuckle.

'They caught up with Davinia at the station,' Cassie explains.

'Did Bellis go to meet her there?' I ask, doubtfully.

Cassie laughs. 'Of course not.'

'They were flying from Gatwick. Was he at the airport?' I stare at James.

'Not Gatwick Airport,' he says, shaking his head. 'Birmingham.'

'Birmingham?' Valerie and I speak at once.

James sniggers. 'We already had all the airports and ports covered, waiting for him to make his move. When Suzanne told us what the plan was, we knew where to find Davinia, but we had an inkling Bellis would be using her as a decoy. He planned to take a later flight from the Midlands.'

'Davinia must have been devastated,' I say with a gasp.

'She was,' James says gravely. 'It was bad enough that her boyfriend let her down, but when she heard she was being arrested for kidnapping and attempted murder, she was totally gobsmacked.'

***

'What's going on in here?' The nurse from earlier bursts into the room, frowning at my visitors. 'You're only allowed two visitors to a bed, and that's during visiting hours, which finished half an hour ago.'

'Sorry,' James says, giving her a gorgeous smile.

She visibly melts at the sight, which only makes me happier that he's mine.

'Right, we'd best be off,' Rob says, getting off the bed and throwing the empty chocolate box in the bin.

'Sorry about these,' Ben says, holding up the fruit basket. 'There are still a couple of apples left and a satsuma.'

'Thanks,' I say, grinning.

'I'll see you tomorrow,' Cassie promises.

They all give me a quick hug and head out the room.

'I must get back to bed,' Valerie says, standing slowly. 'I didn't expect to tire so easily.'

'You need to be careful,' the nurse says. 'Come on, I'll take you back.'

'See you soon,' Valerie promises me before the nurse takes her arm and helps her to the door. James goes over and holds it open for them.

With just Suzanne for company, I suddenly feel the tension mount between us. Without an audience, there's a good chance I'll see her true colours again if this was all an act. Sickness hits the pit of my stomach as I gaze at her.

Suzanne sighs. 'I really am sorry, Libby,' she says quietly. 'I can see now how horrid I was to you, and how much James cares about you. He was in bits when all this kicked off, though God knows how he managed to hold it together at work. I could tell what a state he was in and felt awful knowing I'd been a part of it.'

I nod, swallowing hard. I hate the thought of James being so upset.

'Anyway,' she goes on. 'You did me a favour exposing Oliver Reynolds, and I want to thank you. I also need to apologise properly for what I did and said. You'll be pleased to know that I'm moving to a new flat in a couple of days' time, so you can spend more time with James.'

My heart leaps.

'And I bought you a gift.' She reaches over for the bag James tidied away earlier. 'These are for you.'

She pulls out a gift-wrapped box. A gift-wrapped *shoe* box. I just know it is.

At first, I'm dumbstruck. This all seems so surreal.

'Open it,' she says, eagerly. 'That nurse will be back in a minute to throw me out.'

I snigger. *I'd like to see her try.* Somehow, I can't see Suzanne Harper taking orders from anyone, let alone that lovely nurse who's been looking after me.

She helps me pull at the pretty pink bow and tear at the wrapping paper. I was right, it *is* a shoe box. But not just any old shoe box. This one is a sturdy, brown box with a slightly raised logo on the front, which I run the finger of my good hand across. It's silky smooth and promises something wonderful.

'Open it,' Suzanne urges.

My heart pounds as I do as she says. Inside is a pair of Décolleté 554 stilettos in a nude to black ombre effect with the familiar Christian Louboutin logo smiling up at me. I tear my eyes from the shoes to gawp at Suzanne.

'Are they the right ones?' she whispers.

I nod. It's all I can manage right now.

She beams. 'James lent me some of the money. He said you'd like Louboutins, and he checked with Cassie which ones to get. A couple of the girls from your office had mentioned you admiring them, apparently. I wanted to get you something I knew you'd like so...'

'They're perfect,' I whisper.

'Good.' She's even prettier when she smiles. 'It was such a shame you had to sacrifice your other pair yesterday—although it *did* save your life. I thought you'd need a replacement pair.'

'Thank you so much.' I'm absolutely thrilled that she gets it. Louboutins aren't just a luxury, they're a *necessity*.

'Thank *you*,' she says softly, 'for bringing me to my senses.'

She wraps her arms around me and gives me warm hug. I hug her back, my mind spinning. Suzanne actually likes me. *And* she's bought me Loubes!

A thought crosses my mind, and I stare down at her feet. She's wearing Jimmy Choos—on *both* feet.

'You've had your cast removed,' I say, suspiciously. 'That was quick. How do you feel?'

She draws back from me, biting her lip.

'Stupid, to be honest.'

'What? Why?'

'It was a fake cast.' She grimaces. 'Part of my demented plan to spoil all the fun for you and James. I was just so jealous that you were just embarking on a wonderful new relationship, whereas I'd just made a complete fool of myself falling for a con man.'

'So, you're not still in love with James?' I ask warily.

She shakes her head. 'Nope. We're not compatible at all, I see that now. I just didn't want him to be happy.'

'Oh.'

'When I saw how worried he was about you yesterday, it struck me how much you mean to him. I was just being a selfish bitch trying to come between you. And all you two ever did was help me—he put me up, and you put up with me. I'm so sorry. The cast was just a ploy to get him to cut short his break with you, and to give me a good excuse to stay in his flat for longer.'

For the first time, Suzanne looks truly regretful. And I honestly believe she is.

'Well, at least you can get your shoes on now,' I point out, trying to cheer her up. I gaze at my new Louboutins now.

She giggles. 'Yes, you could say the shoe *definitely* fits now,' she says.

I burst out laughing. I'd never realised Suzanne had a sense of humour until now.

'I think it's time we were going,' James says, returning to the room. 'I presume you two are okay now?'

Suzanne gives me a questioning look.

'More than okay,' I say, smiling.

'See? I told you the Loubes were a good idea,' James says to Suzanne, his eyes twinkling with mirth.

'It wasn't *just* the shoes,' I protest, before we all burst out laughing.

Valerie's allowed home the following morning, but she comes to say goodbye before she goes.

'I want you to take a week off to recover,' she says sternly, 'and I'll be doing the same.'

***

I gape at her. 'What about work?'

'Don't worry, Siobhan's more than capable of running the place in my absence,' she assures me, 'and I'm sure they'll cope without you for a little while.'

'Did you know her dad's in a nursing home that she pays for?' I ask, thoughtfully.

Valerie looks astonished. 'Really?'

I nod, hoping I'm not speaking out of turn. 'He has Alzheimer's and needs constant care,' I tell her. 'Siobhan's mum has arthritis and can only work part-time, so she can't afford a decent home for him, so Siobhan pays. I think she supports her mum quite a bit, too.'

She swallows hard. 'I'm not very good at socialising, Liberty. I tend to keep myself to myself and expect others to do the same. I've always been like it. Maybe… because I was an only child.' She purses her lips. 'No. That's an excuse. I've always been insular. Selfish, I suppose. I need to spend more time thinking

335

of others. After all, if you hadn't been there thinking of me, I might never have escaped...' She trails off, her voice choked, and her eyes filled with tears. 'I'm sorry.'

I put my hand over hers, surprised to notice she's trembling.

'It's okay. We don't have to think about it anymore,' I say.

She nods, wiping her eyes with her other hand.

A thought occurs to me, and I seize the moment. 'Did you also know that Siobhan wants to get married?'

She looks taken aback. 'No.'

'She can't afford to, though, and her fiancé tries to help her out with everything, but he's not on a great wage, either. The thing is...' I chew my lip, trying to suss out her mood. 'They need to get married as soon as they can.'

Valerie gawps at me. 'She's not pregnant, is she? I had no idea.'

'No,' I say quickly. 'But since her dad has Alzheimer's, he might not be around...'

'Of course!' She throws her hands in the air. 'You've only just told me that. I told you I just don't think of these things.'

'It's private, though. All of it,' I add.

She nods. 'Well, I think we know all about confidentiality, don't we?' She gives me a knowing smile. 'I won't say a dickie-bird.'

'Thank you.'

'I will, however, be promoting Siobhan. She's excellent at her job, and I honestly don't know what I'd do without her. I haven't been very nice to her since she walked in on a conversation I had with Davinia. That's how she knew how stupid I'd been, giving money to that awful man. I was embarrassed that she'd discovered how silly I was. She kept it all to herself as I knew she would. I can always rely on Siobhan for anything. She's quite marvellous.'

'You should tell her that,' I say, smiling.

'I intend to.' She bites her lip, thoughtfully. 'Tell me, what do you think of the other women in the office?'

I gulp, hoping she's not expecting all the gossip.

'In confidence, of course.' She must have read my mind.

'Well, Brie's great. Did you know she and Eva used to be models?'

She frowns. 'Well, now that you mention it, I do remember something about that.'

'Eva has some famous contacts, and they both think it'd be a great idea to get some stars in to model fashions for the supplement. People would be much more likely to buy the clothes if famous people are wearing them, and the paper will sell more copies if there are celebrities included. And you could charge more for feature space as they'd sell more products.'

Oddly enough, Valerie looks like she's hearing this idea for the first time. I suppose it just goes to show how little she actually listens to everyone at work.

'I love it,' she says. 'I'll speak to the girls as soon as I get back. In fact, I've been thinking it's time I took a step back. I'll consider giving them their own section.'

'In a more managerial role, you mean?' I ask. 'At their ages, they should be climbing the ladder, shouldn't they? And they've been with the paper for a few years now.'

'Exactly.' She nods, her mind clearly reeling with ideas. 'And don't think I've forgotten about your idea, either.' She smiles. 'I love the concept of a sort of 'fashion agony aunt'. You'd be ideal for the role, and it might bring a younger readership to the supplement, too.'

'It'll be more of a women's magazine than a newspaper supplement when we've made all these changes,' I say with a giggle.

Her eyes light up. 'You're right. We should have a proper, glossy cover—maybe featuring those celebrities you were talking about. That would make it more of an incentive for famous people to take part in as well as heighten our profile.'

'Brilliant.' I want to squeeze her with delight, but we're both still a bit too fragile for that.

'I'm going to take this week to look at each of the girls' roles and see where we can make improvements,' she says. 'Starting with wages, I think. After all, I managed to convince Philip Peerless to pay Davinia an absolute fortune for doing very little. I'm sure I can persuade him that the rest of the department should be compensated for all their endeavours and loyalty.'

'Make sure you get some rest, though,' I tell her, flabbergasted that she's thought of it without any prompting.

'That goes for you, too,' she says, standing up.

We share a gentle hug before she leaves the room.

***

I'm a bit miffed that I have to stay an extra night, but relieved when I'm told I can go home the following day.

I was only being kept in because of the amount of smoke I'd inhaled, although James told everyone it was for bereavement counselling after having to throw my Louboutin out the window. *The git!*

To be fair, Valerie's Manolos were ruined, too, so we both needed to replace our shoes anyway. It's surprising how comforting that thought had been, while reliving those awful moments lying alone in the hospital bed.

'I thought we'd take a trip back to Kent,' James tells me once we get home to my place.

'Really?' I'm amazed he'd want to go back to my parents' so soon after our last visit.

He nods. 'We can leave tomorrow, if you're up to it.'

'Is Cassie coming?'

'Not this time. This is just for you and me, a few days to ourselves.'

My heart leaps. We've never had a holiday together.

'Your parents have been worried sick about you being in hospital,' he goes on. 'They were going to come up to visit you, but I suggested bringing you to see them instead. I told them the fresh sea air would be just the thing to get the last of the smoke out of your chest, and we could pop in to see them and your brothers while we're there.'

'That's so thoughtful,' I say, throwing my arms around him.

We're sitting side by side on the sofa, having a cup of tea. James has hardly let me lift a finger all afternoon, though I'm not complaining. It's surprising how tiring it can be just moving around at the moment.

'And I thought we'd take a trip to Rochester to see how Natalie's getting along with the boutique,' he says with a grin.

My heart leaps. He *so* gets me!

'I'd love to,' I say, squeezing him even tighter.

'I've already told your mum we'll be having a bit of a tour, so she doesn't need to worry about putting us up. We'll be staying at hotels while we're down there, so we won't put anyone out.'

I pull away from him slightly.

'You mean, you don't want to sleep on my parents' sofa again?' I feign surprise, which just makes him chuckle.

'Nope. It's about time I started sleeping in a bed again—my poor back won't stand much more of this.' He winks. 'Besides, we're going to have a proper holiday, just the two of us. *Together*.'

I love the way this man thinks. In fact, it's not the only thing I love about him.

***

Mum and Dad are thrilled to see us when we turn up on their doorstep a couple of days later.

'James is wonderful,' Mum says, while Dad takes him for a tour of the garden. 'He kept us informed every step of the way. We knew what had happened before it got into the press, thank goodness. He's been so worried about you, you know. He was devastated that you were put in so much danger.'

'I know, Mum. He's the best.'

We're sitting in the warm kitchen, drinking tea, and eating cake. I know I shouldn't, but I haven't eaten that much lately, and Mum's baking *is* lovely.

'I could tell by the way he spoke about you,' she goes on. 'He was very professional, of course, and gave us all the details, but he also told me how fragile you looked in that hospital bed. Policemen don't usually report that sort of thing, do they?'

'Well, I think he was ringing you more as a friend than a policeman,' I point out.

'Yes, I know, but even so...'

'I know he cares, Mum. And I feel awful that I put him through so much worry. And you and Dad, of course.' I want to cry. I've been doing that a lot lately.

'It wasn't your fault,' Mum says, astonished. She places a soothing hand on mine. 'You had no control over what happened to you. And I'm glad they have that awful woman behind bars. I hope they keep her there for life.'

I raise my eyebrows. Mum doesn't usually have such strong opinions about people, and I'm quite shocked at how adamant she sounds.

'I think she and Quinton Bellis will be out of the way for a long time,' I assure her. 'The police know what they're doing.'

'That shop of his has been all boarded up,' she says. 'The sign's been taken down and everything. It happened as soon as the police raided it. They took every scrap of paper in there to use as evidence, and then shut the place down for good.'

I'm surprised at how relieved I feel. I'm not planning to go that way while we're down here. I don't want to rake up any more memories—not that I can truly escape them at the moment. Every time I close my eyes, they're there, and even when I'm in the middle of doing something, the thoughts come back to haunt me, but it's good to know I won't see anything of the printers even if I do go that way.

'How's Natalie getting on with the shop?' I'm desperate to change the subject.

She smiles. 'She's very proactive. Ewan said she hasn't stopped. Your dad and I took a trip up there last weekend, just to see what it was like. It's incredibly posh. She has thick, plush carpets throughout, and there's lots of mirrors and glass.'

'It sounds wonderful.' I feel a flutter in my stomach and just can't wait to see it for myself. 'James is taking me while we're down here.'

'I'm sure you'll love it. It's much bigger than I imagined, and Ewan's decorated it with lots of pink and silver, so it's very feminine. Zak went up to lend a hand, too.'

'How is he?'

'Fine. He's still up there. They're keeping him quite busy I hear.'

'Great.' I'm looking forward to seeing both my brothers, but to be honest, I'm even more excited about seeing the boutique and hearing Natalie's plans for it.

Dad and James return from the garden, and Mum immediately gets up to pour more tea for them.

'That vegetable patch is amazing,' James enthuses, coming over to drape an arm around me.

Dad's always liked gardening. I could never see the attraction myself, especially not at this time of year. Even the greenhouse is a let-down, as it's too hot in the summer and too cold in the winter. A total waste of space, if you ask me.

'I'd love to have something like that if we didn't live in the middle of London.' James beams.

'Really?' I can't imagine him in wellies and wielding a shovel, somehow. Although, I have to admit, the woollen fisherman's jumper he's wearing today really suits him.

'Libby's more of a fair-weather gardener,' Dad says, sitting down with his mug of tea.

'Is that right?' James looks a little disappointed.

I just smile, not wanting to upset him even more by admitting that I'm veritably a *non*-gardener, no matter what the weather's like.

We finish our teas and go for a stroll on the beach. I'm wearing a long-sleeved top under a soft, cashmere sweater with jeans and black boots. To be honest, the jeans are only cheap ones, but the sweater was from the Next sale and the boots were from Hobbs, via eBay. I have a thick, black overcoat Cassie insisted on lending me along with her pink and grey Hermes scarf. I still shiver at the cold wind blowing in over the waves. James puts his arm around me as we stroll over the sand.

'Are you okay?'

'Yeah.' I smile at him. I feel so relaxed in his company, despite everything that's happened. I was quite overwhelmed when I first got home from hospital, but the past couple of days spent with James have helped me get my breath back. He's a very calming influence. 'Thanks so much for taking time off to spend with me.'

He squeezes me a little tighter. 'I don't want to let you out of my sight,' he admits. 'I had such a scare when I realised how crazed that woman was. I could have lost you.'

I snuggle into his warmth. 'It'll take much more than that,' I assure him, trying to lighten the mood. It's not like James to be so serious about me.

He says nothing for a moment, making me feel a little uneasy. So, I carry on talking. 'Rob and Cassie are getting very close. She's spending more and more time at his place—or, at least, she was until all this happened.'

She took a couple of days off to stay with me, too. Cassie was incredibly shaken when she heard what had happened to me.

'Hmm,' James says thoughtfully. 'They're in love.'

I nod. I want to say *so am I*, but I daren't. It would be a shame to say the wrong thing and ruin what we have together. But I *do* love James. I'm not sure when I realised it. It just sort of crept up on me. I can't tell him that, though. I just don't want to spoil things if it's not what he wants to hear.

We stop walking, and he turns to face me, a pensive expression on his gorgeous face. My stomach flips. I can't read him. This is either something wonderful or something awful, and the way my luck's going lately, I'm afraid it's more likely to be the latter. Is he about to break up with me?

'Libby. I've told your parents how I feel about you.'

Oh, God!

'And I have their blessing.' He pulls something from his pocket.

My heart pounds.

'I love you,' he says, nervously.

I gape at him, my throat suddenly going dry.

His hand shakes as he unfurls his long fingers and produces a shiny, new key.

'You already hold the key to my heart,' he says. 'How about the key to my door? Libby, will you move in with me?

My jaw slackens and I just stare at the metal object, then at his gorgeous face.

'I don't want us to spend any longer apart than we have to,' he says gently. 'This way we won't have to. Say yes.'

My whole body trembles. I don't say yes. In fact, I don't say anything.

THE END

May I Ask a Favour?

I hope you enjoyed the latest instalment of The Liberty Lawrence Series. If so, I'd love it if you would leave a review at any (or all) of the following sites:

Amazon.com https://www.amazon.com
Amazon UK https://www.amazon.co.uk
BookBubhttps://bookbub.com
Goodreads https://www.goodreads.com
Or anywhere else you like

Reviews are extremely important for authors as they help get the word out about their books and, hopefully, gain more readers. They are also essential for some advertising platforms. I really would appreciate your help.

Thanks so much x

Disclaimer

In the interests of fairness (and not getting sued) the author would like to point out the following:

1. GEORGE CLOONEY IS <u>NOT</u> A CON MAN

People who look a bit like Mr Clooney *may* be con artists—I don't know them all—but are not *necessarily* that way inclined. No inference is made in this book to suggest that *all* George Clooney lookalikes are in any way dodgy. Quinton Bellis is a fictional character (thank goodness!).

2. SANTONI-WEARERS ARE <u>NOT</u> ALL MAD

Davinia Urquhart is a fictional character who happened to favour this brand of shoe. No inference is made in this book to suggest that *all* wearers of these lovely shoes are in any way dubious. Just Davinia, who needs to be avoided at all costs. Actually, as she's fictional, that shouldn't be a problem!

3. CHRISTIAN LOUBOUTINS WILL <u>NOT</u> <u>NECESSARILY</u> SAVE YOUR LIFE

Of course, if you follow Liberty's actions, they might stand a chance of helping you survive, but please don't take it as gospel. Christian Louboutin shoes are *not* intended as lifesavers. However, they will certainly *enhance* your life and your wardrobe, so buy them anyway!

NO SHOES WERE HARMED IN THE WRITING OF THIS BOOK

Trademark Acknowledgement

The following trademarked items appear in If the Shoe Fits... The author acknowledges the trademarked status and trademark owners of the following wordmarks mentioned in this work of fiction:

Christian Louboutin: Christian Louboutin Ltd
Manolo Blahnik: Manolo Blahnik International Ltd
Kurt Geiger: Kurt Geiger Ltd
Karen Millen: Karen Millen Ltd
McDonald's: McDonald's Corporation
Radley: Radley & Co Ltd
Mercedes: Daimler AG
Coke: The Coca-Cola Company
eBay: eBay Inc
Chanel: Chanel International B.V.
Monsoon: Monsoon Accessorize Ltd
Dorothy Perkins: Arcadia Group
Jimmy Choo: Jimmy Choo Ltd
Stella McCartney: Stella McCartney Ltd
Pretty Woman: Uptown Wink LLC
Chloe: Chloe S.A.S.
Vivienne Westwood: Vivienne Westwood Latimo S.A.
iPhone: Apple Inc

BMW: BMW Ltd
Nurofen: Reckitt Benckiser
Airfix: Hornby Ltd
Debenhams: Debenhams plc
Accessorize: Monsoon Accessorize
River Island: Lewis Trust Group
Outfit: Taveta Investments
New Look: New Look Group Ltd
Costa: The Coca-Cola Company
H&M: Hennes & Mauritz AB
Audi: Volkswagen Group
Citroën: Groupe PSA
Next: Next plc
Hobbs: Hobbs Ltd
Hermes: Hermes International
Prada: Prada S.p.A.
Gucci: Kering
Armani: Georgio Armani S.p.A.
Clarins: Clarins Group
Santoni: Santoni Osteria
Rimmel: Coty
Calvin Klein: Calvin Klein
Jigsaw: Robinson Webster Holdings
Joseph: Joseph Ltd; Onward Holdings Co Ltd
Errotha: The Aldo Group
Aldo: The Aldo Group
Christian Dior: Christian Dior SE
Hugo Boss: Valentino, Marzotto

The Devil Wears Prada: Fox 2000 Pictures
Morelli's: Morelli Ice Cream Ltd
Hornby Visitor's Centre: Hornby Hobbies Ltd
Velcro: Velcro BVBA
Rimmel: Coty Inc
Sherlock Holmes: Sir Arthur Conan Doyle Literary Estate
Miss Marple: Agatha Christie Ltd
Cagney and Lacey: Barbara Avedon, Barbara Corday, CBS Television Network
Victoria's Secret: L Brands
Girl Guides: The Guide Association
Christian Grey: E L James

As a courtesy, the author would like to acknowledge the following celebrities mentioned in If the Shoe Fits...
George Clooney
Bear Grylls
Rihanna

And Musicians

REBEL https://www.rebelbaroque.com
Vivaldi
Bach

About the Author
BEA STEVENS

Author of Chick Lit, lover of chocolate (and doesn't think it's pure coincidence that the two sound similar!) Has a penchant for shoes, bags, clothes (the usual necessities), and socialising with friends, family and anyone else who gets dragged along.

Hopes you enjoy her books, get her humour, don't object to her use of British spellings and keep in touch

Please feel free to sign up to her newsletter at:

http://eepurl.com/dnI9bv

And/or follow her on:

https://www.facebook.com/AuthorBeaStevens/

https://twitter.com/beastevensbooks

https://www.instagram.com/authorbeastevens/

https://www.bookbub.com/authors/bea-stevens

https://www.goodreads.com/author/show/17444011.Bea_Stevens

And check out her website at https://www.beastevens.com/

Also by Bea Stevens

BEST FOOT FORWARD
(The Liberty Lawrence Series Book 1)
http://mybook.to/BestFootForward

STEPPING IT UP)
(The Liberty Lawrence Series Book 2)
http://mybook.to/SteppingItUp

RUNNING IN HEELS
(The Liberty Lawrence Series Book 4)
http://mybook.to/RunningInHeels

HERE'S A TASTE OF 'RUNNING IN HEELS'...

I'm so excited to be going back to work—and that's not something I say very often. The girls I work with at the *Daily Chronicle*'s Fashion Supplement are lovely. I've had several get-well wishes from them, cards and flowers, not to mention numerous chats with Fran, Beulah, Siobhan, and even Brie and Eva. I've been through an awful ordeal—someone actually tried to kill me and my boss, Valerie Fulton-Coombes. Imagine that. I mean, I know Valerie wasn't particularly likeable when I first met her, but to try to kill her was a bit extreme—and what about me? *I* hadn't done anything wrong. Anyway, it's all sorted now. The demented woman is behind bars—Davinia Urquhart that is, not Valerie—and Valerie I are both okay. In fact, the whole experience seems to have had an amazingly positive effect on Valerie, who turned out to be really nice. Who knew?

The Tube's packed, as always, but it doesn't bother me today. I'm wearing a powder-blue dress and jacket ensemble by Oasis along with my new nude-to-black ombre Louboutins from Suzanne—my boyfriend, James', ex-wife, *long story*—and a black bag. I'm shivering to death but look amazing! It's November, and I've come out without a proper coat. James would go mad if he knew, what with my recent recovery and all, but I didn't want to hide my lovely outfit. Besides, it gets quite stuffy on the Tube at rush-hour, and I certainly didn't want to be all sweaty when I greeted the office girls.

As if to make my point, a big guy lurches forwards with the jolt of the train. He's holding the grab rail above my head and I'm suddenly treated to a waft of stale BO and a glimpse of the sweat patches under his arms. Whether or not BO is contagious is debatable, but I'm not taking any chances. I use my one free hand to whip out my bottle of J'adore and fumigate myself. The big guy coughs and I inwardly dare him to complain. Better his coughing than my puking any day!

It's a relief when the Tube stops, and I finally get off. Just for good measure, I smother myself in perfume again and take the short walk to the office, grateful for the fresh—if bloody freezing—air.

As soon as I step out of the lift, Fran comes running down the corridor to meet me. She's beaming, her beautiful, red curls billowing around her flushed face as she calls my name. She's wearing a gorgeous, dark green boho-style dress and brown boots.

'You're here!' she shouts, throwing her arms around me.

I'm a little taken aback but get a lovely warm feeling knowing that I've got such a good friend in her. Practically every day since I went away, she's texted me about the changes that are happening in the office, and I can't wait to see it all for myself. I also feel much closer to her now, as we chatted about other stuff such as her dreadful love life, and how she was thinking of moving now that she's had a payrise. And that's another thing. Money. Apparently, everyone in the department's had a rise—even me, and I wasn't even there!

There's a big cheer and a round of applause when I go into the office. Everyone looks up and smiles at me, as they move forwards. I didn't realise they were all so huggy, but they all give me a really warm welcome, even Izzy, though her body feels a bit stiff next to mine. It reminds me that I was absolutely right not to wear a coat. I send up a silent thank-you prayer to Mr Dior.

Valerie steps out of her office and gives me a squeeze.

'It's lovely to have you back, Liberty.'

She looks radiant. Younger, too. She's relaxed and smiling. Even her clothes don't look quite as starchy and severe as usual. She's wearing a dress today, Jaeger, I think. It's not as fitted as she usually wears, and has a cute, sweetheart neckline. It's a sort of teal colour, which really brings out the green inher eyes.

'I'm so happy to be back,' I confess. 'Broadstairs was lovely, but I really missed you guys.'

There are smiles and chatter all around me and a few girls say they actually missed me, too.

'Let me show you around,' Valerie says, graciously, wafting her arm in the air as she leads me away from the crowd.

My heart's racing nineteen-to-the-dozen. 'Ooh, yes please,' I say, beaming, 'I can't wait to see all the changes.'

'Well, there are certainly a few of those,' Siobhan pipes up as the girls all drift back to their workstations.

The large room is still as spacious and airy as I remember, but there are definitive areas now where the girls work in their own sections. There are lovely framed pictures of glamorous models and film stars on the walls. As the girls get back to work, Valerie ushers me over to the corner of the room nearest her office. This whole area seems much larger without the huge table that dominated the room, although a slightly smaller one, which is still quite massive, has been placed farther up the department to one side. The desks that used to line the sides have been replaced with bright white ones that face the middle of the room. Now, matching cupboards and drawers, topped by large work surface line the walls.

The large mirror on the wall and swivel chair in front of it immediately tell me this is Eva's section. She beams up at me from her desk.

'Welcome to my world,' she says, standing.

'Eva, as you can see, is in charge of the hair department,' Valerie says. 'A little bird told me this is her forte.' She winks at me and I giggle, remembering the conversation we had about the girls, while we were at the hospital. We discussed all their various talents, and Valerie realised that they were being vastly underused.

'I'm helping out with make-up and nails, too,' Eva says, but this is my main concern.'

Eva is beautiful, with long, dark, wavy hair and a figure to die for. She has big, expressive eyes and a gorgeous smile. I'd guess she's in her early thirties, and one of the most feminine, classy ladies I've ever met.

'So, you all sort of work together?' I raise my eyebrows, relieved that they're not all segregated and working alone.

'Oh, yes,' Valerie interjects. 'I want to play to the girls' strengths—which often cross over to different departments anyway. But I was concerned not to split everyone up, so they all work as a team, but with their own areas of responsibility as well.'

'We've been promoted to heads of section,' Eva tells me with a wide smile. 'Apparently, Valerie had a brainwave while all that awful stuff was going on and came back and made a load of changes.'

'For the better, I hope?' Valerie queries, a smile teasing her lips.

'Of course. Now we've been assigned defined responsibilities we can plan our own schedules and organise ourselves far better.' Eva winks at me and I get the impression she already guessed who gave Valerie the idea.

'Brie and I are also trying to get a few celebrities in here,' Eva goes on.

'Yes, we're giving the supplement a new look, focussing more on fashion,' Valerie says. 'It will have a glossy cover and better-quality pages as of today, making it more of a magazine than a newspaper supplement.'

'That's brilliant,' I say. 'And you're actually having celebrities come here to the office?' My mind whirls, hoping Eva has links with Jamie Dornan or Brad Pitt. The Hemsworth brothers, maybe? God, I love my job!

'Sometimes,' Valerie says with a shrug. 'We also have a hotline to the photography department, so we can go out and interview the stars on location if we need to. Mr Peerless has removed the restriction on how often we can call on them, providing they're available, of course.'

Mr Peerless is in overall charge of the *Daily Chronicle* and a hard man to negotiate with. Goodness knows how Valerie managed to persuade him to allow this.

'Everyone's going to get a shot at interviewing celebs,' Eva adds, giving me a knowing look.

My stomach flutters. This is a dream come true.

'And over here we have skincare and make-up,' Valerie continues, gliding over to the section opposite.

I don't hear her at first, as I'm busy interviewing Channing Tatum in my head. It's not until Eva clears her throat that I come back to the present and quickly scoot over to where Valerie's standing, talking to Brie.

'Brianna is in charge of this section,' she says, turning to face me.

No shit!

Brie rolls her eyes and then smiles at me. She is absolutely stunning, with short, wavy hair that frames her face beautifully and she's always immaculately made up. She's very slim and elegant, like Eva, and probably around the same age. Both have worked as models in the past, and I think that's how they first met.

'I'm also helping with hair and nails,' Brie tells me, 'but this is my section.'

'Fantastic,' I say.

I notice the lit-up mirror on the wall and guess it'll be getting a lot more use now we're working for a fashion magazine.

'We *are* still a supplement to the *Daily Chronicle,* aren't we?' I ask Valerie.

'Well... yes. Why do you ask?' She raises her eyebrows curiously.

'Well, I was just thinking that there are already enough glossy magazines out there with fashion, make-up and celebrities,' I say, warily. 'I wondered what made us different?'

'That's a good point.' Valerie frowns.

Brie looks a little uneasy. 'We need a USP,' she says.

'Yes,' Valerie narrows her eyes in thought. 'A unique selling point. But what?'

'Well, if we're still affiliated to the local paper, then shouldn't we keep the content local, too?' I ask, quietly thrilled that I've come up with an idea.

'Local? You mean only interview local celebrities?' Brie says with a pout.

'Not necessarily. I was thinking more of tying in with the *Chronicle*'s stories. I mean, obviously local celebs would be a great idea, but what about other celebrities who are *appearing* locally? Like at the theatres and stuff? It's still local news but it's also big-name celebs. And if they might happen to be wearing something that we're featuring in one of our sections, then so much the better.'

'I think we might have to pay a lot more to get a celebrity to wear one of our featured fashions,' Valerie says, doubtfully.

'But we can offer to do their hair and make-up for a photoshoot, can't we? After all, someone has to get them camera-ready.'

Brie's face brightens. 'Of course. And if we happen to use a product that we're doing a feature on...'

'Yes.' Valerie's eyes sparkle with enthusiasm.

'And we can always offer them a bag or a scarf or whatever as a prop?' I add, thinking on my feet.

'I love it!' Valerie clasps her hands together. 'That's what we'll do.'

'What?' Izzy walks over, frowning. She's the eldest of the girls, probably in her late thirties and I can imagine she won't be pleased at the thought of missing out on something. She's very tall and slender, with prominent cheekbones and a white-blonde urchin crop that just accentuates her beauty. I find her quite austere and am a little wary of her, to be honest.

'Brianna will explain,' Valerie says, flippantly.

Izzy narrows her eyes at the boss.

'We're coming to look at your section now,' Valerie informs her, before she even has time to ask Brie what we were discussing.

Huffing, Izzy goes back to her area and we follow.

'This is the nail bar,' Valerie tells me. 'Isobella will be testing new products and getting them photographed as well as writing articles.'

'Ooh, I love having my nails done,' I say with a smile. I was hoping Izzy might smile back, but she doesn't.

Her workstation is next to Eva's, back on the other side of the room, and a peninsular table stands at ninety degrees to the cupboards, narrow enough to sit either side so Izzy can apply or manicure the nails of the person opposite. Two swivel stools are tucked neatly underneath it, and I can't wait to try them out.

'Isobella also helps with hair and make-up,' Valerie goes on, clearly oblivious to the hostile atmosphere.

'Great.' I try to sound excited, but it's totally wasted on Izzy, who scowls at me. She clearly thinks I'm betraying her by having that conversation and not telling her about it, but I can hardly say anything with Valerie right here, can I?

Opposite Izzy is the fashion section, with rails of clothes lined up in front of the cupboards.

'This looks interesting,' I say, turning to smile at the girls.

Thankfully, Valerie takes the hint and we move over to take a closer look.

'Strictly speaking, Kiera and Francesca oversee the latest fashions, Tamara reports on everyday wear, and Alice and Beulah report on evening wear,' Valerie announces, as the girls come closer.

'But we all work together as well,' Beulah points out.

'You'll be helping in this section, too,' Valerie informs me.

My stomach flutters. I wondered where I would fit in with all this, and I'm glad it's in the department with the most girls. I'd love to work with every one of them.

'Brilliant,' I say, smiling.

'It's going to be great fun with you in our section,' Beulah says, grinning.

'However, you will also have your own area of responsibility,' Valerie goes on.

I gulp.

'This is where you will work,' she says, ushering me to the opposite side of the room again. There's just a desk in front of the cabinets, offering no clue as to what I will be doing there.

My entire body sags for a minute. I'm going to be working alone. It's clearly something clerical as I've only got a computer, no interesting equipment, clothes rails, or anything like everyone else has.

Valerie smiles at me, a twinkle in her eyes.

'Remember we talked about an agony aunt's position? Well, as you know that post has recently become vacant and I want you to fill it.'

'Me?'

'Yes, of course. You said you'd like to help people with their problems You also suggested that, instead of the usual personal woes, it would be more fitting to have a fashion advisor, rather than a traditional agony aunt. That's what I'd like you to do. What do you think?'

My mind whirls. We discussed this when Davinia told Valerie how much she hated her job. I meant it when I said I'd like to be in her shoes—well, maybe not those Santonis with the squared-off toe, exactly—but I would want to do it differently. My way. Valerie obviously remembered it all.

'I'd love to do it,' I tell her, my face flushing with excitement. 'It would be a great job. Thank you.' I want to hug her, but it wouldn't be appropriate here with everyone around, so I clench my hands together and settle for giving her a huge smile instead.

She smiles back.

'I'm glad you like the idea, I haven't a clue how I thought of it.'

We both giggle like a couple of schoolgirls, and I can see that almost getting killed has had a positive effect on the boss. She seems much more human today—I just pray that it lasts.

'Siobhan will be working next to you,' Valerie points out, indicating the stunning girl in the corner with the precise, black bob.

I look over at her. Then a thought crosses my mind. So will Izzy, whose desk is to the side of me with Siobhan's opposite, in a large corner section. I really don't think Izzy likes me very much, but I can hardly tell Valerie that.

'It's so good to have you back,' Siobhan says, dragging my attention to the matter at hand.

'It's great to *be* back, I can't wait to get started,' I reply, as she sits behind her large, L-shaped desk overlooking the whole room.

'Siobhan's the department manager,' Valerie announces, proudly. 'Her job is to oversee the whole office and deal with the magazine's editorial issues. You'll still report to her, as usual.'

'Well, I'm glad that hasn't changed.'

'Something else *has* changed,' Siobhan says coyly.

'Really?'

She holds out her left hand, showing me a gorgeous diamond ring that catches the light and glistens on her long, slender finger.

'I'm getting married.' Her face flushes as she tells me, and I whiz over and give her a big hug. I can't help it. It might not be the most appropriate thing to do, but I don't even think about it and just squeeze her as hard as I can.

'I'm so happy for you!' I say, my voice a little higher pitched than normal.

'Thank you,' she whispers.

'Well, I'll leave you to settle in,' Valerie says before returning to her office.

'I mean it, Libby,' Siobhan murmurs once we're alone at her desk. 'Thank you for everything. Valerie told me you'd had a bit of a heart to heart and she's really taken it all on board. We've all been promoted with huge hikes in our pay—some of us more than others.' She looks cagey—embarrassed, almost.

'You deserve it,' I tell her in a hushed tone. 'And overseeing all of us should make you eligible for a medal, let alone anything else. And there's all the crap you have to put up with from Valerie—although she doesn't seem so bad today.'

'She's been like this ever since she came back,' Siobhan tells me. 'She must have Phil Peerless wrapped around her little finger judging by the amount of money she's been throwing around.'

'The office does look brilliant,' I say.

'It's not just the furniture. We all have new computers, and the girls have the latest equipment for their work—she can't do enough for us.'

'Good.' I don't know what else to say.

'Anyway,' she continues, conspiratorially. 'What about you? Any sign of you having one of these any time soon?' She holds up her finger, her ring glinting in the fluorescent lights. 'I don't mean to pry or anything, but Cassie said James had taken you away.

She also alluded that it might be for more than just a bit of R and R.'

Oh, shit! Her face is glowing with expectation, and I know she wants me to give her some good news. But… how can I?